A MAIDEN WEEPING

A Selection of Titles by Jeri Westerson

The Crispin Guest Medieval Noir series

VEIL OF LIES
SERPENT IN THE THORNS
THE DEMON'S PARCHMENT
TROUBLED BONES
BLOOD LANCE
SHADOW OF THE ALCHEMIST
CUP OF BLOOD
THE SILENCE OF STONES *
A MAIDEN WEEPING *

THOUGH HEAVEN FALL
ROSES IN THE TEMPEST

* *available from Severn House*

A MAIDEN WEEPING

A Crispin Guest Medieval Mystery Noir

Jeri Westerson

Severn House

This first world edition published 2016
in Great Britain and the USA by
SEVERN HOUSE PUBLISHERS LTD of
19 Cedar Road, Sutton, Surrey, England, SM2 5DA.
Trade paperback edition first published
in Great Britain and the USA 2016 by
SEVERN HOUSE PUBLISHERS LTD

British Library Cataloguing in Publication Data
A CIP catalogue record for this title is available from the British Library.

ISBN-13: 978-0-7278-8621-7 (cased)
ISBN-13: 978-1-84751-722-7 (trade paper)
ISBN-13: 978-1-78010-783-7 (e-book)

All Severn House titles are printed on acid-free paper.

Severn House Publishers support the Forest Stewardship Council™ [FSC™],
the leading international forest certification organisation.
All our titles that are printed on FSC certified paper carry the FSC logo.

FSC
www.fsc.org
MIX
Paper from
responsible sources
FSC® C013056

Typeset by Palimpsest Book Production Ltd.,
Falkirk, Stirlingshire, Scotland.
Printed and bound in Great Britain by
TJ International, Padstow, Cornwall.

To my husband Craig, who has the patience of Crispin and suffers his own trials. And in memoriam of George, or should I say 'Gyb'.

ACKNOWLEDGEMENTS

Grateful thanks go out to my husband, not just for offering suggestions and helpful thoughts on my writing but in all things; to my agent Joshua Bilmes who keeps Crispin clothed and fed; to Mark Davidson, David Seipp, and Paul Hyams, medievalists all, who offered advice and further reading suggestions on all the complicated medieval English law; to Facebook friend Pat Smith for suggesting the cat; and finally to my readers who keep sharing their love of this strange and distant medieval man who solves crimes. Thank you!

FOREWORD

The idea that a person 'shall not be compelled in any criminal case to be a witness against himself' is a relatively new one. Not that medieval jurisprudence was all that, well, medieval. In fact, it was downright civilized . . . to a point. And in England it was well-reasoned and workable.

By the way, that rule about self-incrimination in English common law became law in the latter half of the seventeenth century, too late to do Crispin any good. Prior to that, silence was construed as guilt. In the 1600s, reason seemed to prevail. But in the early fourteenth century it wasn't about the individual's right to remain silent but the opportunity to speak out and defend yourself.

There aren't any details as to exactly how a criminal trial proceeded during Crispin's time. All we have are the bare facts from the court records, which are interesting enough. Because we don't know exactly what transpired and there were no records of every step and word uttered at a trial as you would see today in court transcripts, I've taken only a few liberties. But the court, as we know it or knew it, was depicted extant. Defendants and juries were specifically *not* 'sworn in' so that they would not be compelled to blaspheme themselves if they lied, assuming they might. And there was no assumption of innocence or guilt. A crime was committed, evidence suggested the accused might be guilty, an indictment or formal accusation was made, and the accused arrested.

Jurors were seated because they had intimate knowledge of the case and came from the immediate vicinity of the crime or knew the accused's character. This is completely unlike today when both of those aspects would get you immediately thrown off the jury.

London was divided into wards, and jurors were culled from those wards where the crimes were committed. Sometimes jurors were important people chosen to be seated in likelihood that they could corral some of these common merchants and laborers who didn't know what they were doing. Unfortunately, that could be stacking the jury. There were a lot of checks and balances in place to try to prevent that, but it did happen with varying results.

A jury, though usually ready with their decision before ever getting to trial, could still be swayed by further testimony or new evidence – or a bribe – but on the whole, trials were pretty quick business, lasting no more than ten minutes. You can see how this might have made for a very short novel.

Despite what bribes *might* have been levied or not, it seems that sixty percent of trials ended with an acquittal. This either speaks about the seriousness with which all parties took the events or it was a clear sign of widespread corruption. And no mistaking, there was corruption, and bribes, and favors gained and meted out.

All that trial by combat or ordeal was done away with by the end of the fourteenth century. You might remember in *Blood Lance* that Crispin was involved in a trial by combat, but this was a different situation of a knight being tried for desertion and cowardice by the court of chivalry. In that instance a trial by combat was certainly appropriate.

GLOSSARY

Abetment	The aiding of a criminal in their illegal enterprise.
Abjure the realm	Banishment.
Assize	A trial or court or the ordinance or edict made there.
Bezant	A medieval gold coin.
Captus in Medio	Latin for 'caught in the middle of.'
Chancery	The medieval equivalent of administrative offices responsible for paperwork.
Chirographer	The officer appointed to produce a legal document (chirographs) to collect fines in the Court of Common Pleas.
Close Rolls	Records kept by the royal chancery office. These were letters issued and sealed by the monarch to grant special rights, titles, grants to persons or corporations. Each year, the chancery would sew these parchments together into one long roll as a record of that year's letters close.
Engross	To produce a legal document in its final form.
Gaol Delivery	The trial of prisoners held in gaol upon charges for which they were imprisoned. It is not delivering a prisoner *to* the gaol, but rather 'deliverance' *from* gaol, albeit to a trial.
Gyb	Common name for a cat in this period, short for 'Gilbert' as one might call a male cat 'Tom' today. The 'g' is a hard g, as in 'go', the 'y' a short 'i' sound.
In Flagrante Delicto	Latin for in 'blazing offense' or caught in the act of committing an offense.

Sometimes referring to being caught in the sexual act.

King's Bench A trial or presentation before the king, following the king wherever he might go in the realm. To cut down on the many cases presented before the king, the Court of Common Pleas was created and stayed in one place rather than having to follow the king's itinerary. That one place was Westminster Hall and later also included the Guildhall in London.

Letters Patent A type of legal instrument issued by a monarch to grant an office, right, or other status.

Liripipe The long tail at the back of a hood, often wrapped around the wearer's shoulders and neck because it was so long.

Mainprise A surety of money, making certain a man will appear in court. A bond.

Nisi Prius Latin, meaning 'unless first.' A *nisi prius* is a procedure to which a party FIRST agrees UNLESS he objects. Also a court of jurisdiction; the original trial court that heard the case.

Outlaw Outside the protection of the law. By three times refusing to appear at one's trial, the suspect is declared an outlaw and can be killed on sight or brought back to gaol and executed without further trial.

Oyer and Terminer A commission that empowers justices to 'hear (oyer) and determine (terminer)' certain cases.

Quinzaine Fifteen of something; people, stanzas, days, weeks, etc.

Stew Brothel.

Sennight One week. Seven nights, or se'n nights.

Small Beer Beer/ale with lower alcoholic content.
Trailbaston Commissions of Oyer and Terminer for violent cases, like murder.
Wain A small cart.

Who can tell truly
How cruel sheriffs are?
Of their hardness to poor people
No tale can go too far.
If a man cannot pay
They drag him here and there,
They put him on assizes,
The juror's oath to swear.
He dares not breathe a murmur,
Or he has to pay again,
And the saltness of the sea
Is less bitter than his pain.

Song Against Sheriffs, c. 1200

'Iff he goth to the law there is no helpe; for trewly law goys as lorsdship biddeth him.'

Preacher sermonizing to the poor,
early fourteenth century

ONE

London, 1389
Wednesday, 14 October

His head snapped up for the second time. Definitely drifting off to sleep. Too much wine . . . as usual.

Crispin Guest licked his lips and settled his chin unsteadily on his hand once more. A horn cup sat at his fingertips. Looking down, he saw it was almost empty. What was left in the jug was, thankfully, just a hand's reach away on the spotty table. The pleasant sounds of others drinking and laughing around him reminded he was in his favorite tavern, and though it wasn't as often these days that he felt morose enough to drink alone, he found a certain comfort in the friendly noises around him, even if he himself never participated in their jovial camaraderie.

A contented lassitude kept his head muzzy, and that was fine. He didn't have to move, didn't have to think. Wasn't that the point of filling himself with wine at the Boar's Tusk?

He'd just about convinced himself that closing his eyes was a good idea when someone beside him nudged his shoulder. He flicked a lazy glance at the unfamiliar profile, ignored it, and settled down once more . . . when it happened again.

He turned to the man in the dark cloak, clearing his throat to give him a rounding, when something hard was shoved at his gut.

'Here,' croaked the shadowed man with a hoarse voice. 'Take it. There isn't much time.'

'What? Take what?'

The thing was shoved at him again, and this time Crispin grabbed it. A money pouch, bulging with coins. His eyes widened and looked down at it. 'What in the name of Heaven is this?'

'Your payment, of course. By my Lady, I thought they said you were smarter than this.'

Affronted, Crispin swiveled to tell the man to shove the coin purse up his arse when the man said harshly, 'The address is inside the bag. Have done with it quickly. It must be tonight. And make it quiet.'

Blinking, trying to clear his head, Crispin took a deep breath. 'You mistake me, sir.'

'No, you mistake me. Do it, or I'll not be responsible for what happens to you. They want her dead and that's an end to it. That's enough silver, I'll warrant, to satisfy any man. Get it done. Tonight.'

'Now . . . wait . . .' It took too long to untangle his legs from the bench, and when he'd freed himself the man was gone. He looked down at the pouch and opened the top. A folded piece of parchment was there, sitting atop a clutch of silver coins. 'God's blood!' he gasped. He hadn't seen that much money in a pouch of his in over a decade.

Turning back to the table, he unfolded the parchment and flattened it out. It read:

> *Elizabeth le Porter*
> *Watling Street between the roper and the eel monger, second floor*

He shook out his head. His shaggy hair stuck to the sweat at his brow. What had just transpired? That man had obviously mistaken Crispin for someone else. A someone who, by all accounts, was some sort of paid assassin.

He looked down into the coin pouch again. This woman, whoever she was, was supposed to be killed and this the payment for it. It was God's mercy indeed that the man had stumbled upon Crispin instead of the real killer.

Crispin whipped his head up, looking around. Did anyone here have the face of a killer? He ran his hand over his cheeks and chin. God's blood, they *all* did. Wait, wait. The man had been looking for a 'type' of man. A man alone, as Crispin was. For a second time, he scanned the tavern, slowly, carefully. There were a few men who were alone. One appeared to be a rich merchant. Another some sort of student. And another . . . dead drunk, his arms pillowing his head.

The fat merchant didn't seem likely, nor the timid student. And what was he to do in any case? Go up to each one, bow with an 'I beg your mercy, but are you, by any chance, a paid assassin?'

There was little choice in the matter. He had to find this woman, this Elizabeth le Porter, and warn her that someone was out to kill her. He could do that much at least.

He grabbed the edge of the table and pushed himself to his feet. Standing for a moment – gauging as to whether or not he could – he shoved away from the table, stumbling over the bench before he righted himself. He looked back regretfully at the jug of wine. Straightening his cotehardie with a tug, he angled his head to crack his aching neck. It was time for the Tracker to do his moral duty.

Sometimes, he really hated that sense of honor.

A light drizzle greeted him as he emerged from the noisy tavern. The cold served to awaken him, and he dragged his hood up over his head. Beyond the clouds, the horizon was streaked with the amber light of an autumn sunset. And just as he wondered exactly how late it was, church bells began to peal Vespers. Later than he thought, then.

His cloak had absorbed the friendly smoke from the hearth, but now the drizzle was drenching it to the odor of wet dog. He pulled it about him and shivered. He crossed West Cheap to Friday Street, skirting carts laden with dampening peat. Their thick, dark smell overpowered. Townsfolk bustled toward the eaves of shops and houses, ducking under their own hoods to get out of the rain.

Friday Street let out onto the pungent Watling, and Crispin stood at the 'T' looking up one way and down the other. Between a roper and an eel monger. He squinted into the mist unsteadily. What he truly wanted to do was get this business over with so he could go home and crawl into bed. Perhaps Jack would have some sort of hot stew waiting for him.

'Good old Jack,' he murmured, smiling sloppily. Why had he left the lad at home while he'd gone off to drink? Oh yes. He had been feeling particularly sorry for himself, for it had been a month since they had gotten a proper client, and the cupboard was bare yet again. He had begun thinking of lost chances, lost loves, and it had somehow spiraled downward into a wallow of pity. Jack had tried to assuage him with watered wine, but they had quickly run out. Poverty stank like a chamber pot.

'Not the boy's fault, though,' he decided, nodding his head. Jack didn't deserve him. He didn't deserve Jack. Only the two thoughts meant something entirely different.

He reached into his hood to scratch at his hair. What was he doing here again? Oh yes.

He staggered forward, checking the signs hanging before the shops. A plump woman with a furred chaperone hood slammed into him. 'Why don't you watch where you're going, churl!' she said, righting herself and inspecting him.

Crispin did his best to bow, but with nearly two jugs of wine in him, it was sloppy at best. 'I beg your mercy,' he said.

She scoffed. 'Drunk!' Pushing past him she ambled up the lane.

He bowed to her retreating figure with a 'Madam!' He watched her move along the muddy street before he swiveled back to survey the signs above the shops. Surely he should be looking for a coil of rope. Ah! There! A *knotted* rope, then. A piece of rope, as thick as a child's arm, hung from a hook above a door, dripping rain-water. Crispin checked and two doors down was a man with eels in a barrel, rolling those barrels into his shop for the night.

In between, was a door with no sign at all.

His shoulder was knocked again, this time by a man in a dark, billowing cloak. The man barely looked up from under his hood and grunted an apology. Crispin bowed with his hand over his heart, but the man continued on. Crispin tried to mind where he was going, waiting as a man pulling a rope leash tied around the horns of a particularly stubborn goat tugged his charge, splashing up mud and water until, with an angry grunt, he got behind the creature and kicked it. It trotted forward and he jogged to keep pace with it.

Once all was clear, Crispin walked up to the blank door and knocked. He waited, but after a time there was no answer.

The eel man had finally moved his barrels and turned toward Crispin. 'You'll never get an answer that way. Go in and up the stairs.'

He swiveled toward the man, a stout fellow in a blood-stained apron. He smelled of the Thames. 'Should I?'

'It's only a covered stair. Private like. It's never locked.'

'Oh. Much thanks.' He offered a jerky bow and pushed the door open. It was, indeed, merely a staircase with arrowslits in the wooden walls to let in the light. Crispin hugged the wall and trudged upward into the darkened passage, slipping only once. At the top of the stair he found another door and knocked.

The door opened, and a woman in a blue cotehardie stood in the doorway. He might have gasped in surprise at her unexpected loveliness, but he couldn't be certain if he truly had or simply imagined it. Large eyes enquired, and the curl of her brown hair lay over one shoulder, picking up the firelight behind her in a golden haze. 'Yes? Who are you?'

He rallied and bowed. 'I am Crispin Guest, demoiselle. Do I have the pleasure of addressing Elizabeth le Porter?'

She leaned against the doorsill and quirked a smile. 'The pleasure, is it?' Her speech was common, that of a merchant or servant, but it didn't detract from her beauty or her bearing. 'Aye. That's me. Oi, Crispin Guest. I've heard that name before.'

'No doubt. I am called the Tracker.'

'Oh! I *have* heard of you, then. Have you come here *tracking*?' It was said with a sly grin. Appealing.

'Well . . .' The money pouch was still in his hand. 'The thing of it is, demoiselle . . . may I come in to talk?'

She stepped aside and he found himself in a modest room, with a warm fire, a table, a coffer, and a sideboard. There was another room beyond with a bed with bed curtains. It was certainly better furnished than his own one-room lodgings. She closed the door, and the play of light touched her face with gold, the contours with shadow. 'Will you have ale?'

Thinking he already might have had too much to drink, he nevertheless nodded. 'If it's no trouble.'

'No trouble,' she said, and moved to the sideboard. She poured from a jug into two ceramic cups. She gave him one while she sipped hers. 'Sit, Master Guest. It is an honor to entertain you in my humble lodgings.'

He did so, gratefully. She sat opposite. It was comfortable in this warm room before the generous fire. He wondered what it was she did for a living, for the room was well-appointed, unexpectedly so. 'Demoiselle, I have strange news to impart to you.'

'Do you?' She seemed more amused by his presence than anything else. 'It's rather exciting, isn't it? A visit from London's celebrated Tracker. And so late in the day.'

He drank down his ale and set the cup aside. Leaning forward, he tried for a solemn expression, but it was difficult when faced with those expressive brows, that playful smile. 'I shouldn't quite characterize it in that way.' He cleared his throat. 'Demoiselle, this may come as a shock. But earlier this evening a man came to me with payment and instructions to find you. To find you and . . . dispatch you.'

'Dispatch me? What does that mean?'

'To kill you.'

The cup lifting to her lips stopped. 'Kill me?' There was shock on her face, but something else as well. He had the impression that perhaps she wasn't all that surprised. 'And . . . *are* you going to kill me, Master Guest?'

He sputtered. 'Of course not! I came here to warn you!'

She sat back in her seat again. 'Well, that is a relief.'

'Do you know of anyone who might wish to do such a thing? And to hire someone to do the deed?'

The smirk was back, and she lifted the cup all the way and downed the ale in one. 'Aye. Maybe I do. They'll not get away with it either! The nerve.' She looked hard at him. 'Tell me, is this the sort of thing that I can hire the Tracker for? But then again, I already know the vile cur what did this. It'd be a fine thing to send the Tracker to him. Leap out of his skin, he will. Teach him to try to frighten me.'

Crispin measured the money pouch in his hand and finally dropped it into the empty pouch at his belt. 'Indeed. And don't worry about payment. I have already been paid.' He patted the pouch.

Her eyes lingered there for a moment. 'Well now!' She rose. 'This calls for more ale.'

Crispin didn't complain as she filled his cup again. She sipped and watched him. He concentrated on sitting upright. 'I've heard quite a bit about you,' she said.

'Oh?' He drank. Either he was reviled for his past or distinguished for his present vocation. It was obviously the latter this time.

'Tell me.' Her voice was like dark silk. 'Tell me of some of your adventures.'

He sighed and sat back, laying his head against the chair. 'Shouldn't you rather tell me whom you suspect of sending an assassin to your door?'

The cup was at her lips. 'That can wait.'

He considered. He should be leaving. After all, he had discharged his duties. But he found himself still sitting. 'As for adventures, there are many. But, er, should we not concentrate on your safety first?'

'But I am safe with you, am I not? Tell me.' She scooted farther to the edge of her seat.

What to say? His first thought was to get her out of her lodgings, situate her somewhere else. But that thought fled through his spirit-muddled mind. Instead, he was awash in her flattery and the eager press of her excitement, her parted lips, her wide curious eyes. He wasn't usually given much for flattery, but a pretty woman offering it, and he in his muddled state . . .

'Well, a time or two I was in fear of my life.'

'You? Afraid? I find that hard to believe.'

'It's true, demoiselle. There are some miscreants that are worth fearing. Caution is always wise. It keeps my wits sharp.'

She leaned so far over she was able to touch his hand, and then her fingers curled around his wrist. 'The tales I've heard . . . you were so brave. Truly a knight.'

'As you know, demoiselle – indeed, as all London knows – I am no longer a knight.'

'And that was brave, too.'

He scowled. 'Treason isn't brave.'

'But you rose above it, didn't you? King Richard thought to best you, send you low. But you made something of yourself. He can't take that away.'

'I beg you, demoiselle, not to speak those sentiments aloud. That is dangerous talk.'

She tossed her head back. 'I heard the stories. How you fought for your mentor, the Duke of Lancaster. You supported him as king. And you paid the price.'

He hated speaking of it. Wanted to rise and take his leave, but the wine was settling hard within him and he couldn't muster the strength. 'That was a long time ago.'

Her hand was still on his wrist, but now it was caressing salaciously up and down his arm. 'Let's have a story, then. Tell me of your last exploit.'

'Demoiselle . . .'

'Elizabeth,' she said shyly.

'Elizabeth. I think it wise that you find other accommodations for the night. I don't think it safe for you here. The man who paid me might discover his mistake.'

'Where would I go?' There was less of a question and more of an invitation in her gaze.

'I . . .' Was he fool enough to offer? Better to put her up at an inn. He had the coin now. But there was something about her earnest expression that stayed the proposal. 'I could . . . stay here . . . I suppose. If you think it fitting.'

She threw herself from her chair to kneel at his feet. 'Very fitting. Ah, you are a gallant knight, Master Guest. Crispin, if I may call you so.'

'Not a knight,' he grumbled, but her compelling gaze caught him, enchanted him, and he leaned over to take her outstretched hands. 'I will do what I can.'

'Will you?' Was she leaning closer? That charming smile softened until her lips were parted most fetchingly. He wasn't certain who moved the rest of the way, but he found himself suddenly kissing her.

As her moist lips meshed with his, he tried weakly to reckon why he *was* kissing her, but with the opening of her lips and her tongue's exploration, he soon left off thinking altogether. His arms encircled her, and he heaved her up to his lap. That was better. He didn't have to lean over in that uncomfortable manner, could get considerably closer to her, fill his nose with the musky scent of her. A familiar heat carved down his abdomen and pooled below his belly with a surprising warmth. She shifted in his arms, and her fingers tugged harshly at his hair, keeping his mouth tight to hers.

Soon eager hands were at his cotehardie, unbuttoning, and lips followed those hands, nipping at his throat. He let her. There hadn't been opportunity of late to indulge in such pursuits.

And he was too drunk to scold himself as to exactly why he shouldn't now.

He stumbled up from his seat, and still kissing, she maneuvered him to the other room, toward the single candle that lit the space with its soft golden glow, to the bed, to sweet rapture, and then oblivion.

His head pounded to the rhythm of the church bells. Fearing to open his eyes lest he vomit, he dug his face into the coolness of the pillow to hide from the sunlight coloring his lids, and he wondered vaguely if Jack was up and making a porridge as he did most mornings. It might settle his stomach. He certainly needed some ale to sluice his dry mouth.

'Jack?' he croaked. Where was that knave? 'Jack!' He opened his eyes and blinked, lifted a hand and rubbed at them.

This wasn't his lodgings on the Shambles under the shadow of St Paul's. Where the hell was he?

He lifted his face from the cold spot of drool he had left on the pillow but let it fall again when the pounding became sharp stabs into the backs of his eyes. *Now wait. Wait. Think, Crispin.* Last night he had gone to the Boar's Tusk and had drunk his fill of wine. Of course he did. And then . . . 'The man,' he rasped. That strange dark man had pressed a coin purse into his hand with instructions to . . .

With divine effort, he pushed himself upright, balancing on his two arms. He looked down. He was naked.

Then he remembered the woman, Elizabeth. He remembered creamy limbs, a long throat, and a sultry laugh. 'Demoiselle?' he said softly. He turned, but the bed was empty. The indent in the pillow told of her past presence. He crawled to the edge of the bed and sat. 'Elizabeth?' he said louder to the outer room.

He swallowed, took a breath, and stood. He wavered there for a moment, wondering what his stomach would decide to do. It roiled but stayed where it was. Grateful, he scratched at his hair and shuffled to the doorway.

'Demoiselle, I . . . I apologize for . . . for last night . . .'

She seemed to be lounging before the hearth, her chemise rucked up to her knees. The fire didn't seem warm enough to keep a chill at bay from all that pale flesh. 'What are you . . .?'

But as his eyes focused, he realized the angle of her limbs was all wrong. He sucked in a breath and slid to the floor beside her.

'Elizabeth!'

Legs lay one way, but her torso was twisted the other. She was looking up blank-eyed to the ceiling. Dark bruises purpled that otherwise creamy neck. He didn't need to touch her to know that she was dead.

TWO

Thursday, 15 October

Crispin pushed his hand through his hair again. He stared down at her body. Her *corpse*, he corrected. What the hell happened? Why couldn't he remember? He knew he had been drunk, but . . .

He fell back into one of the chairs, panting. How could she be dead? Strangled? It couldn't have been . . . it wasn't . . .

He held his trembling hands before his face and stared at them. Surely . . . surely *he* couldn't have done it? Not even drunk could he have done it. Could he?

Dropping his head into his hands, he breathed hard through his fingers. His mind stalled. He couldn't imagine himself in such a state, especially when intoxicated, but there was no other explanation.

Unless . . .

He raised his head. That man. That man from the Boar's Tusk. Crispin's head hurt, but he screwed up his eyes and concentrated. Yes. He recalled it. And gave him . . . 'A bag of silver!' He ran back into the bedchamber and scrabbled amidst the bedclothes that had fallen to the floor. He cast them aside to search for his cotehardie, his belt, his money pouch . . . there! He grabbed the pouch, still heavy from the bag of coins and wrenched it free. He sat back on the floor against the bed, sighing with relief.

But wait. All it proved was that he had been paid a sum of coins to kill this woman . . . who was now dead. It didn't look good for him. Not at all. He lay back against the bed's post and stared at the ceiling. What was he to do? He *had* to get the sheriffs. But tell them what? Tell them he had wandered by and guessed there was a dead body in this room? Tell them he was called by an unknown person to investigate?

Tell them . . . the truth? And hope for mercy?

'Blessed Lord God,' he whispered, 'if there was ever a time

You were listening to me, I beg of it now. What, by Your precious blood, am I to do?'

He sat that way for a long moment before he creakily rose. First things first. Get dressed. The simple act of pushing legs into stockings, buttoning his cotehardie, fastening his belt, served to calm. Dressed once more he approached it logically. He checked the bedchamber first. The window was shuttered and locked. Had it been that way when he had first entered it last night? 'Think, Crispin,' he muttered. He glared at it and seemed to recall the darkness of the room, lit only by a candle. Yes, yes, he was almost certain it was locked. It was closed at least.

He took a steadying breath and crossed the threshold into the main room again. Her body lay sprawled unnaturally before the dwindling glow of the hearth.

He knelt and gently touched her arm, the one farthest from the coals. Quite cold. He attempted to move it. Stiff. Made sense. He had arrived near Vespers and it was nearly Terce now, more than thirteen hours ago.

He touched the bruises gently, so bright against her now especially pale skin. Did she fight her assailant? He examined her hand, the more movable one by the fire. Blood and skin beneath her nails. Yes, she fought. Crispin felt his face and neck. Nothing. No scratches, and equally none on his chest and arms. Relief as he had never known flooded him. It wasn't him. He hadn't done it! Thank Christ for that!

But . . . that still left some unknown assailant that had crept into the room while he slept and she had . . . what? Gone to the door? Opened it in the dead of night?

He shot a glance toward the door. Closed but not barred. But of course not. Only Crispin remained in the room. The assailant had strangled her and left, leaving her for dead to be discovered this way. A husband, maybe? She wore no ring. A lover, who saw Crispin abed and dead to the world? But too much of a coincidence what with the man who had hired Crispin to kill her. Had Crispin been made to be a dupe, to be blamed for the murder? How did they know Crispin would stay, would be in this precarious state? Unless the man who paid him was also her lover.

It was too much for him. He couldn't do this on his own. Sheriffs . . . or Jack?

He fixed his chaperon hood over his shoulders and lifted the leather hood up over his head. Eyes scanning the room, his gaze fell again on her. *I'm so sorry I didn't protect you, Elizabeth. But I swear to you that I will find the one who did this.*

He scanned the room once more, looking for clues, trying to leave it as he had found it. Except . . . He stalked to where he had left his cup of ale. He cast the dregs into the fire, dried it with his cloak, and set the cup back on the sideboard. Just in case.

And now he had irretrievably compromised the room. Whatever investigation ensued from this, the truth was forever tainted.

He shook his head. *He* was the truth. He knew what *hadn't* happened at least. But could he prove it?

When he reached the door, he opened it a sliver and peered down the private stair. No one there. He closed the door silently behind him, tread lightly down the stairwell, and when he got to the bottom, peered cautiously around the edge of the door. The eel monger was busy elsewhere, and he saw nothing of the roper. Hood up, cloak about him, he stole onto Watling Street, feeling as guilty as any thief or ruffian that ever was.

He hurried up Friday Street to West Cheap and went west as it became the Shambles. Farther it changed again to Newgate Market where the gate and prison stood, where the sheriffs could be found. He stopped at the tinker shop. His lodgings were above it up a rickety stair. Jack was up there.

'Oi, Crispin,' called out his landlord, Martin Kemp. He walked out of his shop and laid a polished cup on his outside table, hoping for business.

'Er . . . good morning, Martin.'

'Oh, I see. Just getting in, are you? For shame, Crispin.' Though he smiled the whole time. Perhaps he envied Crispin his unmarried state.

Crispin forgot him and stared down the Shambles toward Newgate Market again. The curve of the road hid Newgate, the prison.

To Jack . . . or the sheriffs?

He snorted at himself. He was no fool. He nodded to Martin, turned on his heel, and trotted up the outside stair to his lodgings. Once he fitted the key in the lock, he pushed through the door.

'I was wondering when you'd get in,' said Jack, busy at the fire. 'First the Prime bells rung, and then Terce, and I thought to m'self, "Master Crispin must be having quite a night."' He chuckled. 'Well, if you're needing it, the porridge is ready. And I even have hot water for your shave if you haven't had one already. Didn't spend the night at the Boar's Tusk, I'll warrant. So who is she, if I might be so bold as to ask?' He turned and nearly dropped the pot with the porridge. 'God blind me, Master Crispin! You look terrible. What happened?'

Crispin collapsed into the chair and slumped. 'God's blood, Jack. Something horrible. I am in very deep trouble.'

Jack set the pot back on the hook over the fire. He wiped his hands on a rag and stood over his master. 'Tell me, master. Tell me how I can help you?'

'If only you were there last night. But no. I . . .' He pushed his hood back and yanked his scrip open. Pulling out the coin pouch, he dumped it on the table. It broke open, spilling silver coins over the worn wood.

'God's blood!' Jack swore. 'Where'd you get that!'

'It was payment . . . for murder.'

'Murder? W-who'd you murder?'

'I murdered no one, you fool. Last night at the Boar's Tusk, I was mistaken for a paid assassin. A man, a strange man with a rasping voice, shoved this at me with instructions about a woman I was to murder.'

'Wait. Why did he hire *you* to do it?'

'He obviously mistook me for someone else. He did not know who I was.'

'By my Lady. So what happened?' Jack grabbed the stool and dragged it across the floor in front of Crispin and sat. He drew up his long legs beneath him.

'I thought it best to warn the poor woman. So I went to the address on Watling, found her, and . . . well, told her.'

'And what did she say? I'll wager she was grateful.'

Crispin raised an ironic brow. 'You could say that.'

Jack stared for a moment before he rocked back, grabbing at his hair. 'You didn't! God's blood and bones, you didn't! Master Crispin!'

He gnarled his hands into fists. 'I was drunk! She was beautiful. I . . . I . . . have no excuse.'

Jack smoldered. 'Well then. No harm done. And you've got this pouch of silver.'

'No, no, Jack. Very much harm was done, for when I awoke this morning, I found her . . . dead. Murdered.'

Jaw slack, Jack's eyes widened to mazers. 'M-murdered? Master Crispin . . . it wasn't . . . you didn't . . .'

'No, thank God. It was not me.'

Jack's hand dropped to his heart and he blew out a noisy breath. 'You gave me a fright.'

'But Jack. I was the only one there. I am still in very great peril. I must go to the sheriffs.'

'You mustn't tell them you was there, sir. They'll muddle it all up. Best make up a story.'

'I can't. I tried every which way to accommodate that, but I can't. I can't lie about it.'

'But sir! Look at the position you are in. Someone gave you money to kill her. And there you were, with a dead body!' He dropped to his knees before Crispin and grabbed his sleeves. 'No one knows, Master Crispin. No one but you and me.'

'And God.' He shook his head. 'I cannot lie. Too many lies I have known, Jack. Too many have brought me low. I cannot live with myself if I forswore my oaths before the King's Bench.'

'But . . . Master Crispin. You do realize that they'll arrest *you* for the murder.'

'I'm . . . rather hoping they won't.'

Jack scrambled to his feet, and his face became nearly as red as his hair. 'But you know they will!' He began to pace across the little room. 'What are you thinking? That they'll be fair to you? That they will find you innocent? They're just looking for an excuse to rid themselves of you once and for all. And the king! Blind me, he'd be happy to hang you. What are you thinking, Master Crispin?' He stopped. 'Wait. You can seek sanctuary. Go to St Paul's.'

'Only guilty people seek sanctuary, Jack.'

'Then . . . escape to Southwark. That's out of their jurisdiction. They can't arrest you there.'

'I cannot run from the truth.'

'It won't matter if they hang you just the same. Oh, master! Why? Why did you lay with that woman?'

'I was drunk,' he muttered feebly.

'You're always drunk!'

Crispin's head snapped up and he narrowed his bloodshot eyes at the boy.

He had always thought of him as 'the boy' but surely that was no longer the case. Jack was seventeen and certainly no boy. He had the makings of a fine ginger beard running along his jaw and a moderate mustache under his nose. As tall as Crispin, perhaps someday he'd be as broad-shouldered, but for now, he was angular and slender, though it belied a strength and agility unmatched by his betters . . . of which there were many.

And Jack glared with a bearing he seemed to have gleaned from Crispin. At least it was suspiciously familiar.

'Aye, I know I'm speaking out of turn,' Jack went on, 'but who else will tell you? Oh the Langtons have been telling you for years and you've ignored it for just as long. But now you're hearing it from me. So. Maybe it's time you stop getting drunk. Look at you. You were once a great man. Aye, we all know it. And you've made yourself into a great man again. You don't need drink, Master Crispin.'

'Jack . . .' He lowered his face. How many times had he gotten himself into mischief because of drink? He had thought of it as his only means of comfort, yet now there was Jack . . . and a chess set, and even a book or two, these days. Yes, he still mourned for the losses of his former life, but the boy – the young man – made sense more often than not, as he always seemed to do.

'What's done is done,' he said gruffly. Embarrassed to raise his head to his own apprentice, Crispin contemplated his fate by staring at the fire. If he turned himself in to the sheriffs it would be the perfect opportunity for them to arrest and try *him* for the crime. 'The only solution would appear to be that we must solve this murder before they hang me for it.'

'But Master Crispin! Haven't you been listening to me? They won't give you the chance to try. They'll hang you and be happy.'

'I won't hide from this, Tucker. I'm surprised you think so little of me.'

'It's not that, master, you know it isn't. I don't want no harm to come to you.'

When Crispin looked up, Jack wore the saddest expression he'd yet seen on him. He reached out to grasp the boy's wrist. 'I know. But knowing me as you have for these past six years, I would think you would understand.'

Jack swallowed a few times. His eyes were suspiciously bright. 'I . . . I do understand, sir. I understand more than you know.'

He nodded. 'Very well. I came first to you so that we could make a plan. Investigate a bit before we go to Newgate.'

'Oh. Then . . . what are we standing around here for? Let's go!' He grabbed Crispin's arm and dragged him toward the door. Jack grabbed his cloak from the peg and whipped it over his shoulders. 'Where to?'

'Back to Watling Street.'

Crispin hung back in the shadows. The working day was in the peak of activity, with apprentices and women carrying bundles of their purchases. Cries from the merchants cast up, one after the other in a chant to compete with the best of any monk's quire.

The roper, wrapped warm in his fur-trimmed cloak, wandered in and out of his shop, positioning coils of rope, and the eel monger was at his barrels. He sported a red hood, with its long liripipe wrapped around his neck this morning to ward off the chill.

Crispin sent Jack alone up the woman's stairwell when no one was looking.

He called on all the patience he had to stand without moving, waiting for Jack to return. His usual stoic nature made no issue of such waiting, but this was decidedly different. He couldn't help but stare at the door to the stairwell until his eyes burned. *Hurry, Jack*, was all he could think.

Finally, the boy emerged and stealthily made his way to Crispin in the gloom.

'Well?' he asked softly.

Jack crossed himself. 'She's dead, that's a certainty.'

'What of the room?'

He shook his head. His sharp eyes darted here and there along the street, making certain there was no one close enough to overhear them. 'As you said it. She did not bar the door after you came in?'

'No. At least I don't recall her doing so.'

'He could have come in that way. Just as easily as I did just now. I saw naught that could indicate who the whoreson was. But naught that implicates you either, master.'

'I must find the man who hired me.'

'How will you ever do that?'

'I don't know.'

'And what about . . .' He thumbed upward toward the stair, hiding his gesture into his chest. 'Won't she begin to, well . . . stink?' he whispered.

Crispin blanched. His stomach was still on the delicate side, and the fact that he had been intimate with her – not that he could remember much – soured his belly. 'You're right, of course. Something must be done.'

Crispin grew silent as he tried to figure out just what *could* be done. By law, *he* should have called the hue and cry. But he feared to be arrested.

He had recognized nothing of the man who had accosted him at the Boar's Tusk. There was no clue as to how to even begin to find him. Unless someone at the tavern recognized him. But he had had his hood up. And Crispin would wager all in that pouch of silver that the stranger had chosen the Boar's Tusk in which to meet because no one *would* know him there.

But Jack was still worrying about the body. He offered various schemes to let the sheriffs know, including writing an anonymous missive and slipping it somehow to the sheriffs in Newgate.

And while he talked, Crispin's gaze followed a young boy, bucket in hand, marching up to the stairwell door and casting it open. Whistling, the boy tromped up the stairs.

Crispin patted Jack's shoulder and pointed. Tucker stopped talking and turned. 'Blind me, master. Should we stop him?'

'No. I'm afraid he's going to do the job we are both too cowardly to do.'

It was a measure of how serious the situation was that Jack

didn't bristle at the remark. Instead, they both watched with anxious anticipation the door that had been left open. Even amid the bustle of the street, they could still hear the boy's merry whistling and then his knock upon her lodgings door. 'Mistress le Por-ter!' the boy called and then opened the door. A shriek sounded a heartbeat later, and then the bucket with its water, tumbled, clattered, and sloshed down the stairs. The boy came running after it, bounding onto the street, looking both ways with wide, terrified eyes. He ran first to the eel monger, grabbing his arm and sputtering his news. The eel monger in turn ran next door and yelled at the top of his lungs to the floor above. A woman opened the shutters and leaned down. Her hand flew to her mouth and she retreated inside.

Crispin looked at Jack. 'And so it begins.'

Crispin waited with Jack in the shadows. He mulled over his own inactions, trying to reconcile what to do with what had already transpired. When the sheriffs arrived on their horses and their men-at-arms on foot, he straightened, and Jack anxiously scoured Crispin's face for any clues as to what he was going to do.

'These are the newly elected sheriffs, are they not?' whispered Jack.

'Yes. The ginger-haired fellow on the white stallion is John Walcote . . .'

'Oi! Is he any relation to . . . to . . .'

'No. He is unrelated to . . . Philippa Walcote's husband Clarence.' Just saying her name caused the bruise in his heart to ache again. He had met her some six years ago, had fallen in love, and had let her go. The pain of it had never left him, though Jack would be the first to tell him he had never tried. He harbored that small portrait of her under his mattress. It was partly the reason he had overindulged last night. And every time he saw the sheriff it only opened the wound again.

'And the other sheriff?'

Crispin's eyes rose to the dark-haired man, whose sallow face was drawn longer and more solemn with its black beard. 'John Loveney.'

'Have you met them yet, sir?'

'Yes.'

Jack didn't probe for more. The boy knew better than to do so.

The sheriffs dismounted and looked up at the building. They instructed their men to await them on the street while the two of them trudged up the stairs.

Crispin hated waiting, but he and Jack did so, both sets of eyes glued to the window above, watching the shadows pass by the slit in the shutters.

'What's taking so long?' he muttered.

'Wait, master. Look.'

The two sheriffs emerged from the covered stair and looked around. The eel monger was nearby, running anxious hands over his apron when they approached him. They conferred for some time, with the sheriff's clerk, Hamo Eckington, writing furiously on his portable desk balanced by straps on his shoulders.

Sheriff Walcote had moved on to an older woman in a fine gown and fur-trimmed cloak. She brushed Crispin with just a whiff of familiarity, but nothing more. Sheriff Loveney had moved on to another man in a dark mud-spattered mantle who was nodding as he spoke.

The poor clerk jumped from one conversation to another, writing down his notes as quickly as he could. But when Sheriff Walcote ticked a finger on his lip in thought and stepped away from the woman who seemed to be correcting Hamo the clerk by pointing at his parchment, Walcote looked up suddenly and spotted Crispin in the shadows.

Crispin straightened as the sheriff threw back his cloak and strode across the muddy way directly for Crispin. Jack straightened too, chin high.

'The vultures gather,' said Walcote, sweeping Crispin and Jack with his gaze. 'What do you hope to do here, Guest? Get yourself hired by the corpse?'

'I might be of help yet, Lord Sheriff.'

'If you think we are going to hire you, think again. I know too much about you.'

'Then surely you know I solve most of my cases.'

Walcote snorted and pointedly turned away.

Crispin tensed. He needed to speak with the sheriffs but

perhaps not on the streets. After they had gathered their information, then he would go to Newgate and relate his own facts. That seemed the safest and most logical arrangement. Oh, they'd fine him, of course, for he had technically been the First Finder and failed to report it and post his surety. He already decided that he would confess to spending the night there and finding her in the morning. After all, it was the truth, and one need stay as close to the truth as one could when dealing with the law.

He signaled to Jack for them to go and it was when he moved out of the shadows that the man shouted. He turned. The eel monger was pointing at him. 'That's the man I saw!' he cried.

And then the woman turned. 'Yes,' she said, adding her voice to it. 'He bumped me yesterday just before he approached that door.'

Crispin froze. He heard Jack swear beside him.

Walcote turned back and glared. 'Guest. It looks like I'll be talking to you after all.' His lips peeled back into a smile. 'Care to come with us?'

THREE

Thursday, 15 October

'Three witnesses identified you, Guest,' said Walcote. He sat at the table in the sheriff's chamber in Newgate, toying with his dagger. Sheriff Loveney stood beside Hamo at the clerk's writing desk, glancing at Eckington's swift spiky writing.

Crispin stood before them, resignation slumping his shoulders. Jack stood somewhat behind, but Crispin could feel the lad's tension peeling off him in waves.

'The eel monger remembered talking to you as you went into the private stair the evening before. And the woman also remembered you bumping into her . . .'

'Because you were drunk,' Loveney gleefully pointed out, apparently reading it from Hamo's notes.

'And the other man also identified you from the street,' Walcote went on. 'What have you to say for yourself?'

'My lords,' Crispin said with a deep sigh. 'Though it was true that I was . . . intoxicated . . . I was in my full faculties. It was all a series of very odd events.'

He stepped forward and, pulling the pouch of silver from his own scrip, he laid it on the table. The sheriffs' eyes widened. 'I was in the Boar's Tusk quite late last night when I was approached by a man who gave me this silver. He told me I was to kill a woman.'

Walcote slowly rose. 'Master Guest, what . . . what . . .?'

'Precisely, Lord Sheriff. Even as inebriated as I was, I could still tell right from wrong. The man escaped me before he could clarify or I could identify him. I thought it most prudent to see the lady and warn her of impending disaster.'

Loveney moved closer, crossing his arms over his chest. 'A fantastical tale.' He flicked a glance at Jack. God knows what he saw there, but he quickly fastened his gaze back to

Crispin's face. 'One can scarce believe it. Do go on, Master Guest.'

Crispin licked his lips. 'Well . . . I told her. And then . . .'

'Then . . . you left?' asked Loveney.

'Not exactly. She . . . she was . . . most seductive . . .'

Walcote and Loveney exchanged glances. Even the stoic Eckington looked up from his careful transcription.

Loveney cleared his throat. 'So . . . when did you leave?'

'This morning. I . . . I found her as you saw her.'

Loveney pursed his lips. 'And you were just going to leave her thus, without reporting it?'

'I was deciding just what exactly to do, Lord Sheriff. I had forgotten about the eel monger having seen me. And the others . . .'

'By St Katherine, Guest! You left her there?'

'My lords, what was I to do? I am now in the very predicament I was trying to avoid. I wanted to investigate it myself before . . . before all this. I know how it looks.'

'It looks mighty bad, Master Guest,' said Walcote, seating himself again. He ran his hand over his clean-shaven chin. 'But not for us.'

'I know.'

Walcote turned to Loveney and threw his hands up. Loveney asked the obvious. 'Did you kill her?'

'No, I did not. I swear by almighty God.'

'Dammit, Guest.' Walcote slammed his hand to the table. The candle wobbled and spilled its liquid tallow from the flame down its long column. 'I do not like traitors. I do not like smug men. In short, I do not like *you*.'

'And we have three witnesses,' said Loveney.

Crispin lowered his face. 'Yes. I understand your difficulty, Lord Sheriff.'

'Do you?' said Walcote. '"Difficulty" you call it. It is not in the least difficult for us. I should swear out an indictment right now.'

Loveney crossed his arms over his chest. 'We must charge someone with this crime. And we would be very pleased – as would the crown – to charge you.'

'I *was* technically the First Finder . . .'

'And here,' said Walcote, scooping up the pouch, 'your surety. Pray tell us, Master Guest, the reason we should not arrest you now.'

There goes that silver. 'I will have a difficult time investigating the murder if I am incarcerated.'

Loveney scoffed. 'You don't have a very good opinion of our common pleas practices.'

'Forgive me, Lord Sheriff, but as you just said, you would be pleased to charge me. If we rely on those witnesses, then I am the one who is guilty. Which I assure you I am not.'

Walcote sat back and jabbed his dagger into the table where it stuck and quivered. 'You were there. You were drunk. And you committed this murder. Three witnesses say so. I will have no difficulty whatsoever getting an indictment.'

'You say you know me, Lord Sheriff. Is it in my character to murder innocent and unarmed women?'

'You forget that you were amply paid, Master Guest.'

Crispin swung away, stalking toward the fire, arms firmly folded over his chest. 'I *can* prove it, my lords, if only given a chance.'

'You mean a chance to seek sanctuary,' said Loveney.

'Only guilty men seek sanctuary,' said Jack suddenly. Everyone turned to look at him, including Hamo behind his writing desk. 'So my master said,' Jack clarified. 'I begged him to, but he would not go. He wants to solve the crime.'

Walcote studied Crispin under narrowed eyes. The new sheriffs were so newly hatched – only a fortnight into their freshly elected roles in fact – that they had yet to work with or interfere in Crispin's cases. But as the former sheriffs had surely told them, Crispin did his job with discretion and alacrity. And was so skilled, in fact, that he often embarrassed the sheriffs when they got it wrong. Though they begrudged him, harangued him, belittled him, there was little denying his proficiency. Crispin could see all of that play out on Walcote's face, and Loveney wasn't far behind.

Walcote grabbed his dagger again, curling his fingers around the hilt until they whitened into a fist. 'This is damnable,' he rasped. 'I don't trust you not to run.'

'And neither do I,' said the other sheriff.

'What if the recorder discovers we allowed him his freedom?'

'I think Master Guest's reputation . . .' Loveney began, and then scowled.

'*We become just by performing just actions,*' quoted Crispin, '*temperate by performing temperate actions, brave by performing brave actions*. My lords, I give you my solemn oath – on my honor – that I will perform my task in all haste and with truth as my lodestone.'

'A brave action indeed by letting a murderer discover his version of the truth,' muttered Walcote.

Loveney winced. 'We aren't allowing this, are we?'

Walcote's face was a study of indecision. Crispin knew his thoughts. They could try Crispin and be done with it. But there was the tiniest niggling doubt that he might just be innocent. And they well knew Crispin was the only competent man to discover it.

'In the interest of justice,' said Walcote with a sly look, 'we will allow a certain amount of latitude. But you report to us *daily*, Master Guest. You are charged with finding the murderer of Elizabeth le Porter. Bring them or their name to us without delay. Should you bolt on us, I swear by all that is holy that I shall hunt you down myself. And I will make certain that a very unpleasant punishment awaits.'

Crispin grimaced as he bowed. 'I understand, my lords. Thank you for your confidence.'

'I have no such thing,' growled Walcote.

Crispin pivoted and directed Jack toward Eckington's desk. 'Tucker, get the names and addresses of the witnesses.' He didn't stop but kept walking from the sheriff's chamber, amazed that he was still a free man and hoping to remain so by getting out of their sight.

Down the stairs, out the arch, and he was standing on Newgate Market, reflecting on last night's events. If he had only awoken. If he had only convinced her to leave!

He felt Jack at his shoulder and stepped out onto the street, with the boy walking beside him. 'Where to first, Master Crispin?'

'I want you to question the witnesses, Jack. And perhaps find others who might have seen someone approach the door later that night. The killer came sometime between Vespers and Terce.

Yes, I realize that is a wide span of time, but someone might have seen.'

'What will you be doing?'

'I need to discover who this Elizabeth le Porter was.'

'Very well. I'm off then, sir. God keep you.'

'And you, Jack. I need not tell you I am relying upon you.'

Jack grinned. 'As good as done, sir.' He sprinted away to the first address. Crispin watched him grimly. He knew the sheriffs would be impatient about this. They wouldn't wait forever.

He looked up Newgate Market toward the Shambles. Why had someone wanted to kill that woman? Did she know something dangerous about someone? Had she threatened someone somehow? And when Crispin had told her about this contract on her life, she had not seemed as surprised as one should be. Even flippant about it. Maybe she hadn't believed him . . . but no. She had, hadn't she? And what's more, seemed to know more about it than she should have.

As for morals, she had taken Crispin to her bed readily enough. She was no stranger to carnal pleasures. It was possible she was a prostitute. But most brothels were situated in Southwark.

He pulled his hood up over his head, bundled his cloak about him, and headed toward Watling Street.

He stood at the mouth of the avenue from Bread Street and gazed down the muddy way, watching the townsfolk at their business. A man forced a pushcart over the muddy ruts. A small boy with a wrapped foot and a crutch sat in the cart atop the pile of what looked like peat, staring glassy-eyed back at the man. A woman with a basket of fish had one in her hand, shaking it toward the shoppers and shouting out the merits of her wares. The silvery body of the fish shone in the fluctuating sunshine, and its dead eyes vacantly perused the shoppers.

Skirting past a man holding a stake with strips of roasted meat hanging from its arms, Crispin walked along Watling. There, just before it became Budge Row was the private door. People passed it with barely a nod, while others pointed, talking in quiet whispers to one another. He trudged forward, crushing fallen autumn leaves beneath his boots. While Jack talked to the eel monger, Crispin would try the other, the roper.

He kept his head down while slipping by the eel monger,

passed the door to the private stair, and stood before the roper's shop. He knocked, and a young girl no more than eight or nine answered. She looked up at him with bright round eyes and dipped into a curtsey. 'Can I get my father for you, sir?'

He smiled. 'Yes, demoiselle. I would appreciate that.'

She reddened at his address, curtseyed again, and left to find her father. Crispin peered inside the door she had left ajar. Coiled ropes of every description hung on pegs. And long lengths of hemp were tied to rings in the process of being twisted together.

His peek inside was suddenly blocked by a man standing in the doorway. 'Good sir,' the man said with a bow. 'I'm Regis Croydone, ropes of every kind.'

Crispin bowed in return. 'Master, I am here to enquire about your neighbor . . . Elizabeth le Porter.'

The man crossed himself. 'Oh a sore thing is that. Are you a relative?'

'No, I am investigating her murder. I am . . .' Should he say? Was it known it was him who was fingered as a possible suspect? The truth was best. 'I am Crispin Guest. I am known in London as the Tracker.'

'Oh, indeed.' By his facial expression it was the 'Tracker' the man recognized rather than the suspect. 'Well. What can I tell you, for I know nothing of the crime itself?'

'You saw nothing? No one going in the stairs between Vespers last night and Terce this morning? Heard nothing?'

'No. We were all snug inside at Vespers and well into the working day by Terce.'

'I see. Would you know what Mistress le Porter did for a living? For whom she worked?'

'As her landlord I would. She was recently a lady's maid, but lost that situation some weeks ago, hence her lodging here.'

'As a lady's maid? You wouldn't know whom she served, would you?'

'I do, for I wasn't about to rent to a young woman alone without references. Who knows what someone like that would get up to? And now I see the folly of it.' He crossed himself again. 'She had worked for the Lady Helewise Peverel. She's a widow, living not far from here in a house on Trinity.'

'Thank you, master. And would you know why she was no longer under Lady Peverel's employ?'

'No. Mistress le Porter would not say and neither would Lady Peverel. But she did recommend her and so I didn't see fit to turn her out. Now I fear the place is cursed.'

'Never fear. London being as crowded as it is, I don't think you will have any trouble renting the space.'

'Let us hope. If I have helped you in your cause, then perhaps blessings will be given to me and mine.'

Crispin bowed. 'You have helped greatly, good sir. Much thanks.' And with that, Crispin withdrew and hurried toward Trinity.

Once he had crossed to Trinity, he enquired of people on the street where the Peverel house was and found it easily. It stood nearly alone, flanked on both sides with a flourishing garden. Autumn-naked trees pushed sharp branches above the garden walls, grasping into the gray sky.

He marched past the empty gatehouse, through to the cobblestone courtyard before the door's archway, climbed the stairs, and knocked. The door was opened by an older man in a crisp cotehardie who looked at Crispin with a faintly enquiring air. 'I beg your mercy,' said Crispin with a bow, 'but is your mistress at home? I urgently require conference with her.'

'And who are you?'

'Crispin Guest, Tracker of London.'

A brow rose only at the mention of his name, but the man bowed and gestured for Crispin to enter. The servant directed him to a parlor brightly lit with window glass and gaily painted murals on its golden walls.

'I will alert my mistress as to your presence, Master Guest.' He bowed again and left Crispin in the warm room. As the man left through a passage, Crispin walked to the wide fireplace. He basked in the warmth, letting his fingers thaw. Even the damp wool of his cotehardie heated through.

He looked around the room. About what he would expect from a rich widow's estate. Fine tapestries, luxurious carvings on coffers and the sideboard. Comfortable chairs with embroidered pillows and footstools. A tall carved post with a flat round platform atop didn't immediately make much sense to Crispin, until the lady swept into the room.

Her generous figure was attired in a green gown with gold embroidery and foliate sleeves reaching down to the hem from her elbows. She wore the modern horned headdress with a gold wire-mesh veil. And a red squirrel with a silver collar and leash was perched on her shoulder. She fed it berries, and it sat, holding a berry in its tiny paws, and nibbled with all its whiskery might. Its tufted ears flicked and swiveled.

'Master Guest?'

He bowed. 'Madam. Do I have the pleasure of greeting the widow Helewise Peverel?'

'You do. Please, Master Guest, sit down. Will you have wine? It is Flemish and quite sweet.'

He paused. It would be impolite not to take some, but he had made his own secret vow to cut back on his drinking. If not for his own sake then to mollify Jack. And then that thought filled him with the absurdity of trying to please a servant.

Before he could reply, a footman was already pouring the wine and offered a silver goblet on a tray. Crispin took it with thanks to his hostess. The servant withdrew to an antechamber and Crispin sipped. It was exceptional wine, but he took only the one sip and set it aside.

The lady urged her pet squirrel onto the platform. The leash, draping downward attached to her wrist, made a glittering bracelet. She put the last of her berries on the platform top. 'Here you are Folâtre, you greedy creature.' She dusted her hands and placed them in her lap. 'Now then. Why should the celebrated and, may I add, quite handsome Crispin Guest come to me?'

He smiled briefly. 'Madam, I fear I come with sad and solemn news. I regret to report that Elizabeth le Porter was found dead this morning.'

The woman was clearly shocked, and she raised her hand to her mouth. 'What . . . what happened?'

'I am very much afraid that she was murdered. I have heard that she used to work for you.'

'Yes, yes. As my personal maid.'

'Can you tell me why she left your employ?'

The widow Helewise fidgeted with her sleeve. 'It was by mutual choice.'

Crispin frowned. Servants spent their lives serving their

masters. And then their children came into the same employment. He couldn't help but voice his skepticism. 'A servant willingly leave such employment?' He looked around in emphasis. 'It does not signify.'

'And yet that is what happened.' Her face hardened. 'What else do you need to know?'

He shrugged it off. 'Can you think of any reason why someone would wish to do her harm? In fact, *hire* someone to do the deed?'

'I . . . can't imagine.' She turned toward her pet squirrel, tapping the platform so that he nuzzled her finger.

Crispin narrowed his eyes. Odd that she believed his tale so readily. 'Madam Peverel . . .'

'I know it is difficult for outsiders to understand. Those who don't know my family and what is here. The troubles.'

He watched her as she toyed with her pet. The squirrel flicked its tail and jerked from edge to edge of its perch. The little bell on its collar tinkled.

'Troubles, madam?'

She jolted from the chair, signaled to the squirrel, and it leapt to her shoulder. 'Come with me.'

She stalked from the room so suddenly Crispin had barely gotten to his feet before she was out the door. They traveled through a corridor and then to another archway. It opened to a small household chapel, closed tight by a gate. She took a key from her girdle and unlocked it, casting the metal gate aside. A statue of the Virgin sat in a lighted alcove, the candle flames flickering on the benevolent carved face. The alcove was also protected behind a gate with a lock imbedded within. Below her was a monstrance, a vial encased in gold, fashioned into radiant beams.

The widow Peverel curtseyed to the statue and knelt on the prie-dieux before the relic.

It's always a relic, he sighed to himself before he knelt at a prie-dieux behind her.

'You see,' she said quietly, 'this most holy of relics came into my family years and years ago. It is the Tears of the Virgin Mary.'

Crispin looked closer, leaning forward toward the gate's bars. Within the crystal vial he saw a small amount of a clear liquid.

'The Tears are precious, not only because they belonged to the Holy Mother,' she went on, 'but because . . . they can heal pain.'

Crispin took a breath. How many relics had he encountered over the years? How many could actually do what was ascribed to them? He kept silent.

'But that is not all.' She rose, took a small key from her girdle once more, and unlocked the alcove. She opened the door and reached for the monstrance. Taking the vial out of its golden cage, she lifted it to the light. Tilting it allowed the liquid to ooze from side to side within its crystal enclosure. 'The Tears of the Virgin . . . it is precious for other reasons. Because . . . it can also make one feel the pain of others.'

Crispin stood beside her. She offered it to him and he carefully took the vial, raising it to the light. The crystal itself was somewhat cloudy, but he could easily see the liquid within. 'How do you mean, madam?'

'You can feel their pain. Not just their physical pain, you understand, but their grief. Their deepest sorrows, regrets, and guilt. It is a two-edged gift.'

He handed it back and she cradled it in her hand, closing her fingers on it for a moment, closing her eyes. When she opened them again, Crispin could see her troubled expression. But before he could ask further, she leaned toward the monstrance again and placed the relic back within its radiant beams and closed the alcove's door. 'Let us come away.'

She cast her skirts aside, and traveled back out of the little chapel, locking it behind them. Pushing through a door to the garden, she walked sedately down one of the gravel paths. She sat upon a wooden bench under a beech. Crispin stood above her. 'You see, Master Guest, this family – and all who live here – are under the onus of the Virgin's Tears. We suffer because we are nigh it. We feel the pain of those around us. Elizabeth . . . could no longer suffer it and begged to leave. I granted her that. Would that I could go, too.'

'Well . . . why not . . . why not surrender the Tears to a church . . .'

Her eyes flicked to his, turning cold. 'I can never do that. The relic belongs to me and my family. We are its caretakers.'

'But it makes you suffer.'

'As our Lord suffered. Can I not do as much in my own small way?' She reached up and stroked the squirrel still perched on her shoulder. It did not try to leap to the trees. Maybe it had learned the lesson of the leash and knew it would be useless to try.

She sighed and looked up into the naked branches above her. 'Are there more questions, Master Guest?'

'No. That is all. For now. I thank you for your time, Madam Peverel.' He bowed and left her there within her walled garden.

He exited by the front door and looked back at the courtyard before he passed through the gate and stood on Trinity again. Strange. And that Elizabeth would have left because of a superstition. She did not seem melancholy to Crispin. But then again, she was out of the sphere of this household. What did that mean? It still did not answer the question as to why someone would want to kill her.

Thoughtful, he walked back toward the Shambles and up his stairs to his lodgings. He thought nothing of the unlocked door, thinking of Jack, until he looked up and spied unfamiliar men assembled in his room.

FOUR

Thursday, 15 October

Jack Tucker re-read the scrap of parchment that Hamo Eckington was kind enough to give him and scratched his head. Eckington had written out the names and addresses of the witnesses, but he had been too long at his task as sheriff's clerk for only *he* seemed able to discern his own spiky hand. Jack well knew where the eel monger was – thank the saints for that! – but as for these others . . .

He thought he could just make out the woman's name – Alison Keylmarsh of Candlewick Street. Might as well try that first.

He walked briskly down the lanes, smiling at the maids as he passed them. When he was lucky, they smiled back. He walked backwards, keeping his eyes and his smile on them until they tittered and hid their grins behind their linen kerchiefs. It wasn't until he turned forward again that he scowled and admonished himself. What did he think he was doing? He had important business to attend to. His master was in peril. It was no laughing matter to be taken lightly.

Yet. He looked back and the maids were still eyeing him. It never hurt to look.

Once he reached Walbrook he studied the parchment again. It said something about 'near the mouth of Walbrook and Candlewick,' the chandler's 'grand' house? He looked up again and spied a shop whose house was the grandest thing on the street. Could that be it? Jack straightened his cloak and coat and marched forward, moving with confidence toward the front entrance. He knocked and postured himself as he had seen Master Crispin do many a time.

When a servant opened the door and looked him over in a disdainful manner as he had also seen servants do to Master Crispin, it only made Jack raise his chin higher. He was proud of that beard he was starting to grow. It was patchy but otherwise carefully trimmed and bright as a robin's breast.

'Master Tucker, apprentice to the Tracker, to speak with Madam Keylmarsh.'

'Apprentice to the *what*?'

Jack deflated slightly. 'The . . . Tracker. The Tracker of London? Haven't you never heard of Crispin Guest?'

'Sounds familiar, I suppose. But what's that got to do with my mistress?'

'I'm here on the king's business. We're investigating a murder.'

'Murder? My mistress has naught to do with that!' He began to shut the door when Jack stepped forward and stopped it with his hand and the strength of his arm.

'Now, now. Your mistress already talked to the sheriffs.'

'Then she has no need to talk to the likes of you.'

The servant tried to shut the door again, but Jack's arm remained locked stiff and he shoved. 'She does if she wants to see justice done. What sort of Christian woman wouldn't want that?'

The servant hesitated. After a moment he said, 'Wait here,' and finally closed the door.

Jack took a breath. Master Crispin sent him on many errands but it had been only lately that he trusted Jack to talk to clients or witnesses. He knew his manner had improved in the last few years. He emulated his noble master as much as he could but even when he thought he had done his best, his low London accent came out of his mouth. There was no denying that.

The door opened so suddenly he jumped. Something like amusement flickered in the servant's eyes, but his face remained passive. 'My mistress will see you *very briefly*.' He walked ahead of Jack after he barred the door again, and Jack walked through the chilly parlor filled with unlit candles. He supposed these were the wares for sale. Fat columns of tallow mixed with beeswax, thin tapers hanging from their joined wicks, squat tallow candles like wheels of cheese, stacked on shelves. He reckoned it was cold in order to keep the candles stabilized.

Instead of another parlor, Jack was taken to a work room where a wide-hipped woman was bending over a desk and talking softly to a clerk, who directed her to scrutinize leaves of buff parchment with lines of figures and tabulations etched down them in columns of carefully scribed black ink.

Jack stood for a long while, hands behind his back and trying not to rock on his heels. Master Crispin had told him many a time not to fidget, to appear at all times calm. The calmer he was the more discomfited would his suspects be and much could be gleaned from a nervous man's speech. Not that Madam Keylmarsh was a suspect, but he supposed the same might hold true of witnesses.

At length she straightened from her bent posture, patted the clerk on his shoulder, and looked up. The satisfied expression she had worn withered when she noticed Jack. With heavy steps she approached him. Jack resisted the urge to take a step back. Instead, he gave a polite bow, sweeping back his cloak as he did so and proffering his foot forward as he had seen Master Crispin do when bowing to great lords and ladies. When he looked up, it seemed to have the effect he was looking for. She settled her face from surprise to pleased.

'And who are you, young man?'

'My lady, I am Jack Tucker, apprentice to the Tracker of London.'

'Such a title for so humble a lad.' She rested her hands over her ample belly and her chatelaine's keys. 'And what would the Tracker's apprentice be wanting of me and my household?'

'My lady, this morning you were questioned by the sheriffs of London regarding a heinous murder on Watling Street.'

She tensed again. He saw it in her shoulders, in her face that had lost its animation and had stiffened to flattened lips and set lids.

'And my master commanded me to personally talk with you about your testimony.'

'And why should your master do that?'

'Because my master is investigating the murder, my lady, and he . . . he . . . relies on his own enquiries rather than on the sheriffs' . . . er . . . clerk's . . . erm . . .'

She waved an impatient hand. 'Very well. Ask your questions. I am a busy woman.'

'So I can see. Chandler, eh? An interesting and quite necessary vocation.'

'Interesting? It might seem so to the uninitiated. But necessary? Oh yes. Which is why it is most busy.'

Jack nodded enthusiastically. 'Oh aye. I can see that. Everyone needs candles, don't they? And so. Madam, can you tell me why you were on Watling at that time of night and, I presume, on your own?'

She bristled. 'The sheriffs didn't ask so impertinent a question.'

'Alas,' Jack said with a shrug. 'My master is most assiduous and likes all angles to be answered.'

'And why, pray, is not your master here personally to ask his questions?'

'As busy as a chandler certainly is, a Tracker is equally so, what with crime what it is these days.' He didn't think a little lie would put him in ill stead. He sent up a small prayer for forgiveness anyway, just in case.

'I should say. It's absurd how much crime there is in this city. Tut. And the king's men do little to curb it.'

'My master does what he can in his own small way.'

'Hmpf,' she sniffed.

'Er . . . and so, madam. You were on Watling Street for what purpose?'

'I was returning from the Shambles. We do much business with the butchers there. For their tallow. Back and forth we go.'

'So late, my lady, and . . . alone?'

'Yes. I often travel alone, and I do my own business. My husband died years ago, but I was right at his side throughout, from the moment we married. There isn't an aspect of my trade that I do not know or handle personally. It takes a stern hand, my lad. Don't forget it. Your master must trust you greatly, for since he has only his results as a commodity, he can ill rely on a feeble servant to accomplish his tasks for him. You should feel grateful.'

'I do, my lady. There's not a day that goes by that I don't pray for the soul of my master for his confidence in me.'

'As you should. Well, then. Is that all?'

'Only this. Did you linger along the lane? Did you see anyone else enter that stair in the time you were on Watling?'

'No. I had no time to tarry. I was making haste back home. I ran into that dreadful man with the scarlet cotehardie. Drunk as a mule, he was. Disgraceful. Slammed into me with barely an apology and in through that door he went. I assume he is guilty of that murder.'

Jack swallowed a hard lump. 'We never assume anything, my lady, for there are circumstances that sometimes present themselves that are not immediately, erm, evident.'

She bristled. 'So *you* say. Well? Is that all?'

'Unless you saw anyone else along the lane. Someone else who might have gone through that door?'

'I was on my way immediately after my encounter with that dreadful man. I hope they hang him quickly. There are enough thieves and murderers in this town. What *has* become of it?'

'Aye. Well.' He bowed again. 'Thank you, madam, for your time. I'll see my way out.'

She had already turned away from him and marched to her own duties.

Jack trudged back the way he had come, and the servant opened the door for him, plainly glad to see the back of him.

'That's one down,' he muttered as he left the courtyard and stood on the street again. He pulled out the notes from the sheriffs' clerk and studied them. The eel monger was closer, so he trotted back toward Watling Street and glared at the private stair door, as if it were the cause of all their woes.

He wrinkled his nose at the smell of the eels as he walked under the eaves and peered into the barrels full of them. He certainly enjoyed a good fried eel, but he hated the sight of them slithering around together like worms in a grave.

The eel monger emerged from his shop and greeted Jack with a wide grin. 'How many can I get for you, lad?'

'Oh, I'm not in the market today, good master. It's Master Hugo Buckton, isn't it?'

The man blinked. 'Aye. Do I know you?'

'No, good sir. I am on an errand for my master. He is Crispin Guest, the Tracker of London, and he is investigating the murder of yon woman –' and he pointed behind toward the stair – 'and has sent me to ask some questions. I am his apprentice, good sir.'

'Ah! Apprentice, eh? Tracker. That's a strange vocation for any man.'

'Aye, that it is. But an interesting one.'

'Find lots of criminals, do you?'

'A fair few, good master.'

The man scrubbed at his stubbly chin and adjusted the hood's liripipe wrapped round his neck. 'I see. Go on, then. Ask.'

'Now I know that the sheriffs talked to you, but my master is very thorough. What can you tell me about yesterday?'

The man grabbed a small bucket of foul-smelling fish, chopped up and running with blood and water, scooped some out with a worn wooden paddle, and dumped it in with the eels. Their furious squirming to eat the morsels kicked up the water. It splashed over the sides with tails whipping out, slithering along the barrel's edge. Jack grimaced, unable to look away.

The gravelly-voiced eel monger shoved the paddle into the foul bucket again and set it down. 'I seen this man. Black hair, sharp snout, clean-shaven . . . and drunk. He wore a leather hood and a crimson cotehardie, blue stockings. He asked about Elizabeth le Porter and where she was. I told him. Up them stairs. He was polite, bowed to me, and went up. Last I seen of him. Except for today.'

'And, good master, did you see anyone else come or go through that stair between Vespers last night and Terce this morn?'

He wiped his hands down his apron, material that had seen far worse, Jack reckoned, with its bloody brownish stains and other filth old and dried upon it. 'Er . . . no. In me bed or up early with me work.'

'Good master, can you think of any reason why someone would want to kill Mistress le Porter?'

He took a knife with a long slender blade from its sheath at his hip and strode over to a board laid out on two trestles. He grabbed a writhing fish from another bucket and slapped it to the board. With expert strokes, he cut up under the gills and sliced off the head. 'She didn't know many on the lane,' he said as he worked. 'Heard tell she was a lady's maid come on hard times.'

'Did *you* know her, Master Buckton?'

'Aye, in a friendly way. She bought eels, I told her good morn, and such like. But er, no. Naught else . . . No.'

Jack scrutinized his fleshy face that had turned away from him. There was dirt on the side of his nose, and his teeth were yellowed. Thick brows hung over his eyes, shadowing their hollows. He couldn't tell if the man was holding back something or if he was just brusque and wished to get on with his work. Jack watched him for a few moments more before he decided to depart. 'If you do think of anything else, sir, can you get a message to me on the Shambles? We're above a tinker shop.'

'Aye. If I think of anything.'

Jack bowed and took his leave. So far there was nothing that could help his master. In fact, it only served to hurt. All they remembered was him in a drunken state. It wasn't looking good.

He dug into his pouch for the list and did his best to decipher the last name. Looked like it said 'Thomas Tateham' on Mercery, but he couldn't make out the rest. Would he have to go back to Newgate? A shiver rumbled up his spine. He certainly didn't want to do that. He'd try Mercery first, see if anyone had heard of this Thomas Tateham.

He headed back up Walbrook to Poultry and thence to where Poultry became Mercery. The various signs hanging before the many shops on the crooked lane gave him no clue. Wool merchants, thread sellers, needle makers, and mercers, mixed in with the occasional poulterer. Even a quill seller. He looked close at the parchment again but he could not identify the scratchings. 'Sarding clerk,' he muttered. He could continue on till it became the Shambles and then Newgate Market, but he wasn't anxious to visit the prison. Instead, he stalked up to the first merchant he saw and bowed. 'Good master, might you know of a gentleman named Thomas Tateham?'

'Eh, boy? What's that? I'm busy.' The man was carefully placing spools of thread into a checkerboard of a tray with its own carved out niches for each of the spools, and he was placing them in order by color. Jack looked on, entranced.

'Erm, I'm looking for a man who lives hereabouts. By the name of Thomas Tateham. Ever hear of him?'

'Naw. Doesn't sound familiar.'

'Oh.' Jack pointed. One color didn't flow with the others. 'It should be a red one there, eh?'

The man turned a frown on him.

Jack stepped back. He bowed and hurried on his way. He couldn't go to each shop, could he? Sighing, he stood in the middle of the lane. *Newgate it is, then.*

He marched forward following a man with a cart laden with bolts of cloth. Another, wheeled alongside the first, nearly blocked the entire passage. That cart carried fuel of bundled sticks. A hen, muddy from the lane, was perched on the bundle nearest the end of the cart, and with its soiled feathers it had a sorry look about it. It eyed Jack with a squinted angry glare.

Jack gestured rudely back at it, and it fluttered once before settling down again and watched Jack unnervingly all the way to Newgate's arch.

He trod in under the shade of the stone, skirting by the serjeants and trotting up the stairs. At the top of the staircase was an arched portico and a door. He knocked, straightening his cotehardie and was grateful to find Hamo Eckington. The clerk looked him up and down. 'What is it? Who are you?'

'Master Eckington, it's me, Jack Tucker. I was here not more than a few hours ago.'

'Oh, yes, yes.' He turned back to the room and his little alcove with its tall desk, shelves full of rolled parchments and books, candles, and oil lamps arranged around him. The man's graying hair flew in all directions out from under his leather cap. He was stoop-shouldered like an old man, but he still had a youngish face. There were careworn wrinkles at his blue eyes and grooves down from his nostrils, but he moved with speed and efficiency.

'What is it you want? The sheriffs are not here if you wish an audience with them.'

'Bless me, no sir. It is with you that I wish an audience. It's this parchment.' Jack pulled it from his scrip and flattened it. 'I can't read this bit here.'

Hamo snatched it from him. 'Little wonder, boy, when you've mangled it so much. No appreciation for the care of parchment.'

'I do have an appreciation. But I cannot read your hand.'

'My hand is as clear as it's always been from the day I learned to write my Latin, when I was a lad of six!' He shuffled into the light of the oil lamp and moved the torn piece this way and that. 'Well that's . . . that's quite simple. It says . . . says . . . hmm.' He slapped it back into Jack's chest. 'You must have smudged it somehow.'

Jack stuffed his hands at his hips. 'If you would be so good as to go back to your original document, I can get the name and proper address.'

'The original document? Do you know how many documents I have since processed?'

'You must have a . . .' Jack waved vaguely at all the rolled parchments. 'A system.'

He poked a finger at Jack's face. 'That's none of your business.' He turned back to his desk. 'Which writ was it? What was the crime?'

'Murder, sir. The victim was Elizabeth le Porter.'

'Oh, that one. Yes, it's here.' He reached up to some cubbyholes above his desk and pulled out a scroll. He laid it on his desk and untied the leather string. Rolling it out, he ran his finger down the writing.

'I'm looking for a witness. I thought it read Thomas Tateham.'

'Tateham. Here. Yes, he is on Mercery.'

'I got that far, Master Hamo, but no farther. Where on Mercery?'

Hamo frowned. He searched again on the parchment. Sliding an inkpot to keep the parchment open, he reached for another smaller scrap of parchment from another cubby. He glared at the scrap. 'But this is . . . highly irregular.'

Jack sighed. He had the feeling that finding this last witness was going to take a lot more work than he wanted.

'Have you found it, sir?'

'No, I haven't found it. It doesn't appear to have this information. It can't possibly be my error,' he grumbled.

'Be hard calling him to witness at the trial then, won't it?'

Hamo looked up. 'Don't take that attitude with me, young man. I don't need you, after all. You need *my* help.'

'So I do. I beg your mercy.' And he bowed quickly.

'Youth today!' He shook his head, staring at the parchment. After a time he looked up as if he had forgotten Jack was there. 'Well? What are you standing about for?'

'Aye, sir. Your servant.' He bowed again. As he turned to go he shook his head, tromping down the steps two at a time. He didn't even want to guess as to how many shops and houses there were on Mercery Lane, but he'd have to visit every single one of them. 'Sarding sheriffs,' he muttered.

FIVE

Thursday, 15 October

'Gentlemen,' said Crispin cautiously. 'To what do I owe the pleasure?'

The two men standing in his lodgings, where they should not be, were younger than Crispin, both dark-haired, with the same pinched noses. He surmised they were brothers at most, kin at the very least. And they were in a great state of agitation. With a quick glance at his room, he noticed that it had been hastily searched. 'What goes on here? My clients generally do not ransack my lodgings.'

The bearded man in a russet houppelande stepped forward, wringing his hands. His clothing was of fine material, his belt smooth leather, and his scrip of the same matching leather with a filigree design etched into it. 'Where is it?'

The second man moved to join him. His face was unadorned, and his houppelande was of dark green, but it was clear they used the same leather workers for their accouterments. 'Do you have it?' he asked breathlessly.

Crispin slowly closed the door, unhooked the frog with the sword, and hung it gently on the peg by the entry. 'Let us begin at the beginning,' he said calmly. 'Who are you and what is it that you seek?'

The men looked at one another. 'We are of the Noreys household. This,' said the man in the russet houppelande, 'is my brother John. I am Walter.'

'And we come for the relic,' said John Noreys. His nervous hand twitched over the hilt of his dagger.

Crispin raised a brow. 'You'll have to be more specific.'

Walter ran his hand through his generous mop of hair. 'The Tears, of course. The Virgin's Tears. Where is it?'

Crispin folded his hands before him. 'The same place it has ever been.'

'But Mistress le Porter was said to have had it. And you were . . . seen . . . speaking to her.'

Crispin's folded hands whipped away, one falling on his dagger hilt. 'Who says so?'

'We were told,' said Walter, chin raised.

Crispin took a step closer, and they both took a step back. 'By whom?'

'We have our sources, Master Guest,' said John. 'Our quarrel is not with you. We merely want the Tears.'

'And yet you go through my personal belongings at your whim.' He scowled. 'It is where it is, and I think you already know that.'

Crispin watched Walter squeeze the handle of his dagger. 'But it does not belong to the Peverels!' Faster than a blink, his dagger flashed free from its sheath. Crispin lunged, grabbed his wrist, and twisted. The blade dropped with a clang to the floor and the man went down on one knee.

The other cried out and leaped toward Crispin, but Crispin jabbed a well-placed fist to the man's nose and he wobbled before tipping over, face bloodied.

Crispin stood and looked them over. 'You are a sorry pair.' He kicked the dagger away to a corner. He stalked to his pantry, grabbed a relatively clean rag, and tossed it to the bloody brother. 'Clean up and behave yourselves.'

He kicked the chair from his table and sat, propping his foot up on the stool, keeping a sharp eye on the both of them.

The first brother sheepishly rubbed at his wrist. 'May I retrieve my knife?' he asked meekly.

'Not yet.'

Walter assisted John from the floor and helped him wipe his bleeding nose. John shook his head to waken his senses. He staggered toward the table and leaned on it.

'If you want to vomit, do it out the window,' Crispin growled.

The man waved his hand and shook his head. Eventually he stood upright, holding the rag to his face.

'Now then,' said Crispin, resting his forearm over his thigh. 'Do either one of you wish to tell me – in a civilized tone – just what the hell you want from me?'

John acceded to his brother, and Walter stood against the

table, somewhat more contritely. He kept glancing at his dagger across the floor.

'We . . . that is, my family, have owned the Virgin's Tears since before we were born. It has always been an important part of our household. Our servants venerated it, as did my family. It held a proper place with us. But some ten years ago, the vile Peverels stole it. Legal claims were made, but none came to fruition. The girl, Elizabeth le Porter, we were told, could come by the Tears and restore it to our family.'

'Why would she care to do you that kindness?'

'For money, naturally. Certain persons were sent to talk to her about obtaining the Tears. We were given to understand that the arrangement had been made.'

'So you paid her to steal it from the Peverels. I hope you understand that this was an illegal enterprise and could very well end with you being tossed into gaol.'

Walter looked at his brother for confirmation. 'No, Master Guest. It doesn't belong to them. We were only restoring it . . .'

'Not according to the law. If you made claims and they were refused then the law recognizes the ownership under the Peverels.'

The man fisted his hands and stomped Crispin's floorboards. 'No! It is not right! For years we have been trying to get it back. We even offered to purchase it.'

'And you think I had it.'

'We were told you had seen the woman. We assumed she gave it to you for safekeeping.'

'And you thought you'd steal it from me.' Frowning, Crispin pulled his dagger. John gasped and took a step back. Walter cringed but stood his ground.

Crispin toyed with the dagger, measured the men, and commenced cleaning his nails with the tip of the sharp blade. 'I have been insulted by your trespass,' he said, keeping his eyes on his hands. 'What do you intend to do about it?'

'Well . . . we . . .'

John pulled the bloody rag from his ruined face. 'We didn't take anything.' His voice sounded nasal and higher pitched than before.

'That does nothing to minimize the violation. You tell me who saw me last evening and I might be amenable to forgetting it.'

'Oh . . . well . . .' Walter and John conferred for some time, whispering hastily.

Crispin sighed. 'Come now. I haven't all day for this.'

Walter blinked and nodded to his brother. 'Very well, Master Guest. But the man we employed . . . just some beggar, certainly . . . goes by the name of Leonard Munch.'

'Lenny!' Crispin ground his teeth. 'That whoreson. Spreading lies about me.'

'You . . . know him?'

'You will find that I know a prodigious amount of people in London. The great and the small.'

'But he . . . he seemed quite . . .'

'I'm certain he did.'

'Well . . . Master Guest, we are still in need of the Tears. Our fortunes have dwindled of late. We need it . . . well, frankly, we need it to sell. It is . . . was . . . quite the most valuable thing the family owned. We are in peril of losing our estates. It is that dire.'

Crispin went back to the methodical cleaning of his nails. 'What's that to me?'

'People hire you, don't they? They hire you to find things.'

Crispin looked up. He sheathed his blade with a snap that startled the two, and he sat up. 'I *find* them. I don't *steal* them.'

'We are willing to pay.'

Crispin got to his feet. The chair fell back. 'Didn't you hear me?'

Walter bit his bottom lip. His eyes darted toward his dagger, and in the next instant he dove for it.

Crispin went after him, but John and his bloody nose was all over him, grabbing him from behind.

With his arms pinned, Crispin knocked his head back, smacking the man in his already bloody nose. But he would not yield.

Walter scrambled for his weapon and held it firmly in his hand when he turned. 'We know you are hiding it for the Peverels. Where is it?'

'You're a fool, Noreys,' he grunted. He stumbled backwards, all the while slamming his head into the man behind him, forcing the man back. He felt the grip weakening. But Walter was coming closer. 'Hold him, John.'

Crispin shoved back. John stumbled backwards still grasping Crispin until they were up against the open window. Crispin slammed him once, twice. The grip finally loosened. Crispin forced his arms upward, dislodging the man's clasp, and he shoved back with all his might. Over the sill went John and, with a cry, he sailed out the window and landed hard to the street below. His cry ended abruptly.

Walter rushed to the window. Crispin grabbed his dagger arm, wrenched it up his back and fell forward, slamming the man to the floor on his face.

'John!' he cried. 'John! Oh God! Oh Blessed Virgin! Is he dead?'

Screams and cries lifted up from the street below.

Crispin kept his knee firmly in the man's back as he peered out the window. 'It doesn't look good.'

'Damn you! Damn you, Guest!' Walter sobbed . . . and bled, Crispin noticed, in swipes onto his floor. 'We only wanted to talk to you!'

'At the point of a knife? That's not how it's done. And now your brother has paid the price.'

'Oh God! You killed him! You killed him!'

'Crispin!'

Crispin turned. His landlord Martin Kemp framed the doorway with his outstretched arms. 'What's happened?'

'Best fetch the sheriffs, Martin. There's been . . . a death.'

Crispin leaned against his stairwell, arms folded. The sheriffs had arrived and not too long afterward came the coroner, John Charneye, and his retinue.

He dismounted and looked over the corpse. He glanced up to Crispin's open window, and finally swiveled his gaze toward Crispin. He strode over the muddy lane and stood before him. 'Well, Master Guest?'

'It was self-defense.'

'He killed him!' cried Walter, pointing a finger at Crispin. 'Without any provocation!'

'Who is this?' asked Charneye.

'The deceased's brother. And trust me, my lord. There was plenty of provocation.'

'Do you wish to press charges?'

Crispin shook his head.

The sheriffs made their way to Crispin. 'You've done it this time, Guest,' said Loveney, adjusting his gauntlets.

'Have I?'

'You'll have to come with us now.'

'Without an indictment?'

Walcote leaned in to him, his face very close to Crispin's. 'You think you are very clever, Guest. But we will get an indictment. Quicker than you think. An Oyer and Terminer commission has been waiting on you for years to satisfy just such an occasion. And a trailbaston to boot. You're coming with us. Now.'

Running steps, boots slapping the mud. And then Jack Tucker was there, holding on to the stair rail and panting. 'What . . . what's happened? Master Crispin?'

'I think I am being arrested for murder, Jack.'

'Again?'

A light sparked in Walter Noreys's watery eyes.

'Much thanks for that, Jack,' he said quietly. 'I . . . I can easily explain away this one. But since this death has occurred they can no longer ignore the other. It's up to you now.'

'Me? Master Crispin, I can't do it alone.'

'Yes you can. Just remember everything I taught you.'

'But . . . Master Crispin! I can't remember nothing! It's all gone!'

He grabbed Jack by his upper arms. 'Tucker, get a hold of yourself. I need you. Think. Observe. Question. You *do* remember.'

Jack wiped at his face. 'Aye. Aye, I suppose I do. But . . . I don't know naught about criminal trials and such.'

'Then get the help of someone who does.' The sheriffs were mounting, and their serjeants were approaching Crispin with fetters. 'Listen carefully, Jack. These brothers, John and Walter Noreys claim that their family owned a relic, the Virgin's Tears, that the Widow Peverel on Trinity has in *her* possession. The same household that Elizabeth le Porter worked for.'

'God blind me!'

'Yes. And further, these Noreys boys said that one of their own hired the le Porter woman to steal the Tears for them. Probably these brothers themselves.'

'*Did* she steal them, master?'

'No. I saw them myself. Madam Peverel showed me. But Jack. Lenny saw me last night. He was working for these execrable brothers. And I doubt there will be much truth from his lips. And the sheriffs will be glad of those lies.'

'Lenny!' He smacked a fist in his hand. 'I'll track him down hastily enough.'

One of the sheriff's serjeants shoved Jack aside and slipped the shackles on Crispin's ankles while another serjeant tied a rope around his wrists.

Crispin took a deep breath. 'Jack, I'm counting on you.'

The serjeant propelled Crispin forward by pushing at his shoulder. Trotting, Crispin was able to keep up and not trip himself. He glanced once over his shoulder toward Jack – who looked very sorrowful indeed – and followed behind the horses.

He felt a little sorry for Jack. Oh, Crispin knew he could easily fight his culpability in the death of John Noreys, but in the case of this other . . .

There truly wasn't much hope for the lad succeeding.

SIX

Thursday, 15 October

Jack walked down the Shambles, head hanging low. How could he possibly help his master now? He hadn't yet found that third witness, and now it appeared that Lenny was added to the list. Lenny, who had worked many a time for Master Crispin and whom his master had set adrift after the spy had wronged him. And now he was set to wrong his master again.

Peverels, Virgin's Tears? What had his master been talking about before his hasty departure?

Get hold of yourself Jack Tucker. He stopped in the middle of West Cheap, allowing carts and people to mill past him. The call of merchants hawking their wares, of a rooster chortling on a nearby roof, of dogs barking and children singing a rhyme, faded to a far place. *Take apart what Master Crispin said*. Elizabeth le Porter worked for the Peverel woman and she had in her possession a relic, the Virgin's Tears. She was supposed to have stolen it for John and Walter Noreys who claim it was theirs – though John Noreys would be explaining himself to God. They were so keen on it in fact that Master Crispin had to defend his life. But Mistress le Porter hadn't stolen it, Master Crispin hadn't found out who in the Noreys household supposedly paid her to steal it, and now a man and a woman were dead.

'These sarding relics,' he muttered. 'No wonder my master would see the back of them.'

He began to slowly walk, thinking out loud. 'So my tasks are fourfold.' He ticked them off on his fingers. 'Find the third witness, get my hands around Lenny's throat, find out what these Noreyses have been up to . . . and keep Master Crispin from hanging for murder. Simple.'

A lad with a spade over his shoulder and dirt smudged on his face stared at Jack with widening eyes. 'Looks like you've got your work cut out for you, mate,' he said to Jack.

Jack smiled and pushed back his unruly fringe. 'Aye. That's a fact. Pray for me.'

The boy saluted. 'You sound like you need it.' The boy pressed on, and Jack found himself on the way to the Boar's Tusk without even thinking about it.

'I've taken after me master more than I thought,' he mused, glancing up at the ale stake and then at the wooden sign of the curled tusk with its faded paint.

He ducked inside and waited at the entrance as his eyes adjusted to the dark. There had been a day when it adjusted immediately so he could do his cutpurse mischief, but he sighed with regret at how age had changed him.

He sat at a far table with his back to the wall and a clear view of the door, just as his master had taught him, and he leaned on the table, scratching his head.

He had a lot to do on his own and no mistaking. A little bit of ale for courage would not go amiss. And as he waited for Eleanor or Gilbert Langton to come and serve him, he scanned the low-ceilinged room, searching the shadowed faces. Lenny wasn't likely to be at the Tusk since he knew Master Crispin frequented it, but there were many familiar faces. The Boar's Tusk was like any alehouse tavern, he reckoned. A man found a tavern he liked and made that his second home.

Eleanor appeared in the back nearest the kitchens, but she was scurrying about, pushing loosened strands of her ash blonde hair away from her face and vainly trying to tuck it back up under her kerchief. She was talking hurriedly to a new servant girl, and Jack stretched his long torso over the crowd to get a good look at her.

A pretty thing. Young, younger than Jack maybe. Long auburn hair, a small mouth, round, pink cheeks. He'd have to find a moment to talk to her . . . Oh what was he thinking! *Priorities, Jack. Master Crispin first, dalliance later*.

His eyes continued to track about the room as his mind whirred on the many problems ahead of him. If only he had help. Who could help? Who knew enough about it all? Certainly no one *he* knew. He sat up sharply. The duke! If he could get a message . . . no. As far as he knew, the Duke of Lancaster was still in Spain. What about his son Henry? No, no. Jack had caused a great deal of trouble to the Earl of Derby a year ago. He wasn't likely to forget it and, in any case, he had his own troubles to contend with. The king had been acting as if he was sitting on ants for the past two years, and in the spring he had finally declared he was done with those lords peering over his shoulder – and one of them was Henry. Richard was king and that was that! Henry had to watch his step if he wanted to stay on the good side of his cousin from now on.

Thoughts of the king made him think of Queen Anne. He had performed a mighty service for her and, in her gratitude, she had saved Jack's life. Might he send a message to her for succor? But no. One could not rely on the beneficence of the nobility. In all likelihood, she had forgotten all about him by now.

He ran his hand through his ginger locks. What else could he do?

Just as he was about to hail Eleanor himself, Jack spotted a familiar face amongst many. There, just near the door and hoisting a horn cup, was the manciple Thomas Clarke. He hadn't seen him since . . . when was it? Three, four years ago?

Jack jolted up and shot between the tables, shoving his way past crowded men hunched over their drinks.

'Master Clarke!' he said, standing over the man.

Clarke turned, cup still in hand, and looked Jack over without recognition. 'Yes?'

'It's me,' said Jack, pounding his chest. 'Jack Tucker. Remember? From Canterbury.' He leaned in and whispered, 'When St Thomas's bones went missing?'

Eyes widening, Thomas Clarke smiled. 'Young Jack Tucker! But look at you, man! When I saw you last, you were a mere slip of a boy. And now you're fully grown.'

Jack felt a hot blush to his cheeks. 'A few years to go, good sir. But it is God's grace smiling down upon me, making me tall. Bless my soul. You're just the man I need in this dread hour.'

'Dread hour? Come, Tucker. Come sit beside me.'

Jack plopped down on the stool and jostled closer to the table.

'Will you have ale?' Thomas poured into another bowl sitting on the table and handed it to Jack.

'Thank you, sir. I am parched.' Jack tipped it up and swallowed one dose after another till it was nearly gone. He wiped his lips with the back of his hand. 'Bless me, the sight of you does my soul good.'

Thomas looked no different from when Jack had seen him in Canterbury all those years ago. He was young, though older than Jack. Like a student, though he was a procurer of provisions for his charges. His brown hair draped over the chaperon hood lying folded on his shoulders. His straight nose and small eyes studied Jack with care.

'Tell me what ails you. Are you still apprentice to that Tracker. Er . . . Crispin . . . something.'

'Crispin Guest, good master. And I am. And a great and gracious master he is. But I am afraid he is in peril.' He gulped down the rest of his ale, and Thomas solemnly poured more. Jack saluted with the cup and drank again. 'My master was on an errand of mercy last night.' He got in close and kept his voice low. Thomas bowed his head toward Jack to listen. 'A man mistook him for an assassin in this very place. Paid him good money to murder a woman.'

Horrified, Thomas drew back. 'God have mercy,' he muttered, crossing himself.

'Aye. So my master went to tell the lady, to warn her and, well. One thing or another, he, erm, fell asleep. And when he awoke the next morning, she was dead. Strangled.'

'Blessed Saint Ives! What happened then?'

'Well! My master was seen by witnesses. They've arrested *him* for the crime!'

'I see. He . . . isn't guilty then?'

Jack scrambled to his feet and drew his dagger. 'Of course not! And I'll slay anyone who says he is!'

Thomas swallowed and looked about nervously. Other patrons cast an eye toward Jack's posturing, no doubt wondering if an altercation was about to break out. 'Peace, Master Tucker. I only asked what any man would.'

Jack frowned, looked at his dagger, and sheathed it smartly. Slowly, he regained his seat and pulled it up again to the table. 'I . . . I apologize, Master Clarke. I might be a bit . . . touchy . . . where my master is concerned.'

'And rightly so. You're a good and honest lad.'

'Thank you, Master Clarke. You see, I am at my wit's end.

For my master and I were investigating the murder to find the true culprit, but the sheriffs went and took my master. I must help him, Master Clarke, by finding the culprit. But I fear they will try him before I can.'

'Hmm. What you need, my lad, is a lawyer.'

Jack brightened. 'Ah. And that's where you come in, sir. Are you still a manciple for law students?'

'Indeed. And I think I know just the man. Come with me.'

Jack stood. 'Where to, sir?'

'To just outside London, to Gray's Inn.'

It was a long and crowded walk from Gutter Lane to Holburn, but it thinned as they left London proper. Only carts with tall beds of hay rolled along the rutted lane, with the occasional rider on a horse trotting through to split the monotony of the open road. A shepherd with a flock of muddy sheep stood off at a distance, staring at Jack and Thomas on the green plain once shops and houses had dwindled. He kept staring as if to plead for . . . something. Jack stared back as he and his companion turned down Chauncler Lane and found a row of three-story structures, limed-daub hatched with dark timbers too numerous to count. New construction was being added to the old and followed along with the same design. Workers hoisted wet daub on mortar boards, while others moved up ladders with solid wooden beams balancing on their shoulders. Sawing and hammering of pegs into holes echoed across the nearly empty plain surrounding the inn's buildings.

Law students and the lawyers who taught them leased out the majority of the inn, for the law was not to be taught inside London's precincts since old King Henry III had declared it so.

'We'll go this way,' Thomas was saying, as Jack took it all in, turning to watch the laborers call to one another. They tramped up a gravel walk that turned to flagged stone until they came to a portico with an arched door. Thomas took a ring of keys from his belt, chose one, and unlocked it. Entering into the shadows, Jack followed, eyes wide and fingers near his dagger.

Thomas's hand fell on his shoulder. 'You needn't worry, Master Tucker.' He gestured with the nod of his head toward Jack's weapon hanging near his right hip. 'This is my domain. There are no enemies here, save the students in the heat of an argument.' He chuckled. Jack relaxed and his hand fell away. The entry alcove opened up to a cozy room with glass panes covering the window in a diamond pattern. Sunlight streamed in, illuminating motes of dust that fell onto the tawny spines of books on shelves. A tall desk, a chair, a small fireplace, scrolls, inkpots, crates, rough sacks full of God-knew-what.

'This is where I do my work, Master Tucker.'

Jack nodded. He didn't know the contents of the books, but what wouldn't Master Crispin give to have a few of them? He had spent precious coin on a book of Aristotle. A small thing but prized. He often read from it when at his ease late at night. Sometimes he'd read aloud to Jack.

'Let us see if there are any still in the hall.' Thomas passed through an arched doorway and to a passage that led to a wide hall. The hammerbeam ceiling rose up three stories, with clerestory windows along walls on opposite sides. The room was bright and warm and still filled with students and lawyers, eating together as servants hustled from one table to the next.

At the smell of the food, Jack's belly growled. He couldn't remember the last time he had eaten.

He hoped Thomas hadn't noticed, but the sharp-eyed manciple gave him a glance. 'I could eat a bite. Could you, Master Tucker?'

'Well . . . if it's the custom . . .'

He sat Jack down, poured him a cup of ale, and pushed a platter with a broken round of bread toward him. 'I will get a servant to bring you meat and pottage.'

'I thank you, Master Clarke.'

The man scurried off. Jack reached for the loaf, tore off a hunk, and stuffed it in his mouth. It was then that he noticed a young man, little older than himself, sitting across the table and staring at him. The man chewed for a moment before he leaned his forearms on the table. His pottage bowl was nearly empty with the dregs of his soup and he was eating a bit of roasted leek. He pushed the pottage bowl toward Jack.

'I'm done. You can have the rest.'

'Oh. That is kind of you, sir.' Jack took it and slurped up the last, licking his lips. He took another piece of bread and sopped up the rest.

'You can't be a student here, can you?'

Jack's face reddened. No doubt he heard Jack's low London accent. No matter how hard he tried, he could not sound like Master Crispin. He had bowed to it long ago, but it did make it hard, sometimes, for him to investigate on his own when lordly people took him for a lowly servant and not the apprentice he was. 'Er . . . no, good sir. I am here at the courtesy of your manciple, Thomas Clarke.'

'So I saw. He called you 'Tucker.''

'Aye. I mean, yes. M-my name is Jack Tucker. I am apprentice to the Tracker of London.'

'Tracker? Bless me, I've heard of that wily fellow. Indicted for treason, wasn't he? Got off with a slap, I daresay. Not the judgment he could have had. He's got angels smiling down on him, I'll warrant. Or devils smiling up.'

Jack bristled but held his tongue. After all, he did not know who these men were or what rank. At any rate, they were all likely far above him. 'He is a fair and generous master, sir, is Crispin Guest. My mentor in all things. And I thank the Almighty every day that he was spared that ignoble torment.'

'Well said . . . from his apprentice. But harken. I didn't mean any disrespect. I simply speak what's on my mind, I'm afraid. We are taught to think quickly, to recall codes of law, to defend our clients as craftily as we can . . . just within the thin border of the law, mind you. I admire your master. He took the sow's ear he was given and crafted a silk purse. And I say amen to that!'

'In that case.' Jack lifted his cup. 'Good health to you, sir.'

The man raised his cup. 'And to you, Master Tucker.' They both drank. The man wiped his mouth with the hem of the tablecloth. 'Where are my manners? I know your name but you do not know mine. I am Nigellus Cobmartin, newly certified barrister for the Common Pleas. I just tried my first case yesterday.' He beamed. His short, blunt nose and cheeks were red, and his gray eyes sparkled. Mousy brown hair neatly combed hung on either side of his clean-shaven face.

'Did you win?'

Nigellus glared down at the melted butter on a wooden plate before him and stirred what was left of his leek in it. 'No. But almost.'

'Oh.' Jack sat back. 'What . . . what sort of case was it?'

'Best not to dwell.' He becrossed himself and Jack, thinking it couldn't hurt, did so as well.

Nigellus looked up suddenly. 'And why are you here, Master Tucker? Are you investigating for your Tracker master?'

'Yes . . . and no. I am investigating but . . .' He looked both ways down the table, making certain no one could hear them. 'But my master is in peril and in need of a good lawyer.'

'Oh! That sounds promising. Tell me.'

'Well . . . I don't like to say. I think that's why Master Clarke brought me here. To find the right lawyer . . .'

'But Master Tucker!' He slapped his chest with both hands, getting greasy butter on his dark merino houppelande. '*I'm* a lawyer!' He slurped up the ale in his cup and settled his arms on the table. 'Tell me.'

Jack stretched his neck, searching for Thomas Clarke. But when he could not find him he sighed and toyed with his cup. Carefully and quietly he explained the situation, and Nigellus nodded solemnly. When Jack had finished, the lawyer put his hand to his chin and sat thoughtfully for a long time. 'Well, Master Tucker, it looks as if we have some time. For it takes a year at least for such cases to come to trial.'

'Oh no, Master Cobmartin. I wouldn't rely on custom where my master is concerned. I fear they will try him just as fast as they can. If they gave me so much as a year, so much as a month, even, they well know I'd find the true culprit and snatch away their chance to hang him.' He shook his head solemnly. 'No, Master Cobmartin. I don't think there is any time to waste.'

The lawyer jumped to his feet. 'Then come along, Master Tucker.'

'What? Where . . .?'

But Nigellus was already walking with long purposeful strides across the hall. Jack ran to the end of the table, rounded it, and hurried to catch up to the man. Jack was taller and his strides soon put him beside the man as they reached the entrance arch.

Jack skidded to a halt and touched the man's sleeve. 'Oh! What do I do about Master Clarke?'

'He brought you here to find a lawyer and you've found one.

I suspect – that wily devil – that he put you at that very table in that very seat in order for you to talk to *me*. He knows how anxious I am to get on with it.' He winked at Jack. 'Come along. To my lodgings. I can take notes there.'

'Will this take long, sir? There is still much I must investigate.'

'Really? I should like to come, too, if it's convenient.'

They climbed the stairs, turned at the landing, then climbed again until they reached a shorter door. Nigellus unlocked it and ducked to enter. Jack did likewise. A small attic room, where the ceiling slanted dramatically. Nigellus had tacked various parchments to the exposed beams and they hung down like pennons from a castle wall. The rest of the space was cluttered with books, scrolls, stacks of parchment, a spilled inkpot, broken quills scattered about, and a small pot sitting in the window that held a weedy rose plant with drooping leaves. The room smelled close of sweat and smoke as if the glass-paned window had seldom been opened.

A bed, whose quilt was covered with more parchment and books, was shoved into a corner, its bedposts nearly too tall for the low-angled ceiling. Indeed, the topmost finials looked to have scraped a few marks into the plaster. The fireplace grate was full of gray ash, and a few disheartened coals glowed pink.

'Make yourself at home, Tucker. Sit.'

Jack looked around. 'Er . . . where, sir?'

Nigellus looked up. 'Dear me. I seem to have an ark of a room; all my rubbish is two by two. Here.' He dislodged a pile of parchment and revealed a stool. He didn't bother picking up the leaves.

Jack pulled the stool along the floor with a scraping sound and sat, gazing at the detritus around them. What was he to make of this? Did this prove the man's dexterity with the law or his mere fumbling with it? He *had* lost his first case. But maybe Jack couldn't afford better.

'What will this cost us, Master Cobmartin?'

'Oh, call me Nigellus. We will be working together. What shall I call you?'

'Erm . . . Jack.'

'Master Jack. Excellent.' Seeing nowhere else to sit, Nigellus pushed the parchments on his bed aside and flopped down, hands resting on his thighs. 'My fee is one shilling.'

'One shilling!' He dropped his face into his hand and rocked his head. 'Master Nigellus, that comes dear.'

'I realize that. Hmm. Perhaps we can come to terms. Assuming I win this case—'

Jack blanched and Nigellus hastily added, 'Why of course I will! Then your master and I will have an agreement that he work for me when I need it. At least until the bill is paid. For a small retainer of say, sixpence?'

Jack nodded. He had at least that much and more in his pouch. He scrambled for it, counted out six pennies into his hand and offered it. Nigellus took it solemnly and dropped it into his money pouch.

The lawyer narrowed his eyes at Jack. 'And now we must get to it. I will need to talk to my client. Is he being held in Newgate?'

'Yes, sir. But I must be back to my own investigating. After all, if I uncover the true killer it will be easier to get my master released, will it not?'

'Unquestionably. Then each to our own tasks, Master Jack! *Veritas temporis filia dicitur*!'

'*The truth is the daughter of time*,' quoted Jack, '*Eventually the truth becomes known*.'

Nigellus beamed. 'Well done, Master Jack. Or should I say, well done Master Guest?'

Jack smiled. 'My master.' But his smile soon faded. 'You must do your utmost, Master Nigellus. I am depending upon you, sir. My master must live.'

Nigellus, too, grew solemn and he rested his hand on Jack's shoulder. 'I tell you truly, Jack, I may seem untried to you, but I have been studying the law, apprenticing under the finest barristers in the kingdom, for many, many years now. And though . . . though I lost my first case, it does not mean I shall be flippant with your faith in me.' He lowered his hand and sighed. 'A trial is a hurried thing. The juries are culled from the *locus delicti*, the neighborhood of the crime, and it is they who are instructed to discover what they can, to talk to witnesses, to sift the truth from the chaff. Now all we have at the moment are witnesses who saw your master arrive. He is the First Finder but he did not call the hue and cry. And finally, he has been known to kill. Even today, and that witness claims he had no provocation. These are all points against your master . . . not the least of which is his past as a traitor.'

Jack shifted his weight from one foot to the other. He never liked discussing his master, and to do so in so cold a manner – as if he were a . . . a *thing* . . . instead of a man – caused an uneasy rolling in his gut. But he listened, because Nigellus was spearing him with an intense gaze, so intense that he could not move or look away.

Nigellus laid one hand over the other and looked up at Jack from under his well-shaped brows. 'You must realize this task will not be easy, and juries typically come in with their verdict within minutes of the trial's beginning. The sheriffs, aldermen elected to their esteemed office, are anxious to show their best faces to the king and to urge their fellow aldermen to someday elect them to the prestigious office of Lord Mayor. To that end they will be doing their utmost to get a swift conviction . . . and a conviction, I'm afraid, means that your master will hang.'

Jack blinked back the tears. Tears did his master no good. He pressed his lips tightly together.

'It will be my task, therefore,' Nigellus continued, 'to prolong the proceedings in order to buy you time. I am already forming a plan as to how to do it, but it is a fine dance between the letter of the law and annoying the recorder of London. For John Tremayne is a man who will brook no foolishness. And much you may have seen to the contrary, I am not a foolish man. So . . . knowing now all of this, do you wish for me to proceed?'

Jack girded himself. He couldn't do it alone and this man, whatever his inexperience, seemed to be a man of conviction and confidence. Jack, much like Master Crispin, relied on the truth of his gut.

He nodded. 'In all haste, Master Nigellus.'

SEVEN

Thursday, 15 October

It was later in the day, well past None, when Nigellus Cobmartin walked in long strides toward Newgate. With the sun on his back it had been a comfortable walk, but there was no accounting for the strange and sudden cold under the arch of Newgate's prison. Perhaps it was all the lost souls who had suffered within its stone walls and had remained to haunt the place. He shivered at the thought, crossed himself, and gave a curt nod to the serjeants.

'Ho, good gentlemen!'

They turned, looking him up and down. His dark houppelande was fairly new and relatively clean, as were his hands, though his fingers were permanently stained with ink. A chaperon hat with a shoulder-length liripipe sat on his head, sheltering his eyes with shadows, and he carried a leather folder bulging with parchments under his arm. He felt, with a little preening, that he looked like a proper lawyer, having sloughed off the mantle of student nearly a sennight ago.

One of the serjeants postured while leaning on his pike. 'Master?'

'I wish to see one of the prisoners, my client.'

'You will have to talk to the sheriffs.'

'Very well, then. Lead me.'

The serjeant looked put out by this order, but he nevertheless set his pike aside and climbed the stairs. 'Mind your head,' he said over his shoulder.

Nigellus ducked when instructed and followed the man. His senses were wide awake, absorbing all around him, the smell, the sounds, the touch of the cold stone against his hand. This was only the second time he had been to Newgate and it felt just as exhilarating as the first, though he tempered his worldly feelings with thoughts of his sacred duty. He called upon the saints and angels to help him on his bold course for he knew that he was but a small cog in the greater wheel of God's universe. And vanity was a trap from which a soul could not easily escape.

But even as he climbed the stairs, he hoped that Master Guest was kept in a small private cell, for Nigellus did not wish to go down into the dreaded dungeons of the place. A cold, miserable habitation it was, where prisoners, both men and women, mingled in the same large cell, where fetid disease ran rampant, where immorality was the stock and trade, where the best men with the best of intentions soon succumbed to the worst that dwelled in all men's souls. No, a prison was a ghastly place, and the briefer the time there, the better.

The serjeant opened a door to an alcove where a clerk was bent over his table and gestured Nigellus in.

The clerk didn't look up as the serjeant retreated. 'Who is it?' he asked, still writing, dipping the quill, writing.

'Master Nigellus Cobmartin to see the prisoner Crispin Guest.'

The clerk stopped writing and turned over his shoulder. He set his quill aside and hopped down from his chair. Moving around a pillar, he stood in an archway. 'Lord Sheriff, a lawyer here to see Crispin Guest.'

Nigellus tried to peer over the clerk's shoulder and could only just catch a glimpse at the dark, bearded man. 'Is there? Send him on, by all means, Eckington. Guest's trial begins Saturday, after all.'

Surprised, Nigellus stifled his indignation. In this Jack Tucker was right. The sheriffs plainly wished to rid themselves of Master Guest. And though they no doubt covered the letter of the law, they would do their damnedest to skirt its soul.

'Very good, Lord Sheriff. Come this way, Master Cobmartin.'

Nigellus bowed toward the sheriff's voice and hurried after the clerk who had not waited for him.

A brazier glowed a gold wash against the stone wall as they reached another arched doorway and came upon a hall of sorts. Tall narrow windows with bars embedded in the stone cast light and cold into the space, hence the large brazier with its roaring flames in the center of the room. The chamber smelled of rot and mildew, and Nigellus thanked a generous God once more for setting him on this path to help the helpless.

To the side was a long table with benches, and at one of the benches sat a man drinking ale from a horn beaker. His tunic was of leather as was the cap he wore. Dry brittle hair stuck out from under it, and his chin and cheeks bristled with dark coarse stubble. The side of his face was bruised with a stripe of dried blood running down from the cap.

He looked up when their steps scratched at the floor.

'Master Melvyn,' said the clerk, 'I have here Lawyer Cobmartin. He is here to see Crispin Guest.'

'Guest has a lawyer?' said the man in a gravelly laugh. 'Little good it will do him.'

Nigellus adjusted his gown. *So little regard for jurisprudence*, he huffed. Had not all prisoners the same prospect under the law?

The man pulled himself from the bench and shuffled forward. His posture was slightly bent and he looked over Nigellus with a sneer of disdain. 'Come along, then.' The keys at his belt rattled as he walked with an odd rolling gait.

Down a corridor they went, the hall growing darker the farther away from the warm brazier they got. Only a few oil lamps burned in alcoves. They reached a door with a grille at head-height and Melvyn slammed his keys against it. 'You've a visitor, Guest. Stand away from the door.'

The man put the key to the lock, turned it twice, and opened it. 'In with you, lawyer. Call to me when you are finished.'

Nigellus's stomach fluttered as he pushed forward. He did not know what to expect of this first meeting with the notorious Crispin Guest, the man who could not seem to be killed. Not even the king could seem to accomplish it. He expected a devil, a dark man, perhaps with horns. He girded himself for whatever he might see.

Taking a breath he rounded the door and peered inside. A simple cell with straw upon the floor. There was a cot with a straw-stuffed mattress, though the straw smelled of mildew. A table and a chair were all the furnishings left in the place. An arrow slit for a window threw a narrow band of light across the wall, and the hearth had a small fire from a pathetic square of peat.

And there, standing before the hearth, was the man himself.

His dark cloak draped around his stooped shoulders like a shadow. He was of medium height, with intense narrowed eyes of gray slate, and black hair hanging well below his ears. His nose was straight and sharp and his mouth curved down in a frown. There was dried blood and fresh bruises on his square chin. He had a patrician air about him of tarnished nobility, which the man had certainly earned.

No horns, however.

Heavy shackles harnessed his ankles, but perhaps they had nothing to do with his natural stillness.

Guest turned at Nigellus's step. 'Who are you?' he asked with a roughened voice. The predatory eyes studied him relentlessly, following his every move.

Nigellus bowed. 'My dear Master Guest,' he said breathlessly. 'I was retained by one Jack Tucker as your lawyer. I am your servant, Nigellus Cobmartin.'

At the mention of his apprentice, Guest's whole demeanor changed. The dark suspicion of his pinched face suddenly relaxed. The resigned set to his jaw fell away, replaced by eyes shining with light and warmth. The transformation took the lawyer's breath away. 'Jack? He . . . retained you? And how much did that cost us?'

'You mustn't worry over that, Master Guest. You have more pressing concerns, I daresay.'

'I *must* worry over it. For Jack must have enough income for his upkeep when I am gone.'

'Really, Master Guest. I find that line of thought an insult to my abilities at the bar.'

'Forgive me. But I do not know you.'

'Well, allow me to say that I have had excellent training at Gray's Inn from some of the finest legal minds in London.'

'How long have you been practicing law?'

'For just over a sennight.'

'Good Christ.' He turned back to the fire and warmed his hands.

'Master Guest, we haven't any time to waste.'

The animation he had seen only moments before in Guest's eyes faded. 'I believe it is all a waste, Master Cobmartin. Are you familiar with the details?'

'Master Tucker was most thorough. But I should like to hear it from you.'

Guest sighed and turned back only enough to stare at Nigellus. He offered him the chair with a nod and Nigellus bowed, strode forward, and took it. He laid his folder on the table, took out ink and quill from his scrip, and blew his warm breath onto his fingers, readying to take notes.

Guest looked him over with a snort and turned to the fire once more. Still shackled but seeming unperturbed by the heavy irons, he told his tale plainly, adding no embellishments, and Nigellus dutifully took it down in his swift and thrifty hand.

'So you see, Master Cobmartin,' he said when he'd finished, 'I fear – unless Jack can uncover the culprit forthwith – that there is very little for you to do.'

'It is clear, Master Guest, that you do not know the law as intimately as I do. For there is very much indeed to do. The witnesses must be beaten down – oh, only in the sense of a verbal sparring with logic and rhetoric as my weapons. Nothing physical, certainly . . .' His gaze scanned Guest's bruised chin once before he turned back to his parchment. 'And the recorder must be appeased with eloquent argument. The sheriffs equally pacified so as to appear robust without actually being proved wrong. And most of all, I must find a way to convincingly stall the proceedings so that your apprentice can do his proper investigating and find the true culprit.'

Guest slowly turned and measured Nigellus with an unusually intense scrutiny. One side of his mouth gradually drew up in a lop-sided grin. 'I see Jack chose well.'

'I hope I have earned your confidence, too, Master Guest. For there is much to accomplish.'

'Hmm.' He shuffled away from the fire, manacles clanking on the stone floor before he dropped heavily to the cot. 'What would you have *me* do, Master Cobmartin?'

'Well . . .' Nigellus glanced around the small cell. 'There is little for you at the moment, Master Guest. I need not tell you all of the obstacles you are up against, not the least of which is your . . . unfortunate past.'

A brow rose, but he made no comment.

'These witnesses will be our bane. Master Tucker tells me he is having trouble finding one of them, but this might prove to our advantage. Tell me, you were unacquainted with the victim prior to your congress with her the day before?'

'I had never heard of nor met her.'

'But you felt compelled as a matter of honor – even in your, er . . . less than sober state – to attempt to warn her.'

'Yes.'

Nigellus dipped his quill and jotted down some notes. 'That goes very well indeed, Master Guest. It shows a certain level of rectitude.' He took a few more notes and then looked up. Guest's gaze was steady. He sat upright without slouching, hands laid on his thighs in a posture of readiness as if he would bolt from his seat at a moment's notice, manacles or no manacles.

'I take it you cannot claim benefit of clergy?'

He released an airless chuckle. 'No.'

'Pity. Very well. Let me explain the procedure, then. You will be tried before the Common Pleas at the Guildhall. There will be a presentment, which is a formal presentation to the court regarding the offense. Jurors are being selected now by the sheriffs within the Bread Street Ward. They will be amongst those with a relevant knowledge of the crime and those who are acquainted with you personally as a judgment of character.'

For the first time, he saw Guest shift uncomfortably.

'The jurors will be familiar with the case and the testimony before the trial convenes, you understand. For all intents and purposes *they* are investigating the crime and will be fully familiar with the details such as they are. They merely witness to the facts as presented. But we may call further witnesses to add to the facts they have already heard. Now. This is very important. I am not permitted to speak for you during the trial. My purpose is to instruct, to gather evidence, and to teach you to present it. *Ita lex scripta est*. It is you, not I, on trial. And so *you* must defend yourself, Master Guest. Silence is acquiescence. Silence is guilt. You are expected to speak.'

'I will.'

'Good. *Vérité sans peur*, eh? You mustn't be afraid to speak the truth. Now, though it is also true that witnesses for the defense are discouraged, they can be permitted if the recorder is willing to entertain them. And it is then that I am permitted to question the witnesses. But remember, both the jury and the judges have already been acquainted with the crime and testimony and may have already decided the case *before* the trial.'

'I have been on trial before, Master Cobmartin.'

Nigellus caught the sharp edge of Guest's comment. 'Oh . . . oh y-yes, of course. However, a trial for treason is a different kettle of fish than a trial for murder, though they are very similar—'

'Let us hope the outcome is far better this time.'

'Oh indeed, Master Guest. That is my wish also.'

He waited, but Guest had nothing to add. He merely stared at Nigellus with a penetrating glare.

'Take heart, Master Guest. I have no intention of losing this case. London would be the poorer for it if they hanged you.'

'My sentiments as well, Master Cobmartin.'

'Of course. Have you, er, anything to add? Anything at all?'

Guest edged forward, leaning his forearms on his thighs. 'I discovered that Elizabeth le Porter's former mistress is the owner of a relic, the Virgin's Tears. She claimed that Mistress le Porter left her employ because of that relic; that it was mutual. But of that I have my doubts. Especially after Madam Peverel's rivals, the Noreys boys, came to my lodgings. They claim Mistress le Porter was paid to steal the relic, which was clearly still in the possession of the Widow Peverel.'

'But now, these Noreys men. You said before that they ambushed you?'

'They ransacked the place and lay in wait for me in my lodgings.'

'That does show a certain level of culpability on their part. And they threatened you?'

'They jumped me with their knives drawn. I was lucky to escape with my own life.'

'Though John Noreys wasn't as lucky. That is a shame. Did you bring charges?'

'I didn't see the point.'

Nigellus huffed down at his parchment. 'But my dear Master Guest, it would be a stronger case for your character to prove that you hold dear your honor.'

'I consider it *dis*honorable to have to prove my honor so!'

Nigellus stared at him for a long moment. Laymen. They did not understand the law at all!

'Well, be that as it may. Though it may have little bearing on your murder charge, this is certainly something with which you can cast doubt upon your having committed the crime, and wave a flag of proof for your statement that some unknown person had paid you to murder Mistress le Porter.'

'But why try to murder her if they had already paid her to steal the thing . . . which she hadn't done? Was it because they were afraid of her? That she might tell? Or was she extorting them?'

'Ah. I see. How clever your mind is, Master Guest. You pick at the marrow to get every last morsel.'

'Indeed,' he said, eyes narrowed in distaste. 'But will it not be a problem of logic, then, to try to prove Walter Noreys guilty of murder if he is also supposed to be guilty of hiring her to commit larceny?'

'Not if it can be proved. Casting doubt is our flagship, Master Guest. To *think* you guilty is not enough for a jury to convict. They must be certain. And if Walter Noreys proves an impediment to that, then we must bless his interference.'

'We will see.'

'Indeed we will. For now I shall assist Jack Tucker where I can prove useful. And you, dear sir . . . well. Your prayers will suffice.'

'Let us hope so. And Master Cobmartin, please remember: *It is possible to fail in many ways . . . while to succeed is possible only in one way*.'

'Quite true, Master Guest, quite true.' He rose. 'I shall endeavor to succeed.'

They bowed to one another, and Nigellus went to the grille in the door and called for the guard.

Nigellus was still thinking of his unusual encounter with Crispin Guest as he set out for Newgate bright and early the next morning. Were the tales of the man true? He hardly seemed the devil as so many had said of him, nor did he appear to be a saint . . . which he had also heard. Crispin Guest was a man of contrasts. There was talk that he was a combative man – and the bruises on his chin proved that. If he had not gotten them from his altercation with John and Walter Noreys, he had received it by fighting the guards at Newgate.

It was also rumored that he was ill-mannered and untrustworthy. Clearly those were both falsehoods, for the man that Nigellus had met was the most tactful of gentlemen, and Jack Tucker was certainly not his apprentice for the money. Guest must therefore be trustworthy and fair-minded, though a little gruff in manner, perhaps. To teach a boy of the streets Latin and to read and write was not the mark of an injudicious man. No, Guest might have been a traitor, but he was a most unusual one. Therefore the good Nigellus had heard – his honesty, his charity, and his piousness, for there was always some sort of relic Guest was associated with – must be credited to him as well.

That crafty Thomas Clarke. He must make an effort to thank him for putting this case in his path.

Nigellus traversed the curve of the road, his thoughts assembling in order to talk with the man again before the trial commenced, when he beheld Newgate, its stoic walls and tall gate with its crenelated battlements, its portcullis. It was still early yet – Prime had rung – but guards walked both atop the wall and below, their faces lit by torches whose flames whipped in the wind.

Before he could take another step he heard shouting at the gate and he looked up to observe the running about of the guards and serjeants of the prison. Smelling the excitement, Nigellus hurried forward and stood unobtrusively until he was able to ask a guard what the shouting was all about.

'A woman's been found strangled, up Catte Street, by Milk. Dreadful thing.' And he rushed off to take his station. Horses were brought forth and soon the dark-haired Lord Sheriff appeared and mounted up, kicking the flanks of the beast to urge it up Newgate Market.

Hands suddenly grabbed Nigellus from behind and he twisted around, staring into the blunt face of one of the sheriff's serjeants.

'You! Come!'

'But I—'

'You're a lawyer, are you not? Don't deny it, I seen you yesterday.'

'I shall not deny it. But what would you need with me?'

'You can write, can't you? The sheriff's clerk is otherwise occupied with Sheriff Walcote. Sheriff Loveney will need a clerk.'

'See here—'

'Do you argue with me?' said the serjeant, tightening his grip on his cudgel.

Nigellus swallowed. 'Of course I will help the Lord Sheriff,' he said quickly. 'You need only ask.' He clutched his leather case tightly to his breast and anxiously set out down Newgate Market, keeping the sheriff in view and another eye on the serjeant behind him, whose club was kept at the ready.

EIGHT

Friday, 16 October

Not so much refreshed as resigned, Jack Tucker returned to the Boar's Tusk the next day. This was not a job he was willing to do alone, not when the stakes were so dire. He pushed through the heavy doors, marched down an aisle between long tables, and pushed the drapery to the back door aside. Walking across the courtyard to the kitchens he came upon Ned. 'Just the lad I was looking for.'

Ned was a stringy fellow of uncertain age. He was older than Jack but considerably younger than Master Crispin, and he had said he had worked for the Langtons since he was a small boy. His messy hair, spotted face, and sorrowful brows gave him a hang-dog expression even when he was merry, but Jack had always taken to him. He might not be the hottest poker in the fire, but he was fair-dealing and knew a good jest or two.

'Eh? What you want, Jack?'

'You. I need your help. How would you like to be a Tracker's apprentice's assistant?'

'A what?'

'Come on. We've got to talk to Gilbert.' He began pulling Ned toward the kitchens but Ned held back. 'He's not in there. He's in the tavern.'

'I didn't see him.'

'Then he's in the mews. Come then.'

He led Jack down the stairs to the dark cellar where the tuns of wine and ale rested in the coolness. A candle glow indicated Gilbert's presence and they headed in that direction. He looked up. His congenial face always cheered Jack. The Langtons were both faithful friends to Master Crispin and, truly, he was lucky to have them.

'Why Master Tucker. What brings you here? Crispin with you?'

'I bring you dark tidings, Master Gilbert. They've arrested my master, and I must in all haste find the true culprit or he will hang. I beg you, let me take Ned with me to find a missing witness.'

'What? Slow down, Jack.' He set down his bucket and faced the two. 'What is that you said about Crispin?'

Jack repeated the facts. He felt all jittery inside, as if ants were crawling over him. He needed to get on with it, to help his master. For he also needed to find out more about those Noreys brothers, *requiescat in pace*, and those Virgin's Tears. There had been a day when he could have gone to the Abbot of Westminster for that last bit, but old Abbot Nicholas was dead these past two years, and though the new abbot, William de Colchester, was more disposed toward his master than he had been previously, Jack didn't know if the cleric would readily take to Jack.

'And so I need Ned's help. I can't go door to door all by m'self. If I could but borrow Ned for the day, good master . . .'

'Well, seeing that it's for Crispin. What say you, Ned?'

Ned scratched his messy thatch of hair. 'What would I have to do?'

'You ask – politely, that is most important – if any in the household have heard of or know the whereabouts of Thomas Tateham. And if they have, to tell me immediately.'

Ned looked from Gilbert to Jack. 'All right.'

Jack grabbed his arm and tugged. 'Then come on! God keep you, Master Gilbert!'

'And you, Jack! My prayers are for Crispin this day.'

Jack tore from the Boar's Tusk and hurried up Gutter Lane before he turned and found himself alone. 'Where is that sarding lad?' Ned lumbered up from behind a man with a stack of tied twigs on his back. 'Ned, there is no time to tarry.'

'I just thought of something,' said the dark-haired boy. 'You get paid to do your master's bidding. What about me?'

'Do you mean to stand there and *haggle* with me? Of all the ungrateful . . .'

'Master Crispin never done naught for me. I have naught to be grateful for from him.'

'Why, Ned! I never knew you were such a greedy knave that you wouldn't help your fellow man out of good Christian charity.'

He ticked his head. 'For shame. Go off with you, then. I can do it on me own.'

'Now, Jack. Don't be like that. It's just that . . . here's a day's wage I might lose, you ken?'

Jack narrowed his eyes. 'Very well. I get a farthing for my work and I will gladly sacrifice it for my master's sake. Good enough?'

Ned ducked his head and nodded sheepishly. Jack dug into his scrip, pulled out the quartered coin, and handed it over. 'There! Now will you come along!'

Ned perked up. He smiled as he stuffed the quartered coin in. 'Aye, Jack. Let's to it.'

They headed up West Cheap to Mercery and Jack stopped them. 'Now, Ned, you take that side of the street and I'll take this side. Tho-mas Tate-ham,' he pronounced clearly.

'But we don't know his vocation.'

'Naw, lad. If I knew that, me job would be made easier.'

Ned saluted Jack and trotted forth to the first shop.

Jack watched him go before he turned and hurried across the street, stopping before he was run down by a man with an empty wain. The cart rattled swiftly by and he darted forward, marching up to the granite step below the door. He knocked smartly and waited.

A woman answered, wiping her hands on her apron. Her nose and cheeks were red and chapped. 'Yes?'

He bowed. 'Good day, mistress. I am looking for a Thomas Tateham of Mercery Lane.'

'There's no one here of that name.'

'Would you know of this man by name or by profession, good mistress?'

She frowned and shook her head. 'No. It isn't familiar.'

Jack sighed. 'I thank you.' He stepped down. The woman gave him a nod and closed the door. He looked up the street at all the doors, the shops, the people. 'Best get to it, Jack.'

But after an hour of talking to not only those at the shop doors but to their tenants, he had no luck. Jack had climbed many ladders that day and still he had more to go. He cast a glance across the street. Ned was not nearly as efficient and had lagged behind, but he was doing the job, bless him.

Jack moved on to the next house when he heard a shriek. All motion on the street stopped save for a few dogs on leads. Everyone seemed to be halting in their steps, listening. And then the shriek happened again.

Jack took off running toward the sound. He cut down another lane and then another. People were gathering round a woman, a maidservant it looked like, and she was sobbing on the arm of a burly man. She pointed behind her, and those closest to her tried to discern what she was yelling about.

Jack tapped a man beside him on the street, motioning for him to come with him. He and Jack went and yet another man followed. Up the stairs and they found an open door. A woman lay across her bed, head hanging over the side, eyes wide and bulging. Her throat was painted with dark bruising.

Jack crossed himself. 'God blind me,' he muttered.

The others stayed back, but Jack approached cautiously. He reached out and touched her arched neck and knew he would find no pulse. His fingers encountered cold flesh. His hand moved to the jaw. He tried to move the head but found it tight. He touched one of the arms with its twisted elbow.

'Lad,' cried one of the men. 'What are you doing?'

'Investigating,' said Jack. He tried to move the arm and found it still pliable. The staring eyes were only starting to cloud over.

More men burst into the room. 'Here! What are you doing?'

He turned to the gathered crowd and drew himself up. 'I am Jack Tucker, apprentice to the Tracker. And I am merely examining the body. She's begun rigor which means she's been dead nearly six hours.'

'Who did he say he was?' asked one man of another. The others started to murmur.

'Said he's the Tracker's apprentice.'

'Who's the Tracker?'

'That fellow what did that treason all them years ago. Now he catches murderers, doesn't he?'

'I never heard of no Tracker.'

'Yes you have, Roger. That surly man. With them relics.'

'Oh. *Him*.'

'What's he do with relics?'

'Finds 'em. When they're lost or stolen. He finds murderers, too.'

There was general agreement and head-nodding . . . until, 'I never heard of no apprentice.'

Jack whirled on them. 'I'm Jack *sarding* Tucker! I'm always with Master Crispin.'

'Heard it was a young boy. Shorter than you.'

'I've been with him six years. I'm seventeen now.'

'Ooooh! You mean Crispin *Guest*!'

'That's what I've been saying!'

The first man grinned and thumbed toward Jack. 'That's the Tracker's apprentice, that. Jack Tucker.'

Jack huffed and decided to ignore them. He motioned them back and scanned the room. The window was unbroken. One shutter was open. He went to the window and gingerly looked over the side. No ladder. No scratches as if a ladder had been placed and removed. The room was in fine shape, in fact, no ransacking for goods, no thievery. Though there were two goblets set out, and the half-eaten leavings of cheese and fruit.

It was around Terce now so that meant she had been murdered between sunrise and Prime. She and her murderer's little meal was an early mixtum or late-night supper.

He made his way toward the table, and the men opened a path for him. He peered into the goblets. Yes, there were the dregs of wine in one, and the other still had a portion. He picked it up and examined it, sniffed it. And was suddenly aware of his audience.

Slowly pivoting he took in the men's faces, all anxiously watching. 'Erm . . . has someone gone to fetch the sheriff?'

The crowd looked at one another but were unable to determine if in fact someone *had* gone for the sheriff until one hearty soul volunteered.

'Gentlemen,' said Jack in a stern voice. 'It is best you all leave these lodgings now so that the sheriff and the coroner can do their work. If anyone is a witness to what might have transpired, if you saw anyone enter or leave these premises since yesterday, you should expect to stay and give your testimony to the sheriff.'

They grumbled and made their slow progress to the doorway.

Jack offered up a relieved sigh as they ambled out and made a slow perusal of the room, noting this and that, before he, too, followed them out.

When he descended the stairs and stood on the street, the crowd left a wide berth around him. He also waited for the sheriff, calming himself with assurances that he was doing just as his master would have wanted.

When the sheriff arrived and his sharp gaze landed on him, Jack wasn't as certain at his decision to stay.

Sheriff Walcote dismounted and strode forward. 'You're Guest's apprentice, are you not?'

Jack bowed. 'Y-yes, Lord Sheriff. Jack Tucker.'

'I don't care what your name is.' He pushed past Jack.

'She's been dead six hours at most,' said Jack.

The sheriff's foot was only on the second tread when he stopped. He swiveled his head and glared. 'What did you say?'

'I've . . . I've been up there. Investigating. She's been dead—'

'Who gave you the authority to do so, Tucker?'

He straightened his cotehardie. 'Well . . . my master—'

'And who gives *him* the authority?'

'It . . . it's just that . . . people call on him to—'

'That's what I thought.' He climbed again and gestured curtly to his guards toward Jack. They bore down on him.

'Wait, good masters,' said Jack, backing up. The crowd opened up for him and he was slowly being backed into a fence. 'I done nothing wrong!'

'Come here, you.' The serjeant lunged. Jack ducked. It was true, he wasn't as short as he used to be, and sometimes his taller height was a disadvantage, but he was just as agile as ever and by pivoting on his hips, he easily slipped the man's clutches. But another moved in. Jack stood his ground before he felt the fence at his back.

Two more guards lurched toward him. He rolled backwards over the fence, legs high in the air, until he landed upright and took off running.

He heard them scrambling lamely over the fence behind him but didn't look back. The courtyard narrowed to the tight span between two shops and he jumped over the fence before him. He ran full tilt down the street and turned at Catte. Still pumping arms and legs, he made the tight turn at Milk Street and came up short. The other sheriff and his men were crowded round another house, one reputed to be a stew, though such bawdy houses were not allowed on this side of the Thames.

He froze and stared at the proceedings, blinking. Until a hand came down on his shoulder. His first instinct was to twist away and run, but the hand tightened and the friendly voice of Nigellus Cobmartin stopped him. 'Master Jack? What are you doing here?'

'I could say the same of you. What *are* you doing here?'

'Well, it was the strangest thing. As I was coming to Newgate to see your master again – and he gives you his prayers, by the way – an alarm had gone out. The sheriff was being called to investigate the murder of a woman.'

Jack turned away to stare up to the second floor of the shop around which everyone was milling. 'Here?'

'Yes. I was intrigued because of the manner of this alleged murder. She was supposed to have been strangled.'

Jack frowned. '*Here*?'

Nigellus huffed a breath. 'Yes. Why do you—?'

'Because . . . I have just come from another crime . . . of a woman who was strangled.'

'What?' He grabbed Jack and pulled him away from the crowd. 'Are you certain?'

'I sarding well am. I was nearly nabbed by Sheriff Walcote's men just for doing my own investigating.'

'And where was this?'

'Just off of Watling.'

'And there is another here.'

'Aye.' Jack's eyes reflected the same gleam that sparkled in Nigellus' gaze. 'There's someone strangling women in London . . . and it isn't my master!'

NINE

Friday, 16 October

Jack and Nigellus found themselves back at the Boar's Tusk, hunching low over their cups.

'You say that the woman you saw was six hours dead?'

'Aye,' said Jack, eyes sweeping the room, making sure ears were not attuned to them. 'At the most, by my best reckoning.'

'I know not how long the woman on Catte Street was dead. And then there is Elizabeth le Porter, dead now more than a day.'

'Someone is killing these women. It can't be a coincidence.'

'Young Master Jack, I dare to agree with you. But how to make the sheriffs see the light? Or the recorder?'

'But if them women were killed by someone else, then surely they must release my master before ever there is a trial.'

'Possibly. But there are witnesses that put Master Guest entering the le Porter woman's lodgings.'

'But six hours ago my master was already in gaol.'

'Yes. It certainly looks better for your master.'

'That house is said to be a stew, Master Nigellus.'

'Indeed? Well. And what of the other woman off Watling?'

'I know not. I neglected to get her name. I was in fear of me life and limb.'

Nigellus rubbed his chin.

Jack sipped his ale, hoping for inspiration. 'That settles it. I've got to find this killer. He's a danger to all good and wholesome women in this parish!' He got halfway to his feet before Nigellus tugged him back down.

'I think you are forgetting something, Jack. What of the man who hired your master to kill that le Porter woman?'

Jack slumped. 'Oh, aye. Blind me! That don't make sense to the rest of it. Why hire Master Crispin if he could just do it himself?' He leaned on his elbow and dug his fist into his chin. 'He plainly did not want to be seen.'

'Yes, one reason surely.'

'They'd had a falling out. He could not get close to her again. Or . . . he was being hired by another to do the task, and to take all suspicion from him, he'd hire a third party.'

'That is devious, Jack.'

'Nigellus,' he said, taking up his cup and taking a hearty quaff, 'I can tell you, I have seen some strange things in London. Very strange. And this is getting to be just as strange.' He took another drink. 'As my master would say, "unpack the facts, for it is usually simpler than we thought." And so, the facts are these.' His fingers wrote them down on the sticky table. 'Fact one: My master was hired by an unknown person to kill a woman. Fact two: That woman was supposedly hired to steal a relic. Fact three: The relic was *not* stolen. Fact four: Them that wanted it, the Noreys household, tried to kill my master to get it. And so, it seems to me, that I must first concentrate on these items and get to the strangulation deaths of the other women later. But oh! If we can prove to the sheriffs that those murders happened outside the possibility of my master's having done it, he will be freed. What to do first? Dammit!' He slammed his hand to the table and suddenly noticed a maiden standing at his elbow with a sweating jug of ale cradled in her hands.

She was young, younger than Jack, with a sweep of auburn hair just barely contained in her linen kerchief. Her small mouth was hitched in a smirk, and her bright hazel eyes were softened by a spray of dark lashes. A small upturned nose was stippled with a mask of freckles over the bridge and across her cheeks on pale, smooth skin.

Jack might have stared for longer than was polite. He wasn't certain but he only snapped out of it when Gilbert blocked his view.

'I see you've met my niece, Isabel. This is the lad I was telling you about, lass. Jack Tucker. He's Crispin Guest's apprentice.'

Her smirk softened to a smile and she gave a curtsey. 'Master Tucker.'

'Demoiselle.'

Isabel grinned. Her animated smile radiated brilliance and sunshine, two things lacking in the Boar's Tusk's dark interior.

'So then,' said Gilbert. 'Where's Ned?'

Jack stared at him for a long moment before he remembered and slapped his forehead. 'God blind me! I clean forgot! Er . . . Nigellus . . . I'll, er, be back.' He jumped up from the table and darted out of the dim tavern.

Hitting the street at a run, he returned to Mercery Lane in no time. And there was Ned, standing at the head of the street, looking around for Jack. When Ned spied him, he came trotting over.

'There you are. Well, I done my side of the street.'

'And? Don't keep me waiting, Ned.'

'Nothing. No one's heard of him. You'd think at least someone might.'

Jack scratched his head. 'I'm beginning to think this man does not live on Mercery.'

'Or that's not his name.'

Jack stared at Ned.

Shuffling his feet, Ned kicked at a stone. 'Or so . . .' he trailed off.

'Ned!' Jack grabbed him and the man stiffened, eyes round. 'That's *exactly* it! God blind me! I should have knowed it the first. He gave a false name, man! And, for all we know, a false address. There's something about him. But what?'

'How will you find him now?' He rubbed his arm where Jack had grabbed him.

'Ah me. That's just it, isn't it? How do I? Well, it makes no matter now. I have other tasks I must complete. I thank you, Ned. You can go back to the Boar's Tusk now.'

Ned shrugged and turned, waving his farewell.

Jack took a step forward before he looked back. 'Oi, Ned!'

Ned jerked back, his messy hair flickering in the wind.

'Erm . . . about that Isabel.'

Ned offered a salacious grin. 'She's a pretty thing, isn't she?'

'Well, I wondered is all.'

'Wondered what?'

'What she's doing there?'

Ned sauntered back. 'Well, it's like this. The Langtons don't have no children. And his brother just died. Hasn't been a mother in years, as I hear tell it. So the girl come to live with Gilbert. She's the heir, isn't she?' He hiked up his belt. 'Might give her the nod if she's inclined.'

'The nod?' Jack slapped his shoulder. 'Here now! That's the Langtons' kin you're talking about. They're like family to me.'

'I don't mean anything sordid in it. It's just that . . . if they don't have no heirs and if she's the heir, her husband stands to inherit an alehouse. And that could be me as much as any other man.'

Jack frowned. 'I reckon so,' he muttered.

'See you, Jack. Thanks for the farthing.' He marched on, leaving Jack standing in the road and watching his friend leave.

So she was now the Langtons' heir. He had to admit, she was the fairest lass he had seen in a long time. So fresh and young. And a good disposition, even though the Fates had dealt with her harshly. God-fearing, she must be. Must have her own patron saint.

A goose honked loudly and nipped at his calf. 'Ow! Sarding bird.' He leapt out of the way, and the goosegirl snickered at him. He took himself to the side of the road and pulled his cloak over his shoulders, protecting the coat from mud. Time to find these Noreyses.

Another quick visit to Eckington and his notes and he found the Noreys household on Lombard. Jack slowed when he approached what was most certainly the house, with its front entry draped in black. Of course. There had been a death . . . at Master Crispin's hands.

Now think, Jack. You can't go marching in announcing you're the Tracker's apprentice. They'll know who the Tracker is . . . and I'd not be welcome.

Why else would he have cause to be there, asking his questions? The only one who would need to ask would be, 'The sheriff,' he muttered aloud. 'I'll be just another clerk to the sheriff. That will do.' But he had no quill, no parchment, or ink. Who did he know nearby that might have such things? He grimaced. 'God blind me,' he mumbled. He'd have to try it. He couldn't go all the way back to their lodgings on the Shambles, wasting precious time. He'd have to gird himself and go.

He stomped his way toward the London Stone and to the lodgings of one of Master Crispin's more notorious friends, John Rykener. He found the place atop a wick maker, the highest attic room with a ladder leaning against the wall as its only access.

Jack grabbed a rung at head-height and began to climb. When he reached the top he rapped on the shutter. 'Master Rykener! Are you at home?'

He heard a shuffling within and at length the shutter opened. A man of about Crispin's age with shoulder-length brown hair and sleepy eyes peered out. He yawned wide and rubbed his sleep-blurred face. 'Jack Tucker? To what do I owe the pleasure?'

'Master Rykener. I am in a bit of a hurry. Might I borrow from you a quill, parchment, and ink?'

He stared for a moment before bursting into laughter. 'What?'

'Master Rykener, my need is dire. Do you have the items?'

'Yes, of course. Come in.'

He stepped back to allow Jack to climb in through his window. It was even more cramped than Cobmartin's room at Gray's Inn, but Jack stood in the center and tried not to look around too curiously. Though he couldn't help but notice a coffer lying open with numerous women's gowns spilling from it. Mercifully, John was attired as a man today, or at least a man in a shift. Jack supposed he must do his sleeping during the day as he mostly plied his trade in the evening as a whore. It would explain why he was still sleepy and shuffling about so late in the morning.

John rummaged through another coffer and bundled the items in his arms. 'I don't suppose you will share with me what you are about, Master Tucker.'

'It is on Master Crispin's business, you can be assured of that.'

'Oh, I wasn't questioning the purity of your motives, Young Jack. Not at all.'

He hadn't meant to huff his repugnance aloud, but John slid his gaze toward him nonetheless and frowned.

Rykener pressed his small mouth together and said nothing as he handed Jack a scroll, a worn goose quill, and a small pot of ink. Jack stuffed them in his scrip and turned to go.

'I know you don't like me.'

Jack paused on the windowsill before turning back.

John tossed his head and sighed. 'You don't approve. That I sleep with men. That I swive them.' He looked Jack in the eye. 'And I shall never ask for your approval, for I do not need it.

But I am Crispin's friend. I have been loyal. And I will always be there to help him if he needs it. And I hope you realize that the same goes for you. Whether you welcome it or not.'

Master Crispin *had* needed it, only last year when Jack himself was imprisoned by the king. Rykener had stepped in and had taken Jack's place, helping to solve the crime and ultimately freeing Jack. Master Crispin even later confirmed that it was Rykener who had purchased the bed Jack now enjoyed.

It wasn't as if he wasn't grateful – though he couldn't remember if he had actually thanked John – but that he had felt supplanted and by a man whose enterprise and manner he did not respect. Yet John was all the things he said he was. Yes, he was a whore servicing men and dressing as a woman, but he was also a trusted and loyal friend to his master and that made him the same to Jack. Perhaps he was a sinner, but the Church taught that so was the state of all men.

Jack scuffed the floor with his boot, watching his toe kick up a bit of straw. 'I . . . I thank you for that loyalty, Master Ry – John. My master needs it more than anything right now. He is in prison awaiting a trial for a murder he did not commit.'

John gasped and touched his hand to his mouth.

'Aye. It's a sore thing and I am doing me best. But . . .' He couldn't finish that sentence. He swallowed down a lump in his throat and nodded. He hadn't meant to speak. He meant to take his leave, hurry away to do his master's bidding. But the words, some that had been buried deep in his heart and soul for long years, seemed to leave his mouth without his consent.

'When I was a boy,' said Jack, the words sticking to his tongue, 'I . . . I was in one of the . . . stews.'

John's eyes widened. 'Oh, Jack.'

Lip trembling, Jack wiped at his eyes. 'Aye. Well. I saw all manner of men. Rough men. Harsh. Some worse than any task-master could be. I learned things . . . I never wanted to know. I prayed for God's forgiveness. I still do.'

John lowered his hand from his mouth and sat on the edge of the bed. He gazed at Jack a long time before he spoke. 'I knew boys in the stews. Strange *I* was never one of them.' Steady, his voice was soft and seemed to match the sudden stillness of the room when it had been full of urgency and panic before. Jack was almost soothed by his tones. 'But, Jack,' he went on, 'the coarse men that patronize those places, that act on their vile needs. Jack . . . I was never one of those men either. I never have been, never will be. Though it is true I favor . . . men – *adult* men, and God knows why – I wasn't one of those who hurt you long ago.'

Jack swallowed. He did not raise his eyes to Rykener but he did note his words, turned them over, worried at them like a rosary.

After a long time when there were no sounds in the room but their breathing, he finally spoke, touching the bulge of items in his scrip. 'Thanks for these things, John.' His voice was tight and rasping. 'And as a proper Christian and a proper friend, I will try to . . . to treat you with the respect that you've earned.'

John cocked his head, studying him. 'As I do you, Jack,' he said quietly. 'But I meant what I said. You know I would do anything for Crispin or you. You need only ask.'

'And if necessary, I shall. God's blessings on you, John.'

'And to you, Young Jack. For all your toil.'

Jack bowed curtly but before he could leave, John spoke again. 'You don't need to ask God's forgiveness, you know. You were not to blame.'

Jack said nothing. He might have nodded or merely inclined his head. But he quickly hurried out the window and down the ladder, leaving Rykener's place behind. Back he went to Lombard and the great house that belonged to the Noreys family, wiping his face, drawing slower breaths to calm himself.

How could he *not* blame himself? *He* had chosen to enter the stews. Was starving to death more noble? Or stealing a purse? 'That was so long ago, Jack,' he whispered to himself, watching servants and masters mingle on the streets. Long ago but sometimes like yesterday. He never meant to speak of it to Rykener, but there was something about the man that invited honesty. He was likable, despite his profession. And more importantly, Master Crispin trusted and favored him. Could Jack not do the same?

Before he reached the Noreys house, he shook himself free of his memories. There was only his investigation. There was only Master Crispin.

He raised his chin, took on the officious manner of Hamo

Eckington, and knocked upon the door. As soon as the door was opened, Jack pushed his way through and stood in the entry. The servant scuttled up to him with a sour look on his face. 'Here now . . .'

'I haven't time to waste,' said Jack with a clipped tone. 'I am from the sheriffs of London, and I have questions to ask.'

The servant was in his middle years, and there was the hint of gray amongst the brown locks that hung in waves just under his ears. A mushroom cap of a nose – round and big – sat pride of place in the middle of a clean-shaven face with its wide chin and small eyes. His cotehardie was worn but clean. 'This is a house in mourning, master. Please. Have a care.'

Jack's better nature came through and he blinked at the servant, almost giving in. But he recovered and took on a haughty mantle once again. 'Aye, I am aware. But the law does not wait. I must speak to the head of the house.'

'Could it not wait a day, good master? My master suffers so and I would not see him suffer for the world.'

As a loyal servant himself, Jack appreciated the man's pleas, but his own master naturally took precedence and there was little time to waste. 'You would have me return to the sheriffs empty-handed when they sent me themselves? That I cannot do.'

The man sagged and nodded. 'Then please, wait here.' The servant hurried through a doorway, and Jack rocked on his heels watching him go. Good Christ. He didn't believe it would work but here he was! Just as Master Crispin said. Look like you belong and everyone will curry to you.

He looked around. The place had a shabbiness about it. The tapestry which should have been repaired some years ago, with its frayed edges and moth-eaten portions, hung as it was. A glass pane hadn't been replaced with new glass but with a wooden shingle. Something was certainly amiss in this household.

Presently the servant returned and, with great dignity, he bowed and asked Jack to follow him. They passed through an archway to a parlor. The room was fairly large but stark and full of echoes. Jack was certain there should have been more furniture. Yes, there were places on the wall that were lighter, rectangles free of years of smoky fires, that seemed to mark the presence of a sideboard that was no longer there. And a coffer. A missing tapestry, perhaps, on another wall. There were a few chairs with cushions, a small table. But that was all.

A man in his middle years with a dark beard brushed with a host of gray stood at the hearth. His dark gown was floor-length and he wore a simple cap.

The servant announced, 'Master William Noreys. And the sheriff's envoy, a Master . . . Master . . .' Stricken, the servant cast a worried glance toward Jack.

Jack bowed to Noreys. 'I am Jack Tucker . . . with the Lord Sheriff's office.' He looked around, wondering what next to do and, inspired by his lawyer friend, he decided to busy himself. Clerks were always looking busy, and no one paid them any mind as they generally worked in the background. No one watched a clerk as they would a mason or a blacksmith.

He pulled out his parchment, inkpot, and quill and set them on the small table. Uncorking the ink, he dipped in the quill and touched the nib to the parchment's surface, writing some Latin nonsense. 'Now then. I must first beg your mercy at this unfortunate time, good master. On the, er, death of your son.'

Stoically, the man sat. The servant hurried to bring him wine in a wooden goblet. Noreys clutched it to his chest but didn't drink. The servant brought Jack a cup as well. Tempted, but reluctant to be diverted from his duty, Jack simply set it at the head of his parchment.

'That man. That man they arrested,' said Noreys tightly. 'He killed my son.'

'About that. It is the opinion of the sheriffs that Master Guest was defending his life.'

'How can that be? Why would my sons attack a perfect stranger?'

'Why indeed? Yet they *were* in his lodgings.'

'That . . . can be explained, I'm certain.'

'As I understand it, Master Noreys, your sons were there to extract an object from Master Guest that they believed he harbored. Might you know of this object?'

'I haven't a clue, Master Tucker. Walter would not say, and now he is quite distraught.'

Jack nodded. 'It is said, Master Noreys, that your sons wished to obtain a holy relic. The Tears of the Virgin.'

He turned slowly toward Jack and rose, legs straightening without his seeming to make them do so.

'How did you know of that?'

Momentarily stumped, Jack set his mouth in a firm line. 'It is the Lord Sheriff's office,' he said simply, as if that should satisfy all enquiries.

Noreys glared for a long moment before his shoulders sagged and he moved again to the fire, dragging his feet in their long-toed slippers as he went. Jack noted the repairs in the man's gown when the hearthlight struck the material; the patches, the stitched seams. So they *were* in need of funds.

'Yes. It is true. My sons are headstrong and moved on their purpose without telling me. They . . . they hired a maid to steal it. The shame. Is not our family undergoing enough shame and degradation? And now my son . . .' He choked and ran a hand over his face.

'*Requiescat in pace*,' said Jack, crossing himself with the quill still stuck between his fingers. 'So you were unaware that your sons were plotting this theft?'

'Of course I was unaware! I never would have allowed it.'

'And they believed she took the relic.'

'Yes.' He gnawed on a knuckle and turned his face marginally toward Jack. 'Did she?'

'No, master. As it happens, Elizabeth le Porter – the maid in question – was murdered most foully.'

He snapped around, eyes wide. 'Murdered?'

'Aye. Do you have any idea who might have had cause to murder her?'

He held up his hands, clearly overwhelmed by this information. 'Wait. Wait.' He reached behind him and found the wall. He clutched at a tapestry. Jack saw it sway above him and wrinkle with the force of his grip. 'You . . . you are suggesting that someone in *this* house . . .'

'Master Noreys, with all that has recently transpired, it is not outside the realm of likelihood. *Plausible impossibilities should be preferred to unconvincing possibilities*.'

'I don't care about your plausible impossibilities! You're insulting my family. Who are *you* to be dictating to *me*? Only a clerk.'

'The sheriff's clerk,' Jack hurried to add. This was quickly getting out of hand. He rose, taking his time to fold the parchment and cork the ink pot. 'Master Noreys, it looks to all be in order then. I shall trouble you no more. But there is one thing.'

Seething, Noreys glared, mouth turned down in a dark frown.

'Why was it so important to obtain this relic?'

'By the Mass!' Noreys shook his head. 'It is a valuable relic. It belonged to my family.'

'That is not how the law sees it.'

'Then devil take the law!' He wiped the spittle from his beard and gestured around the room. 'You see the state of things, Master Tucker. We are in deep financial straits. Even if we possessed this most precious of relics, we would only turn around and sell it, for we are in sore need of funds.'

'Your business, sir? What's become of it?'

'Some sour transactions. Too many of them. Too much spending and gambling by my sons . . . and now . . .'

Jack stuffed his scrip with his belongings and shuffled toward the door. 'I believe that will do, Master Noreys. And God's blessings on this house.'

'It will take the Almighty's intervention to save us now.'

Jack headed for the archway when an older woman, holding a kerchief to her reddened nose, stepped through. 'Husband,' she said, casting a wary glance at Jack. 'I heard raised voices. What is amiss?'

He strode toward her, taking her hand and patting it. 'Nothing, my love. Nothing at all.' He looked passed Jack. 'My wife, Madam Madlyn.'

Jack bowed. 'Forgive this intrusion, madam. I was just leaving.' He clutched his scrip to his side, walked through the entry, and out the door to the street. He didn't stop until he reached Poultry. 'God's blood,' he swore. 'That's a sorry lot if ever there was one.' He wondered if his deception was a sin. He supposed it was lying. But as Master Crispin often said, lying for a good cause wipes away the sin. Or so he hoped.

What have you learned now, Jack my lad? He walked slowly down Poultry and found himself on Mercery again. That they did indeed try to hire the murdered girl to steal the relic. But why hadn't she? He supposed it was loyalty to her former mistress.

Hard, slapping footfalls behind him made him turn just in time for a man to grab him. Jack wriggled away and managed to draw his knife and crouch into position to fight.

'Hold, good clerk,' said the panting man. He was young and wore a russet houppelande. His nose was pinched, his bearded chin sharp. 'I . . . I overheard you speaking with my father.'

Jack's eyes flitted over the man, taking note of it all. 'You are Walter Noreys.'

'Yes. Is what you said true? Is the maid . . . dead?'

'Aye. No thanks to you.'

He drew back as if slapped. 'W-what do you mean by that?'

'Do you not think your knavery had put her in harm's way? That *you* might be responsible for her death?'

'Me?'

'Was it not you who hired her to sin by committing thievery?'

'I . . . I . . .'

Jack waved a hand at him in disgust. 'What is it you want?'

He shook his head, having the decency to look contrite. 'If what you said is true then I have much sin upon my head. But then so does that knave Guest, for he is keeping the relic for himself.'

'He isn't, you fool. He never had it. And neither did Elizabeth le Porter. It is where it has always been. In the Peverel household.'

'But . . . that cannot be!'

Jack turned his back on him. 'Get you to your own household chapel, Master Noreys. You are in sore need of prayer.'

He walked away, and the man did not follow. He was surprised she was dead, then? That was one item checked off his list. He wondered if the same could be said for *John* Noreys. But of course, the dead do not testify. Could he have been up to more mischief than even his brother Walter knew?

But now to the Peverels, for he had to see this damned relic for himself – He crossed himself and sent a prayer of apology upward. 'Now Master Crispin's got me doing it,' he muttered. Jack had always had the utmost respect for relics, unlike his recalcitrant master. But being in the company of his master and encountering more relics than he had ever heard of did paint it all with a different brush.

The Peverels were on Trinity and so he made his way, cutting down some narrow lanes, passing Watling till he was on Trinity and looking for the house. After asking a merchant or two, he found the place. Deciding to be himself, he knocked upon the door. When it opened, Sheriff Walcote stood in the passage. Before Jack could say anything, he lunged forward and grabbed Jack. 'Now I've got you, you knave. How would you like to occupy a cell right next to your master? Two murderers.'

'Murder, sir? Never!'

'Someone is strangling the women of London. I think it is two someones.'

Appalled, Jack pulled back. Walcote squeezed Jack's arm, but Jack wrenched to the side and pulled free of his grip. He leaped onto the street. Behind him he heard the sheriff call to his men to capture him.

Jack ran hard and didn't look back.

TEN

Saturday, 17 October

Crispin watched the shadow pass by the high barred window in his cell for the third time. His hand went to his empty dagger sheath, and he made a sound of disgust. The sheriff had his dagger. Thank God his sword was at home. But he was ready for whatever it might be that lurked at his window; bat, bird, rat . . .

He startled slightly at the sudden appearance of a cat's face popping through the bars.

He peered closer. 'How the devil do you get way up here?'

The cat blinked at him, mewled, and then leapt down. Immediately the black and white cat slid its sinuous body against his shackled leg. 'Tart,' he grumbled and bent to pick him up. He looked into its black mask with its white blaze, its large yellow eyes. 'Just what brings you here, Gyb?'

The cat purred, and Crispin absently pressed it to his chest and stroked its soft head. 'You're not supposed to be breaking *into* prison, my friend, but *out* of it. But I'd welcome you if you free this place of rats.'

The cat suddenly bounded from his hands and dove under the cot. A scramble, and then it emerged again with a twitching brown rat in his jaws. Crispin chuckled. 'Never have any of my requests been so smartly obeyed.'

The cat found a place on the hearth and proceeded to disembowel his prey, eating most of the center of the creature and leaving the head, feet, and tail behind. Once done, he sat, carefully licking and grooming its white paws.

'At least someone's eating their fill.' He kicked the remnants into the fire, wincing at their smoldering smell, and crouched before the feline. 'Whatever brought you into my den, puss?'

It looked up once from its grooming, blinked, and returned to swiping its head with its dampened paw.

Crispin rose, stretching his back. 'Well, I don't suppose I mind a little company. It does get dreadfully dull here.'

He glanced at his own barren plate on the table. His belly growled from its emptiness. He'd protested when the gaoler wanted to charge him for his meals. He had already paid a mainprise. Surely that should cover it, he had argued.

And still he starved. He had thought those days were over. Well. For the most part.

Besides their arguing over his surety, Melvyn had been particularly obstinate and delayed bringing him his meals, when he deigned to do so. Little wonder after Crispin had hit him on that first day he was brought in. Melvyn had made a most inappropriate and rude comment that Crispin would not allow. He got in one good hit before the other gaolers took Crispin down. Still, it had been worth it.

He turned with surprise when the prison door opened again. But it was not Melvyn or any of the sheriff's men pushing their way through and threatening him but that lawyer again, Nigellus Cobmartin. Crispin greeted him with a nod.

'Master Guest, I trust you are well.'

'As well as one can be in Newgate.'

The lawyer formed a conciliatory smile on his lips. 'Forgive me for not returning sooner. I was delayed. Do sit, Master Guest. May I call you Crispin? It is such a worthy name, is it not? The name of a humble saint and martyr.'

'I am no saint, sir, and, hopefully, no martyr. "Crispin" I am. It is my name. You have my leave, Master Nigellus.'

'Good, good.' He busied himself with his papers, trying to keep them tidy . . . and failing.

'Has there been any word from Jack?'

Nigellus frowned. 'We met just the other day. And though the circumstances were abominable, it might serve you. Two women were found strangled.'

The horror of it struck home. 'God's blood.'

'Yes, though it is a tragedy, it proves *you* were not the culprit. There appears to be a devil loose in London who likes to strangle young women.'

'Or likes to hire someone to do so.'

'Hmm.'

'What has Jack to say about it?'

'Well, that is the trouble, Master Crispin. Sheriff Walcote likes Jack as the culprit, and the boy is currently *in cognito*.'

'The damned fool sheriff.'

Nigellus shook his head. 'Yes. But I think your apprentice is quite resourceful, and so I would not fear for his whereabouts.'

'I don't. Jack can care for himself.'

'Someday I should like to hear how you acquired the lad.'

Crispin offered a lopsided grin, remembering. 'It's a long tale, Master Nigellus. And I hope fervently to have the time to tell it.'

'The trial starts today, Master Crispin. Noon.'

The cold words clutched his heart with equally cold fingers. His breath left him for a heartbeat before it returned.

'Forgive me,' said Nigellus. 'That was abrupt.'

'No, for it is the truth. Why so soon? I have known many a trial to take a year or more to be seen at the King's Bench or Common Pleas.'

'Your Jack seems to think that the sheriffs are most hasty on the matter in order to convict you, for surely with enough time Tucker can solve the crime on his own.'

Crispin nodded. 'It never ceases to amaze me the diligence with which the sheriffs fervently labor for my disposal. I shouldn't be surprised and yet I am. Do you think a bribe would do me any good?'

'If these are the circumstances I should think not.'

'Not that I have the funds. And so we start today. I do not see that we have much more than what we started with.'

Nigellus laid a hand on Crispin's arm. It was strange comfort from a man he did not know. 'We will do what we can. Since I have not heard from Master Jack I must resort to my first tactic, that of delay. The trial will begin, you will begin to speak – and make it lengthy, Master Crispin. Spare no lexicon. And I will put forth new writs that must be addressed. In this, we will gather more time for the witnesses *we* desire and the story that *we* want told.'

Crispin rubbed his jaw and looked down at the cat who was now dedicating himself to rutting his head against Crispin's calf.

'What have we here?' said Nigellus. He bent down to pet the cat. 'Oi, Gyb. You are here for good luck, eh?'

'*Good* luck would be an interesting change of pace,' said Crispin.

'But you *have* good luck, sir. For *I* am on the case! And I am already forming a tale of these strangled women. Remember, my good Crispin, that I need only inject doubt into the minds of the jury. They must *know* you to be guilty, not *think* it. With doubt, there will be room for them to question their own facts. Now, I should like to hear in your own words what you intend to say.'

'Now? Recite my testimony?'

'Yes. Since I cannot speak for you at the trial it is best we rehearse your speech now. Now is better than later.'

'So I see. Well then.'

Crispin launched into his speech, but Nigellus stopped him from time to time to help him clarify this point and blur that one. Crispin began to feel a certain level of confidence in the man that he just might know what he was doing.

After Crispin seemed to satisfy him, Nigellus looked around. 'Have you no meat and drink? This is insufferable.' He moved to the door and called for the gaoler through the grille. 'Gaoler! Food and ale for this prisoner. He needs his strength for the trial ahead.'

It took some convincing – and a coin or two – but the gaolers brought Crispin some actual meat, cheese, bread, and a jug of ale.

Nigellus took the cat from Crispin's arms and insisted he sit to eat and Crispin did. The meat was cold, but that didn't matter. The cheese had a skin of mold on it, but he trimmed it off with Nigellus' knife. He ate and drank heartily of the ale. They had only given him water for all that silver he had surrendered to the sheriff, and the ale tasted good to him.

'Will you be in the courtroom?' asked Crispin, mouth full.

'Yes. I must observe and be on hand to submit my writs, to keep my eye on the witnesses and jury, and to question witnesses myself. If there is anything amiss with the jury, I can usually spot it and take that as well to the recorder.'

'Is it to be the one judge or several?'

'It is hard to say. You are on the cusp, Crispin. You are an important personage, enough to warrant several judges, while at the same time . . . of little importance these days, if you understand me.'

He snorted and tore off a piece from the loaf, stuffing it in his mouth. 'Yes, I get your drift.'

'In any case, we might do better with the one judge. John Tremayne has always been a fair-minded man. You could do worse.'

'Indeed I could.'

The bells from the nearby church tolled, and Crispin paused in his eating. He set the scraps down and wiped his hands on the cloth provided. 'Sext, Master Nigellus. Should we make ready to depart?'

He nodded, looking toward the door. And it was then they both heard the footfalls. 'The Guildhall is half a mile from here. I shall be with you the whole way.'

He gave a half-smile and bowed to the man as the door whined open. Crispin moved forward, and the cat followed. He turned toward the cat as he stood in the doorway. 'You are free to go, Gyb. No one's keeping *you* here.'

The cat, with tail raised high, strolled out the door and trotted down the stairs in the opposite direction. *Well, there's one prisoner freed*, he thought. *Perhaps it's a good sign.*

Crispin followed the sheriff's serjeants down the stone stairs with difficulty. The iron shackles weighed heavily on his steps. Nigellus followed close behind him. As he came out into the sunshine of Newgate's arch, an assembly of people stood out in the street. Strangely silent, they watched as he did his best to keep up while Sheriff Loveney mounted an awaiting horse and trotted ahead. The serjeants surrounded Crispin and marched him down Newgate Market. The people, still silent, turned and walked with them, serving as a noiseless retinue, until one woman called out from the crowd, 'God's blessings on you, Crispin Guest!'

His head snapped sharply in that direction. Another shouted from behind, 'Me and mine are praying for you!'

That set the crowd to murmuring with other calls for God's blessings upon him. The sheriff twisted on his saddle and scowled at the crowd, telling them to disperse, but it only seemed to gather more people as they traveled toward Milk Street and made the turn.

Crispin lost his breath. 'God's blood,' he murmured. This crowd. They weren't out for his blood as he suspected they might be. They were here *for* him! In support. His eyes tracked the people, faces he did not know. Men, and women carrying babes or dragging their children beside them with clasped hands. They offered their silent gazes. It was an entirely different sensation from those crowds from court some twelve years ago. They had jeered him then, truly out for his blood and he had expected to give it. Yet these humble people . . . where did they all come from? Who were they? Surely he had not touched this many lives in the nine years since he had turned to his present occupation.

He memorized the worn faces, the cheeks pressed against wimples, the beards, the razor-stubbled chins, the dark and weary eyes. They were the ordinary folk of London. They were the lowly. He had been far above them once, but now he was one of them. And they knew it, too. They had accepted it far earlier than Crispin had done in all his years of foot-dragging. He couldn't deny it any longer. He *was* one of them. And if die he must, at least the crowds would be on his side. A generous mercy from on high.

The sheriff and his men turned down another lane and found a grand structure, half-timbered with a stone arched portico and a wide square. The Guildhall. The sheriff's horse clopped over the cobblestoned courtyard. The crowd widened to cover the courtyard's edges, leaving a wide berth around the sheriff's men. Sheriff Loveney dismounted, his scowl deepening. 'Keep these people back,' he growled at one of his serjeants.

'Yes, my lord,' he said, clasping his pike tightly and lowering it at an angle.

The sheriff flicked a glance back at Crispin. 'I don't know how you managed to stir them up, Guest, but there had better not be trouble.'

Crispin said nothing. He shook his head in disbelief, taking in all the people and wondering if he was worthy of such patronage.

The sheriff led the way through the entry arch. Crispin followed, felt the footsteps of Nigellus behind him. They walked through a corridor until it opened into the great hall.

The sheriff announced, 'Crispin Guest, the accused, coming into court!'

The blood surged within him. Crispin longed to *do* something, to fight. But his only weapon would be his voice. He surveyed the room. The recorder of London, John Tremayne, sat on a raised dais on a great bench with a high back. He was alone.

Before him, a wooden rail, or, Crispin supposed, a bar.

Across the room were nine men, two rows of them on long benches. The jury.

The serjeants marched Crispin to the center of court just below the dais and pushed him up against the bar with the jury behind him. He faced the judge even as Nigellus slipped into court and stood a moment with the others who had managed to get inside to watch the proceedings, until his lawyer made his way through the crowd to find a seat at a desk next to the clerk.

Scanning further, Crispin noticed the eel monger, Hugh Buckton, standing uncomfortably, wide eyes looking about. He wrung his tunic hem in his hands. And not far from him, Regis Croydone the roper, searching the room curiously. And Alison Keylmarsh, the other witness.

But no Helewise Peverel nor Walter Noreys.

There were others there as well, no doubt waiting for their own trial today. Crispin's was not to be the only one before the senior circuit judge. But how to stall *his* trial and his sentence?

Crispin took a deep breath, trying to calm his nerves. This was significantly different from his treason trial. For there, it was plain what was to happen. He had said nothing. He had not wished to implicate any others and knew he was guilty. He greatly feared the grim punishment – that of drawing and quartering – but he well knew he had no choice. Not until Lancaster spoke up and spared his life. At that trial, he had been exhausted from days of torture that could not extract the other names in the conspiracy. He had expected his execution to happen immediately, set his mind and aching body to it. He had not expected the reprieve that had come like a wash of rose water.

Today, however . . . today, in all truth, he did not know what to expect.

The sheriff took the seat at the right side of the recorder and settled himself in.

'Let us commence,' said the voice of John Tremayne. Crispin stopped his musings and turned his attention to the man on the dais. 'Will the clerk read the indictment from the sheriff's calendar? And I must say, this shortened calendar perplexes me.'

He sent a glance toward the sheriff, who merely resettled himself on the bench.

The clerk took up a parchment and read in a loud voice: 'The information given to John Charneye, Coroner, and to John Walcote and John Loveney, Sheriffs of London, that a certain Elizabeth le Porter lay dead of a death other than her rightful death in the Bread Street Ward, in the parish of St Anthonine. Thereupon they proceeded thither and having summoned good men of that Ward, they diligently enquired how it happened. The jurors say that Crispin Guest of the Shambles did enter the rent of Elizabeth le Porter and the following day she was discovered dead. The witnesses Hugh Buckton, eel monger, and Alison Keylmarsh, widow, chandler, say on their oath that when on Wednesday, after the Feast of St Calixtus, fourteenth October, after the hour of curfew the said Crispin did enter the rent of le Porter and she was found dead the following day, Thursday fifteenth October. Being asked if they suspected anyone else of the said death besides the said Crispin, the witnesses say no. The corpse was viewed, and the neck appeared blue and inflamed.'

Crispin had heard trials before, but to hear his own circumstances told in such stark language even gave him pause.

He straightened when the recorder said, 'You have been accused of the crime of murder of Elizabeth le Porter of Watling Street, London. How do you wish to plead?'

In a loud, clear voice, Crispin replied, 'Innocent.'

The crowd murmured, some even tried to cheer, but Tremayne stared them down.

'And how do you wish to be heard, Guest?'

'By jury.' He glanced across the hall to the seated jury who had, no doubt, already made up their minds.

'Very well,' said Tremayne. 'Let it be known that today, on the seventeenth day of October, the twelfth year of the reign of our sovereign King Richard, the trial of Crispin Guest commences. Before the witnesses speak, does the prisoner have ought to say in his defense?'

Crispin discreetly cleared his throat and bowed to the assembly. 'If it pleases the court, my lords, jurymen, I do.'

'Then speak, Master Guest.'

His eyes tracked over the jury again. 'On Wednesday night, I was approached by an unknown person and was delivered a message and a pouch of coins—'

'How late Wednesday night?' interrupted the sheriff.

Crispin glared at him. 'Late. Near Vespers.'

'And in what state were you in, Master Guest? Would you say you were cognizant of your surroundings?'

'I was drunk,' he answered harshly. The jurymen mumbled.

He took a breath and raised his chin. 'I was drunk,' he said softer. 'But I was aware. Aware enough that when this person made his heinous proposal to me, I was stunned and felt suddenly responsible for its consequences. I—'

'What did this . . . *alleged* . . . person ask you, then?'

If you would stop interrupting me I'd get on with it! He breathed slowly. 'He told me he was hiring me to murder Elizabeth le Porter.'

The gasps from the jurymen and the audience told him that he should have parsed out that particular phrase better than he had. He flicked a glance toward Nigellus perched at a desk beside the clerk. They both furiously took notes.

'And you took the money and that's what you did,' said the sheriff. 'You murdered her.'

'No! That is *not* what I did. He thrust the money pouch upon me and before I could rise to challenge him, he departed. When I found the name and address of the woman inside the pouch, I thought the only course was to warn her that someone had contracted for her demise. She needed to be notified, protected.'

He wiped the sweat from his upper lip and continued.

'I immediately set out for Watling Street. I found the door to the private stair, encountering the eel monger. I knocked, but he told me to go up, which I did. I knocked again and this time Mistress le Porter answered. She bid me enter and I told her my tale. She did not seem frightened by this aspect—' And even now he wondered at it. Did she not take it seriously? No, it seemed she expected it. Or treated the threat like a naughty prank. She knew this person then. Knew them and did not fear them. But she was wrong. If anyone but Crispin had been hired . . . wait. What if the man had *deliberately* chosen Crispin, knowing he would go to her to warn her? What if that was the plot all along? She would know this man who hired him. It was merely a threat that the man well knew would never be carried out.

Yet she *was* murdered just the same . . .

Suddenly Crispin looked up. He had stopped talking in his musings and the sheriff and the recorder were both glaring. He cleared his throat again.

'She, er . . . she felt no fear at what I related to her. Instead, she was most hospitable. Offering me wine.'

The sheriff leaned forward and with a scowl asked, 'Did you have relations with her?'

The audience gasped again and murmured. Damn the man.

'I . . . I was seduced by her charms. And I . . . soon fell asleep.'

The sheriff sat back, a self-satisfied smile on his face. 'I see.'

Crispin had not meant to mention that part. Nigellus had instructed him not to, but thanks to the sheriff, Crispin's shaky reputation was that much more tarnished.

'My Lord Sheriff,' said Tremayne, cocking his head toward Loveney. 'Perhaps it would be more expeditious to simply let the accused speak. His testimony will, after all, be corroborated by the witnesses.'

Loveney snorted, settled in his chair, and waved a hand at Crispin to proceed.

'When I awoke the next morning, I found her dead. Strangled. It was not I who did it. I had slept through her murder, God help me. I cannot forgive myself for that. But it happened as I said.' He took a deep breath. He knew the next part would tarnish him further in the eyes of the jurymen, but against Cobmartin's judgment, Crispin opted for the entire truth. 'And . . . because of my former difficulties with the office of the lord sheriff, I . . . stole away. Without saying anything, without alerting anyone. For the simple reason,' he said louder over the murmuring of the crowd and the jury, 'that I wanted to investigate the crime myself before turning myself in. Nothing would be gained by incarcerating me before I could help. Before I could find the knave that did it. Alas. I had not the time before I was nabbed by the sheriffs and was forced to abandon my pursuit. My apprentice has picked up the gauntlet and is investigating even as I speak, and I have no doubt that soon the true criminal will be found. And yet here I am in this unusually *speedy* trial. One wonders why it made it to the calendar rolls so quickly.'

The sheriff leaned forward again. 'It is on the sheriff's calendar,

Guest. You have no business questioning that. But that is beside the point. You were the last person to see her alive. All the witnesses say so.'

'Clearly not, Lord Sheriff. For surely that was the real murderer.'

The audience laughed and all the sheriff's sneering could not make them stop.

'But I contend *you* are guilty,' said Loveney loudly over the crowd. 'And further, I contend that your apprentice perpetrated two more murders merely to hide the scent of your own, for two women were also found strangled in London, not too far from the first.'

The crowd gasped and the rumble of murmuring grew louder.

Crispin glanced at Nigellus. It had been the lawyer's plan to submit a writ, claiming Crispin couldn't have done the crime so similar to the other murders, and here was the sheriff destroying that very tactic.

Nigellus wore a stunned expression. But he soon shook it off, sent his parchment to the floor, and furiously wrote on a new sheet.

'My lords,' said Crispin above the rising voices, 'what cause would I have had to kill that woman? She was in the other room, I was in the bedchamber. I was not angry with her. On the contrary. I worried over her wellbeing. To have strangled her would have taken great strength and determination, both of which I did not possess at that hour. And further, she fought her assailant. Under her nails was blood and hair. I haven't any marks upon me.'

Tremayne leaned forward. 'What's that you say, Guest? What about her nails?'

'I inspected her as I am used to doing at the scene of a murder. I go through similar motions to try to detect who the assailant might have been. You might call it a routine inspection. If, for instance, a man is stabbed to death, I look at his hands and arms to see if he resisted, to see if there are cuts to his skin, defensive wounds. If he did not, then there might be cause to believe his assailant was someone he knew and trusted. Or that he was surprised from behind. Or a few other factors. If someone is strangled, they fight. They strike their assailant. Dig into him. His face, his arms. She fought. The evidence was beneath her nails.'

Tremayne huffed, but he blinked, looking thoughtful. 'What

does John Charneye say?' He waited but the room remained silent. Looking around, his face appeared puzzled. 'Where is the coroner?'

The bailiff bowed. 'He . . . doesn't appear to be present, my lord.'

'What sort of trial is this? I should like to ask him if he has ever heard of such a method.' He sighed impatiently. 'We shall have to adjourn this trial while we wait. The accused is to remain here. Someone fetch some food and drink. You jurymen may wait here as well. Lord Sheriff, best call for the next trial on the sheriff's calendar so that no time will be wasted.'

Loveney's face contoured to an unusually meek expression. 'The next is also a trailbaston trial.'

Tremayne screwed his lips tightly. 'Then . . . the *next* on the calendar.'

'And that one, too.'

'For the love of . . . Lord Sheriff, know you not that it is your sworn duty to make certain the coroner is present for a felony trial of violence?'

'Yes, my lord.'

'Do you realize that we should have finished at least ten trials today alone? And by this delay you postpone justice for all and sundry?'

'Yes, my lord.'

'Ah, well, as long as you *know*!' He paused before all but lunging at the sheriff. 'Then go *get* him!'

'Yes, my lord.' He signaled to a serjeant who ran from the hall to comply.

'Then I suppose,' sighed Tremayne, 'we wait. This is obviously going to take longer than it should.'

Crispin glanced at Nigellus who seemed satisfied and gave Crispin an encouraging nod.

ELEVEN

Friday, 16 October

Jack managed to evade the sheriff. He sat on the roof opposite the tinker shop, crouched low in the shadow of the chimney. He couldn't go home. The sheriffs knew where he lived. He couldn't believe they would arrest him for those murders, but wasn't that just like the sheriffs? Didn't care who the real culprit was. They only wanted their writ done and over with. Never mind that the wrong man hanged for it.

He tapped his lip. Where to go? It wouldn't be much better going to the Boar's Tusk, but at least there were places to hide there. It seemed his only alternative. He had to remain free or he couldn't help his master. And, of course, himself, for they would never bother looking for another culprit once they had Jack.

He slid backwards and up over the peak of the roof and down the other side. He landed in a heap in the back courtyard of a poulterer's, scattering the hens and surprising a spotted dog who, rather than call the alarm, trotted forward and placed his forepaws on Jack's chest, urging him to play. He patted the dog on the head and edged toward the fence.

'Good dog,' he said, climbing one leg then the other over the wattle fence. 'We'll play another day.' He put his finger to his lips and the dog obliged, merely wagging its tail and panting with a wide smile and a lolling tongue. If only the sheriff's men would be as cooperative.

He trotted, keeping to the shadows and staying amongst the crowds, taking the long way around to Gutter Lane. Once he slipped through, he kept on trotting till he got to the tavern but decided to keep going until he could get around to the back into their courtyard by the kitchens. He hopped up to the wall and dropped down to the other side, never looking where he was going.

He noticed the person too late, grabbed hold of them, and rolled along the ground. When he landed on top, he felt the soft pliant body against his own before he opened his eyes and beheld wide hazel eyes and a snub nose.

'Oh! Blind me! I beg your mercy, Mistress Langton!' He scrambled to his feet and leaned over to help up Gilbert's niece.

Flustered, she took his hand and when she regained her feet she stared into his eyes for a long moment before brushing harshly at her cotehardie and apron. 'Master Tucker. You took me unawares. I wasn't expecting . . . such an abrupt entrance!'

'Forgive me. Are you hurt?'

She rubbed at her elbow with a wince but shook her head.

'I have hurt you. Curse me for my impetuosity! My master is always berating me for that. Here, let's have a look.' She allowed him to take her arm. She had untied and discarded her long cotehardie sleeves in her work, so he pushed up the sleeve of her white linen shift, gently turning her arm. 'You might have a bruise there. Is it very painful?'

She slowly took her arm back, rolling down the sleeve and cradling the elbow. 'No. It will be fine. Why were you climbing over the wall?'

'Oh. Well, it's a long tale, one for Gilbert if he's about.'

'He's below in the mews. I'll take you.'

'No need, lass. I know the way.'

'But he doesn't like strangers to come below.'

Jack offered a sunny smile. 'I'm no stranger here, lass.'

She raised her nose haughtily. 'Nevertheless. Come with me.' She moved forward, brooking no argument with her posture. Clutching her skirts, she raised the hem over the mud. She ducked through a door at the back of the stone foundation of the tavern and he followed. There were perks to following her, of course. He noticed how the apron strings cinched her waist, saw the swing of her hips and the plump of a round backside. So preoccupied was he at his observation that he nearly missed a step and stumbled.

She gave him a scolding look back over her shoulder and he straightened, offering her a serious expression.

'Uncle Gilbert! Here's that boy to see you again. Jack Tucker.'

Gilbert popped out from behind stacked barrels. 'Well, Young Jack. What's the word?'

'The word, Master Gilbert, is not good. I am being pursued by the sheriffs for murder as well.'

'What?' He grabbed Jack's shoulder and pulled him deeper into the room. The three of them stood within the nimbus of a small candle on a table. Gilbert set his jug aside. 'Tell me!'

Jack pushed his hood back and ran his hand through his curly hair. 'It's like this, Master Gilbert. I was helping to investigate a murder – another woman strangled. And I thought to m'self, "Aha! If I can prove the knave what done this, it will set my master free." But the sheriff saw it different. Thought it was me doing the deed to throw the sheriffs off the scent of my master. I swear by my soul, Gilbert, that I'd never do such a thing!'

'Oh, lad, I know that. Everyone what knows you knows that.'

Jack nodded, relieved at the words.

'They're after me. I can't go home. I'm asking most humbly if I can stay here. Well hidden, of course. I don't want no trouble for you and yours.' He glanced back at Isabel, nodding to her.

Before Gilbert could speak, Ned ran up, catching himself on the doorway. 'Master Gilbert. The sheriff is here to see you.'

'The sheriff?' He exchanged looks with Jack. 'Jack, my lad. You go hide amongst the barrels. You know what to do.'

Jack sprinted away into the shadows. The smell of musty wine and stale ale was stronger amid the weeping barrels. He almost shimmied into a tight place between them but thought better of it. Isn't that the first place they'd look? He glanced upward to the top of the wide tuns and began to climb. Carefully, he hugged the barrel's sides with his thighs, dug in with his fingers, and pulled himself up. He flattened himself across the top just as the sheriff stalked through the doorway.

'You are the tavern keeper,' bellowed Sheriff Walcote.

Gilbert bowed. 'Aye, my lord. Gilbert Langton.'

'I am aware that you know well Crispin Guest and his miscreant apprentice. Is that boy here?'

Gilbert shook his head in all sincerity. 'No, my lord.'

The sheriff moved closer, shoving his face close to Gilbert's. 'Do you know that if you are lying I can arrest you as an accessory . . . to murder?'

'My lord, I give you my solemn oath. That boy is not in my tavern.'

The sheriff snorted, eyes narrowed. He turned his gaze to Isabel, who cowered next to her uncle. 'What about you, lass? Have you seen that boy? Remember, it is a sin to lie and believe me, you would not want to be tossed to the fires of Hell for the likes of that knave.'

She looked up at Gilbert with eyes bright as bezants.

Ah, Jack, you're doomed! She's such an innocent creature. She won't be able to lie. And he didn't want her to. He didn't want her to suffer for him. The sheriff might even strike her, and he could not have that sin on his soul. He flattened his hands on the barrel, getting ready to rise, when he heard her in a clear voice say, 'No, good my lord. I have seen no one.'

'Jack Tucker? Hard to miss. Tall boy with bright ginger hair? You say you haven't seen *him*?'

She looked the sheriff straight in the eye and never wavered. 'No, my lord.'

The sheriff scowled, looking for all the world as if he might draw back his arm and hit her anyway. Jack didn't know what he would do if that happened. He'd surely jump on the sheriff's back and beat him . . . until he was torn off him by the serjeants and either beaten to a pulp himself or thrown in gaol, dead for sure.

But Walcote did nothing more than spin on his heel, march up the steps, and was gone.

Isabel crept up the stairs and slowly peered out. She turned back. 'You can come out now, Master Tucker.'

Jack jumped up and slid down the side of the barrel, landing squarely on his feet. He rushed up to Isabel, eyes tracking over her face. 'You were as brave as a saint!'

She smiled charmingly. 'It's easy to lie to a villain. He deserves no less.'

'Demoiselle, I am ever in your debt.' He bowed.

Her smile had not faded. 'I'll remember that.'

'Here now,' said Gilbert, a worried look to his face. 'You leave Jack be. Will you stay here in the mews, Jack?'

'For tonight at least, Master Gilbert, if it contents you. Tomorrow I must continue to investigate for my master. But, er . . . might I trouble you for a scrap of food and mayhap a little ale? It's parching work, tracking.'

Gilbert laughed and put his hand on Isabel's slender shoulder. 'Of course, lad. Now stay out of sight. There are too many eyes who would love to get their palms greased by the sheriff.'

Jack took his advice. And later, Isabel brought him a tray of meat. He would have liked it if Isabel had stayed to talk with him, but Eleanor came looking for her. She gave Jack a squinted eye and Isabel scurried away. At nightfall, he wrapped himself in his cloak, tucked himself into a dark corner, and promptly fell asleep.

Come morning, he stretched, ate the hardened bread from the night before, drank the ale in the jug, and prepared himself to depart. His hand was poised to grab the latch when the door suddenly yanked open. He might have made an unmanly yelp, but Isabel only looked a bit startled. She stood there, a basin of water held in both hands, with a towel draped over her shoulder. 'I thought you might like to wash. Before you left.'

'Ah, demoiselle. I thank you.' He took the basin from her and retreated back down the steps. He placed the basin on the table, and by the time he turned, she was there, offering him the towel.

He unbuttoned and rolled up his coat sleeves and sluiced his face. He wiped his cheeks and brows with the cloth, then dipped his finger in the basin to brush his teeth, scrubbing them dry with a corner of the towel. 'I thank you, demoiselle . . .'

'You can call me Isabel. I mean . . . after all. I heard that you and Master Crispin are here often. It . . . it seems foolish to remain formal under those circumstances.'

'Aye. I agree. You . . .' He stepped closer, looking down at her. Her hair was combed and parted in the middle, partially covered in a brightly clean linen kerchief. 'You can call me . . . Jack. That wouldn't go amiss.'

She raised her eyes to him once, before lowering them. She hid the action by gathering the basin and crumpled towel. 'Where do you go now?'

'Well, there is a house to which I must go to and question the people inside.' He sighed. 'But I am vexed that the sheriff might be waiting for me there. God's blood! But I *must* talk to them people!'

'Could I . . .' She bit her bottom lip. 'Could I help?'

A 'no' was on the tip of his tongue. But as he thought about it – took in her angelic face, its fresh purity – he thought about what the steward of the household might say to *her*, to a pretty, young face. 'Well now. That's a thought, demois— Isabel. But we must talk first to Gilbert. He may not wish for you to help me. It's dangerous work, sometimes. Oftentimes, I am running for me life.'

'I can run,' she said. She raised her face to his, hazel eyes bright.

Slowly he returned her smile. 'I'll wager you can at that. Come, then.' He urged her forth, and he followed her up the stairs and into the warm tavern. Eleanor was taking coins from a patron when she looked up and spied them. Her brows immediately lowered and she clutched the coins in her fist, grabbed her skirts, and marched toward them.

'Uh oh,' Jack muttered. He straightened his posture to greet her, and when she was before him he bowed formally. 'I thank you, Mistress Eleanor, for succoring me last night when I sorely needed it. I will convey your generosity to Master Crispin.'

'None of that now,' she said, smacking his shoulder. 'Don't you try that on me, Jack Tucker. I know what part of London you are from, no mistaking. What are the two of you doing together?'

'Begging your pardon, madam, but we are not "together", as you say. Mistress Langton here was merely leading the way. We wish to talk to you and Gilbert if it's convenient.'

She drilled her glare into him before she raised her chin and bellowed, 'Gil-bert!'

It was early and there were few patrons, but heads turned. Gilbert rumbled up, looking the trio over. 'What's amiss?'

'Are you aware that your niece is consorting with Tucker, here?'

He laughed. 'The lad isn't 'consorting', my love. He's a guest. And she is being properly hospitable.'

But even as the words left his mouth, Isabel drew forward. 'Uncle, Jack needs my help. He cannot do his job to help his master and I offered to go with him.'

Gilbert drew back, looking at the two anew. 'What?' He shook his head, his jowls jiggling. 'No, lass. That's not proper work for the likes of you.' And then he swung on Jack. 'Did *you* propose this to her?'

'Well . . .' He looked from one angry adult to the other. 'Well . . . she . . . she understands my predicament, Master Gilbert. She offered. It seemed like a good idea . . . at the time. But I know there are dangers. And so, as I said, Isabel—'

'"Isabel" is it?' muttered Gilbert.

'I told her we must ask your permission. And I see you will not grant it. No harm done, then.' He bowed to Isabel. 'I thank you for your kind offer, demoiselle. But I must try to do this on me own. Thank you Gilbert, Eleanor, for your hospitality. God grant that I will be safe tonight.' He swept them all with a glance. 'Farewell, then.'

He pivoted on his heel, tossed his hood up over his head, and strode to the door. He hovered in the doorway, looking both ways down the street to see if the sheriff's men hid there. He pulled the hood down lower to shadow his face, ducked his head, and plunged into the street. He had to get into the Peverel household somehow. And then he'd have to go back to those places where the women had been strangled.

He took the roundabout way to Trinity Street and stopped at the corner, peering around the edge of a shop. The street was filling with shopkeepers, shoppers, and other townsfolk. He saw no livery and gave a sigh of relief. He was about to step out to the main thoroughfare when a man came out of the shadows. A serjeant. He wore the sheriffs colors and he was scanning the street. Jack drew back around the corner and pressed his back against the wall. God's blood! Just as he thought. They were lying in wait for him. How was he to get in now?

A hand suddenly on his arm caused him to whip around, knife drawn.

'God's blood! Isabel, don't do that! What are you doing here?'

'I came to help.'

'Your uncle changed his mind?' Her eyes flicked away. 'He didn't!' Grabbing her arm he marched her back down the lane. 'You're going back, do you hear? Your uncle is a man of honor and if he says no, no is what he meant.'

She wrenched her arm away and stood her ground, hands at

her hips. 'You don't tell me what to do! Everyone has my best interests at heart! Fie! When my father died, all my relatives were *so* solicitous, all trying to tell me what to do, which way to turn. Looking to get their hands on his money, more like.' She leaned back against the wall and bit at a nail. 'When my mother died all those years ago,' she said quietly, 'I took over the duties of mistress of the household. It wasn't as if I was a simpleton. I was ten! And I did it right well. My father told me so. Did the books . . . with his help. But now that he's gone, I couldn't very well shift for myself. And I couldn't run the cooperage on my own. Uncle Gilbert was the only one who gave me a place and put me to work, without thinking first about what he was to gain from it. He never mentioned my dowry, never tried to take it. And by all rights he could have. But of all of them, he's most like my father, is Uncle Gilbert. Though he's never had a child, never knew what willful beasts we can be, he's been kind. I do as he says *because* he is kind to me. But I am myself and for many years *I* decided. I'm fifteen, after all. I've used my own head for years.'

Jack studied her. 'Willful beast' was right! But more like a . . . a cat, going her own way. He couldn't help but smile and turned away to hide it. 'But no one wants a shrewish wife.'

'I'm no shrew. I'm . . . resourceful. I've survived my mother's death and now my father's. And I'll go on. And I'll be obedient to my aunt and uncle because of their kindness. But not in all things.'

'I'm an orphan, too,' he said quietly, half an eye on the street around them. 'Master Crispin took me in. He lets me have me own mind, too, though I obey him because he's clever and knows the ways of the world. But you being a girl, well. That's not the same, is it? Your uncle is a fine and honorable man. It's well and good to have your own mind – you'll need it when you run the Boar's Tusk someday. But for now, you are his niece, his ward, and you must obey. Scripture teaches us that the woman must heed the man of the house. *In the Lord woman is not independent of man.*'

'. . . *Nor man of woman*, so it also says.'

'Ah, lass. You know your Scripture.' *Too well*. 'Harken. The point is, you must obey your uncle as if he were your father.'

He folded his arms over his chest, thinking. The fact of the matter was, she was here now. And he needed her. The rest could be sorted later. 'Very well. You must deal with your uncle and accept his punishment for your disobedience.'

She appeared sullen and cast her eyes downward.

'But I do need you, Isabel. And I thank God for your presence.'

Brightening, she lifted her face to his. Something in his chest shifted, thumped. He blinked it away and looked back toward the corner. 'The sheriff's men are expecting me alone. But with you, they will not be looking too close. I hope. Will you . . . will you go with me?'

'Yes! That's what I'm here for.'

He secured his hood and helped her adjust her kerchief to cover more of her face. With head down, he wove his arm in hers, and plunged onto Trinity. They walked at a steady pace. Jack glanced up carefully from under his hood toward the sheriff's man. The serjeant's gaze swept over them and continued on, searching. Jack sent up a prayer of thanks before they approached the Peverel household. He knocked and waited. With the sly movement of his other hand, he crept Isabel's kerchief *back*, revealing more of her face. She looked at him questioningly when the door opened.

The steward noted Jack first and then Isabel, where his gaze fastened.

'We are here to see the mistress of the household,' said Jack urgently.

The steward gave him only cursory attention. 'And whom shall I say calls?'

'The Tracker's apprentice.'

His head snapped toward Jack and appraised him anew. 'I see. I was told by the sheriff's men to alert them should you come to the door.'

'I beg you, sir, do not. For we are here on an errand of mercy. To discover a foul murderer. An innocent man's life hangs in the balance. And the sheriffs care nothing for that.'

The steward's level gaze measured them. He nodded. 'This I know. Word has it that the Tracker himself is being tried for a murder this very day.'

'I knew it! I knew the sheriffs wouldn't wait. Do you see that, sir? Who gets a trial two days after they're arrested, eh? Only a man the sheriffs are trying to put away. Do you see how urgent is my cause, sir?'

'Then make haste inside. For the sheriff's serjeant is looking this way.'

Jack dared not look over his shoulder. Instead, he grasped Isabel's arm tightly and shoved her inside, following quickly on her heels.

The steward told them to wait in the foyer and they stood. Jack was still clutching Isabel's arm and quickly released her. 'Sorry,' he mumbled.

She looked all around the foyer and then settled her gaze on Jack. 'This is like my father's house, but his was much smaller.'

'If you had such fine things, why did you come to Gilbert's to live? Could they not have come to yours, taken over your father's business?'

'Uncle Gilbert doesn't know the coopering trade and neither did I. Not enough of it. My father needed sons, but got only me. The household items were sold to pay his debts and the rest – what little there was – was granted to my nearest relative – my uncle. He put it away for my dowry.'

'Then you are blessed indeed. Well, I mean . . .'

'I know what you mean. It could have gone worse for me. Uncle Gilbert and Aunt Eleanor are good to me.'

They stood in silence for a moment before she asked, 'Why did you pull my kerchief back when you were so careful to push it forward before?'

'Ah. Well, I knew the steward would be distracted by your beauty.'

She made a little gasp, eyes wide.

Jack felt his cheeks warming. 'And . . . it worked.'

He said nothing more, but he felt her sharp gaze upon him.

The steward returned and told them to follow. Jack sensed Isabel behind him and now he felt like a proper fool. You didn't just blurt out to a lass that she was a beauty! Of all the addle-pated things to do! You were supposed to woo her slowly, carefully. That's what Master Crispin had told him when he had asked about it.

Wait. *Was* he wooing her? She was no wench to bed for a simple tumble and then leave behind. This was Gilbert's niece. She was untouchable. At least in the carefree manner of his master with women.

But what if she *was* for wooing? A man had to settle down someday. And she seemed like a good prospect for a man like Jack. Surely his master would approve. But what of Gilbert?

He tucked those thoughts away for later consideration when they passed through a solar into a garden. A woman sat at her embroidery stand. A red squirrel with a bejeweled collar and silver leash was perched upon her shoulder, gnawing on an acorn.

'Madam Peverel. The Tracker's apprentice, Jack Tucker.'

Jack raised his brows. He had not given his name but realized that the sheriff's serjeant might have mentioned it. Either that or his own infamy was tied to that of the Tracker's.

Madam Peverel looked up for only a moment, taking him in and then Isabel, before she returned her attention to her embroidery. 'I have already spoken to your master, Master Tucker. Why are you here?'

'Madam, my master is in great peril. He was only seeking the truth in the matter of the death of Elizabeth le Porter but he was accused of her murder instead. Please, madam. To save him I need answers.'

Slowly she put down her needle and turned in her chair. The squirrel hopped down to her lap, where she stroked it absently. But being an excitable creature, the squirrel could only rest but a moment before it leapt to her shoulder and then a platform. 'What can I tell you that I did not already tell your master?'

'Indeed, madam. What?'

They both fell silent, each staring intently at the other. But Madam Peverel blinked first. 'This is an unusual occupation you and your master have chosen,' she said, picking up her needle again and giving her embroidery her attention.

For several silent moments Jack watched her stitch. His breathing was so harsh he was certain the steward, whom he could see just beyond the doorway, must have heard him.

But her façade had cracked. Her fingers trembled and she laid them down on the linen of her stretcher stand. 'Perhaps . . . if you shared what you know, Master Tucker.'

'Very well. I know that John and Walter Noreys hired Mistress le Porter to steal your Virgin's Tears.'

Her eyes were like two furies swooping down with murder in their hearts. She rose so abruptly the squirrel chittered and leapt down from the platform. But the leash made its escape impossible. 'How *dare* they! I shall call the law down on them.'

'The law of God has already fallen upon one of them, for John Noreys is dead. My master . . . killed him in self-defense.'

Isabel made a sound of shock behind him, but he heard her stifle it behind her hand.

It took a long moment for Madam Peverel to hastily cross herself. But it looked more as if she wanted to say, 'Good riddance.'

'The Noreyses, madam. Who are they to you?'

'Miscreants. Devils, apparently. Did one of them kill Elizabeth?'

'That . . . has yet to be determined. Why would they kill her if they had clearly hoped that she had done the deed they hired her to do?'

'I cannot know. Only if . . . if she had not done what they wanted, might they wish to silence her so that she would speak to no one of it?'

He nodded. 'That is my contention as well, madam. Would you be willing to testify as to their character?'

'I most certainly would.'

'Oh, madam! I would be grateful to you for such a boon! Thank you.' He bowed and made ready to leave when something gnawed at the edges of his thoughts, poked and prodded. It was as if his master was speaking to him over his shoulder. Had he not heard him enough over the last six years when interrogating a witness?

He stopped in mid-step and abruptly turned back. 'Madam, may I ask one thing more? Are you . . . are you quite sure that she *didn't* steal the Tears?'

Her murderous expression was back. 'What kind of question is that?'

'Well . . . a thorough one, madam. One my master would expect of me. You see, there has been many a time when an object – say a jewel in a ring or on a chest – was stolen and replaced with a duplicate. So that the owner would not know it was missing. Is it possible that something like that could have occurred?'

Not only was Madam Peverel staring at him, but Isabel's mouth had dropped open as well.

Madam Peverel rose and fisted her hands over her belly. 'I see nothing can be done until you are satisfied. Come with me, young man.'

The squirrel made a leap for her shoulder and was content to hold on with its tiny claws. She stalked ahead, and Jack and Isabel followed.

They pursued her down a long corridor to a chapel door. She unlocked it and opened it for him, showing him the chapel within but not inviting him inside. 'There, on the small altar, is the monstrance containing the Virgin's Tears.'

Jack peered into the gloom and saw the gold of the monstrance gleam from the single candle flame. Behind a locked grille was the golden casket containing what looked like a phial no bigger than a man's palm filled with some clear liquid. The casket sported golden radiant beams, made of gilt wood or metal.

Jack's eyes widened. He marveled at such things and was grateful that he had a chance to observe these most precious of objects so closely, even though his master was not as enamored. Indeed, his master would doubt its authenticity, disdain the qualities attributed to it. Often he'd question why God would allow these items and their power into the greedy hands of man.

'It is there,' she said, 'as it has ever been.'

Jack pushed his awe aside and took on the mantle of his master. 'Very well, madam. The Noreys family believes it belongs to them.'

'It does not! Years and years ago my departed husband – a blessed man – obtained it for me. But wretched have I been ever since, for it only brings grief to those around it. You know the tale.'

'Forgive me, madam, but I do not.'

Absently, she stroked the fluffy squirrel tail lying upon her shoulder. 'The Tears can heal, but they also confer the pain felt by others upon those around them. In this household, we greatly suffer the pain of the heart as well as the body of one another. It was why Elizabeth left me. She could no longer bear the grief of others.'

'That is a sore thing indeed.'

'Yes. But it is my burden to bear for the sake of our Lord, who suffered for our sins.'

'Aye. That is the truth of it.'

She pulled the door closed again and smartly locked it. With her hands clutching the keys, she glared down her nose at Jack. 'Well? Is there anything more? I fear I have helped you little in your cause.'

'No, madam. I shall obtain a writ to have you come to the Guildhall for my master's trial.'

'Then God speed you on your way, young man.' It was a firm dismissal.

'Thank you, madam.' He bowed and Isabel curtseyed.

They all retreated together down the passage. At the solar, Madam Peverel went one way back to the garden, while Jack and Isabel went the other, back toward the entrance where they were greeted by the steward. Jack tapped his chin in thought, absently stroking the few hairs there. 'Master Steward?'

The man stepped closer. 'Yes?'

'Have *you* ever seen the relic in the chapel? The Virgin's Tears?'

'Oh yes. Many a time. On Sundays the household take communion there.'

'I see. Have you ever observed it closely?'

'Well . . . I supervise the cleaning of the chapel. I am always present when the scullion cleans the altar and scrubs the floor.'

'Have you ever noted a change in its appearance?'

He frowned. 'I do not understand your meaning.'

'Have the tears in its phial ever looked different to you? Fuller? Emptier?'

He shook his head, still frowning. 'No.'

'And Master Steward, are you aware of the relic's power?'

He gave a wan smile. 'My mistress exclaims that it has properties to force those around it to feel each other's pain.'

'Aye. That's what she told me.'

The steward looked carefully around and slowly shook his head. 'I have never felt this of my person. At first, I thought it was a fault of mine. I prayed on it. I fasted. For I felt that I somehow lacked the empathy required of my faith. But after hearing the same from the other servants, I concluded that the tales must be false.'

'Hold. Are you saying that—' He looked around, too, hoping Madam Peverel was well and truly ensconced in her garden. 'Are you saying,' he said softly, 'that none of the servants in this household *did* feel the pain and suffering of one another?'

'Not in the sense you mean. Of course we are sensitive to each other's grief – living in common as we do – but we did not suffer what it is said the Virgin's Tears confer.'

'And how long have you served in this household, Master Steward?'

'More than ten years. After my father. And before the master died.'

'Were you here, then, when the Virgin's Tears were brought into the house?'

'Yes. My father oversaw the construction of the altar's grille and monstrance. It was a very great honor.'

'But you *never* felt this suffering attributed to the Tears?'

'No, as I have said.'

Jack frowned. He looked back down the corridor toward the chapel, he glanced back toward the doorway leading to the garden, then up the stairs toward, he presumed, the bedchambers. Something definitely was not right.

His final glance was toward the front entrance. 'Master Steward, is there another way out of here?'

'Yes. It's in the back.'

'Can you take us there? I would confound the sheriff's men for as long as possible.'

With a jerk of his head, the steward motioned for them to follow. They passed through a narrow door, down some stairs, through the warm kitchens with their savory smells of smoke and roasted flesh, and out the back garden. A wall surrounded it but another locked door was there in the wall, which the steward unlocked and stepped out of. He hastily looked around and came back. 'It is clear, Master Tucker. Will you help my mistress? This death has affected her so.'

'I will do my best, sir.' He nodded his thanks, took Isabel's hand, and darted out the door. It was closed and locked behind him, and he found himself in an alley. 'Come on.' Still holding her hand, Jack trotted away toward Walbrook and didn't slow until he saw no signs of any man who looked to be in livery.

He dropped Isabel's hand and smiled. 'I thank you for that. It was most useful. And now to get *you* back to Gutter Lane before Master Gilbert finds you missing.'

'This is an unusual occupation you have.'

'Aye. I sort of . . . er, tumbled into it. But it's a fine way to use your mind. My master is one of the cleverest in all the kingdom. He's schooled, he is. And he's taught me plenty. Oh, not just reading and writing, but of the philosophers and history. And arms. Master Crispin . . . he's an unusual man.'

'Is it hard being a Tracker?'

'Well.' He puffed out his chest a bit as he walked. 'It's taken me years to learn the skills of my master, and I improve every day. It's a lot to learn, though. You have to learn to truly *listen* to what your witnesses say. As my master says, it's what they *don't* say what says the most.'

'Jack,' she said thoughtfully as they slowly made their way up to Poultry Street, 'I've been thinking about what Madam Peverel said. Just as you say, I listened to her words. And if the murdered woman left because she felt too keenly the grief of others . . . when no one else in the household felt it . . . what does that mean?'

Jack smiled. She *had* listened. He liked this Isabel Langton. Liked her pretty face, her sparkling eyes, and the fact that there was something more than just a silly maid's notions behind them.

'Well, one of two things. First, that Elizabeth le Porter *did* steal the relic. Or . . . Madam Peverel was lying.'

TWELVE

Saturday, 17 October

Crispin had eaten, grateful to the recorder for ordering that he be brought food, but now he waited with everyone else. The crowd was leaning against the walls, and even the sheriff was fidgeting in his seat. The jurymen sat and laughed together on their benches, passing a jug of ale between them.

Crispin asked permission to confer with his lawyer near the dais and that, too, was granted.

The lawyer leaned forward and said quietly, 'It is going well, Master Crispin.'

'Indeed? I thought the opposite.'

'Oh, no. For look where we are now? We await the coroner, the jurymen are at their ease with food and drink, and the crowds are docile. What will the coroner say?'

'He will say that he has heard me make the same statements and that they have proven his cases more times than he can count.'

'And that will also prove for your favor.'

'But what of the witnesses and jurymen? Will they not be angered at the delay and cause me harm because of it?'

'For the most part, they have already decided. You just might have turned their minds.'

'Let us hope so. Where is that damned man?'

But the serjeant had felt Crispin had spent enough time with his lawyer, and he pushed him away back to his place before the bar with wary eyes upon him, while everyone else milled and waited for the coroner to arrive.

'This is damnable,' said the sheriff suddenly. His growl quieted the room. 'If the man cannot be found then we should return the prisoner back to Newgate. I have better things to do than wait in this courtroom the whole day.'

The recorder, who had been sitting at a table with his own

meal, raised his head. 'And so you would have been had the coroner been here in the first place. It is nearly two of the clock, Lord Sheriff. Can you not wait a half hour more?'

The sheriff sighed pitifully. 'I suppose,' he huffed.

But the wait wasn't necessary, for the doors opened and the coroner, John Charneye, was announced.

He moved in next to Crispin. He gave Crispin a cursory inspection and then turned to the dais. 'Forgive me, my Lord Recorder. If I had known I was required I would have attended you.' His statement was for the sheriff though he did not glance his way.

Tremayne set his cup and his food aside, wiped his mouth and hands on the tablecloth, and moved toward the bench. He sat, arranging his gown around him. 'Now then,' he said, 'the court will reconvene. Jurymen, assemble yourselves.'

They set down their ales and crusts of bread and sat properly on the benches, settling in.

Tremayne then nodded to the coroner. 'My lord,' he said, 'Crispin Guest has been testifying on his own behalf, and made the statement . . .' He turned to Crispin. 'What did you say, Master Guest, before we were forced to await the coroner?'

'I said that to have strangled her would have taken great strength and determination, both of which I did not possess at that hour. And further, she fought her assailant. Under her nails was blood and hair. And I haven't any marks upon me.'

'There,' said Tremayne. 'Master Charneye, Master Guest claims that he has proposed this . . . this *method* of examination to you before and that you have used it to great effect. This examination of the nails for blood, skin, and hair. And to look upon the assailant to see if he had any validating marks that would indicate he was the culprit. Is this true?'

'My Lord Recorder, my Lord Sheriff.' The coroner bowed to both. 'While it is true Crispin Guest has mentioned such to me, I have found little use in the matter.'

What the devil? Crispin gripped his empty scabbard and pressed his lips tight. *He's perjuring himself!*

Tremayne leaned his arm on his thigh. 'Do you mean to say that you have never used this method to catch a miscreant?'

Charneye shuffled his feet. 'Well . . . there . . . was a time or two.'

Crispin let out the breath he was holding.

'But certainly not every time.'

'My lords,' Crispin interjected. 'May I question the witness?'

Tremayne sat back with a scowl and waved his hand in acquiescence.

Facing Charneye, Crispin squared with him. 'My Lord Coroner, in those instances where this method did not prove true, was there a significant time elapse between the discovery of the body and the catching of the guilty person?'

Charneye's brows dug into his eyes. 'I don't . . .'

'Long enough for scars to heal, my lord,' Crispin clarified.

The coroner snorted. 'I . . . suppose.'

'Then this being a legitimate form of examination and investigation, would you say that the same can hold true for this instance?'

'It could,' he acknowledged grudgingly.

'And did you detect blood, skin, and hair beneath the nails of the deceased?'

Charneye took a deep breath. 'Elizabeth le Porter was found to have such evidence under her nails.'

Crispin tore open his cotehardie and the chemise within, showing his chest to the coroner. 'The crime occurred only three days ago. Are there any marks upon me?' He further pushed up his sleeves, showing his untouched arms.

The coroner's gaze swept the room, from the rapt and slack-jawed faces of the jurymen, to the crowd, and finally back to the sheriff and recorder. He smiled grimly. 'No . . .'

The room erupted in cries and exclamations.

'However . . .' he shouted to be heard above the noise. The serjeants strode the room with their cudgels, glaring at each man and woman to be still. 'However,' the coroner went on. 'Since you were the only one to have been seen entering the room and you did not call the hue and cry I would still conclude that you are the culprit.'

The crowd guffawed, made unpleasant noises, and shouted down the coroner.

Crispin's gaze flicked toward Cobmartin, but the lawyer didn't look happy.

God's blood.

'Very well, very well,' said Tremayne. 'The court of the Common Pleas thanks you, John Charneye for your testimony. There are more trailbaston cases before us today. Please await us in yon chamber.' He pointed to a door at the back of the crowd.

Charneye didn't so much as glance back at Crispin as he swept out of the room, indifferent to the trouble he had caused. *And after all the help I gave him. Ungrateful whoreson.* Crispin shook his sleeves down in place and proceeded to re-button his coat.

Tremayne resettled himself in his seat. 'I think it time we talk to the witnesses.'

There was a scramble at the door. Some of the crowd were pushed aside, squawking and complaining at the harsh treatment, until the cause of the commotion made his way to the front. Jack Tucker stood straight and tall, chin raised. Crispin's heart flooded with relief on seeing him there. What a presence the boy seemed to have these days. Crispin saw something of his own posture and gestures in him, and little wonder when they spent nearly all their waking moments together. But he could not read his face. Did he bring good news or not?

He gave an acknowledging nod to Crispin before he slowly crept around the crowd toward Cobmartin.

Tremayne signaled to the clerk and after consulting his parchments announced in a clear, loud voice, 'Will Leonard Munch come forth?'

Crispin snapped his head around and scowled as Lenny pushed his stoop-postured way through the crowd and stood next to Crispin. Perhaps he saw Crispin's hands contract into fists and that was what made him take several steps away from him.

Lenny's eyes darted here and there throughout the room. His greasy sparse hair hung from the edges of his bald pate down to his shoulders. His crooked nose twitched. Crispin stared at the bunched and crusted flesh where his ear used to be before the sheriff had it hacked off for thievery.

Tremayne looked him over. 'Have I seen you before, Master Munch?'

'Well, m'lord.' Lenny's voice was parchment dry and vinegar sharp. 'It's possible. I, er . . . have had dealings with the sheriffs from time to time.'

'Hmm,' said Tremayne. He folded his arms over his chest. 'Proceed.'

'Well . . . I seen Master Guest coming out of that poor woman's lodgings. Staggering and distressed he was. And angry.'

Crispin glared. 'You lying son of a whore.'

'Oi! You see that, my lord? As angry as a dog pissed on by his brethren.'

Tremayne tensed his jaw. 'You say you saw him *leaving* the premises?'

'Aye.'

'You are the only witness that says so. No one else has testimony of this kind. What time was this?'

'It had gone midnight. Oh, he was in a foul mood! *Murderous*, you might say.'

'My lord,' said Crispin. 'I submit to you that this man is lying.'

'Listen to him!' said Lenny, throwing a hand in the air. 'Just because it shows him as the guilty knave he is, he claims *I* am lying.'

'He wants his ill-advised revenge on me,' Crispin went on. 'We used to work together, he and I. I would pay him to be my spy, but I sacked him for his thievery. He has been in gaol many a time.'

'As have you!' cried Lenny.

'Both of you! Be still!' They both clamped shut their mouths and looked toward Tremayne. 'I will not have this in my court room. You!' He pointed a finger at Lenny. 'The prisoner says you are lying. And by my contention I believe it, too. Can you prove, Master Guest, that he is lying?'

'He's moving his lips.'

'Master Guest,' warned Tremayne.

'Call as a witness my landlord Martin Kemp. He saw me return not at midnight but in the morning. The time was just after Terce.'

'I need bring no witness,' said Tremayne. 'He's a thief. He has been brought to me before. Why he hasn't been hanged is a very good question. This witness is dismissed and to be disregarded.'

'My lord!' cried Lenny.

'Do you wish to be thrown in prison? I would gladly do so for your perjury.'

Lenny shook his head and fell silent.

'Serjeant, remove this man.'

The serjeant seemed only too happy to do so, and the crowd jeered and threw stubs of bread and apple cores at him as he was shoved none too gently toward the entry.

'Give me another witness, one I can use,' muttered Tremayne.

The clerk mussed his parchments and drew one toward his face. 'Hugh Buckton, eel monger.'

The man had short chestnut colored hair, a round shaven face, and a blunt nose. His green cotehardie was mostly clean, and he again wore a red hood with its liripipe wrapped tightly around his neck. Nervously, he shuffled forward, wringing his thick fingers. He bowed to the judge and the sheriff. He gave Crispin a sideways glance, almost apologetically.

'Now then,' said Tremayne, leaning back against the bench. 'Tell us what you saw on Wednesday last.'

'My lords. I, er, I was tending to my shop. It was time to close and I was wheeling my barrels back inside. It's heavy work. The barrels are full of water and eels. I had just gotten the last one in – near Vespers, it was, since I had just heard the bells at St Anthonine's. I seen this man . . .' – he gestured toward Crispin, but kept his eyes averted – 'I seen him knocking on the door of the private stair. You see, my lord, it is an outside stair but is enclosed all around with a door below. But it isn't locked. He . . . he was in his cups, that I could tell, and I told him he need not knock, but to go up. Which he did.'

'How well did you know the deceased?'

'Not well, my lord. But I did note that she had callers from time to time. Men.'

'Indeed.' Tremayne lifted his drooping eyes to Buckton. 'What manner of woman was this?'

'Begging the court's mercy, my lord.'

Shocked at the outburst, Crispin turned to face Jack Tucker addressing the recorder.

Tremayne didn't appear to like being interrupted. 'Who are you?'

'I am Jack Tucker, my lord, apprentice to the Tracker . . . to Crispin Guest.'

'You are not a witness.' He shook his head at the clerk. 'He's not a witness?'

The clerk desperately shuffled his parchments. Nigellus Cobmartin whispered to the clerk and seemed also to signal Jack.

'I cannot find . . . cannot find . . .' said the clerk.

'Never mind,' said Tremayne. 'Tucker, you say? Why are you interrupting the testimony of this witness?'

'Because this man don't know the whole story about Elizabeth le Porter. And *I* do.'

THIRTEEN

Saturday, 17 October

Jack looked up with a solemn face toward John Tremayne. He longed to tell his master that all would be well, but even with the information he wished to impart, he knew there were still too many unanswered questions.

And that coroner had done them no favors.

'My lord,' Jack began, clearing his throat and fitting his thumbs in his belt. 'According to the information I obtained in my capacity as the Tracker's apprentice, I have discovered that Elizabeth le Porter was once employed as a lady's maid to Helewise Peverel, widow on Trinity Street, and had recently left her employ. And further, that Walter and John Noreys, brothers, living in the family household on Lombard Street, did hire Mistress le Porter to steal a certain relic owned by the Peverel household, the Tears of the Virgin Mary.'

The crowd gasped. Jack took courage from it.

'The Noreys brothers were unsuccessful with this enterprise,' Jack continued, 'as Mistress le Porter failed – or *refused* – to do as requested. My lord, I submit to you that more witnesses be called. That of Walter Noreys and Madam Peverel, and that the Tears of the Virgin be brought forth as evidence. And I further submit to you that there have been two other murders of women in London, strangled, all too similar to that of the murdered Elizabeth le Porter on Friday last. Murders my master couldn't possibly have committed.'

Tremayne clutched his knees. 'And so we have heard.' He angled toward the sheriff. 'Though you, Lord Sheriff, have accused this man here,' and he gestured toward Jack.

Jack took a step back, mouth open in shock.

'Perhaps it is time to talk of these murders,' said Tremayne.

The door burst open and Sheriff Walcote pushed his way through. He scoured the crowd and spotted Jack. He raised his arm and pointed a finger. 'There you are, you murdering miscreant!'

'Oh! Time to go!' said Jack, and he threw himself into the crowd opposite the sheriff, and amid screams and shouts, scrambled toward a window.

'Stop him!' cried Walcote.

'God's teeth!' shouted Tremayne. 'Stop! Stop all of you! Tucker! You there!'

Jack was halfway out the window when he turned sharply.

'This is all madness,' grumbled Tremayne when the room quieted from the uproar. Jack was still hanging halfway to freedom, but there was something in Tremayne's tone that halted his progress. The sheriff's men, with pikes and swords drawn, had entered the chamber, and Tremayne motioned for them to stand down. 'We will get to the bottom of this. But for now, we will adjourn this trial for the day. There is more here than meets the eye. I want Tucker, Guest, and the sheriffs in that chamber. Now!'

The crowd didn't like that they were being pushed out by the sheriff's men, but Tremayne stomped off the dais and entered through a door to a smaller chamber just behind the raised area.

Nigellus looked up at Jack with a grateful smile and a nod, and Jack slowly pulled himself down from the sill. *Well, that's done it*, he mused. He looked toward his master, and Master Crispin was giving him a sly grin. Jack felt better about it then, but when he glanced at Walcote he shrank again. The sheriff was staring at him with murderous eyes. That didn't bode well. But at least he would offer enough doubt all around, just as Nigellus said he needed.

When they assembled in the chamber and the door was closed, Tremayne turned on all of them. 'Just what the hell is going on? I have never presided over a trial as mad as this.'

They all tried to talk at once. Tremayne silenced them with a wave of his hand. 'Sheriff Walcote. You begin. Why are you after Jack Tucker here?'

'Because he's a murderer!'

'No I'm not! And you know it . . . my lord.'

'Then what were you doing at the scene of the murder of that woman?'

'You mean like all them other people crammed into that room off Watling Street?'

The sheriff puffed and said nothing.

Jack gestured to his master. 'Master Crispin and I investigate crimes. My lord, you *know* we do. It's what pays our fees. It's how we make our living, one honest and true. If you had only asked me instead of sending your men after me . . .'

'I can do what I like with my men,' countered the sheriff, face growing red.

'But that don't help no one—'

'Jack.' Master Crispin's soft voice interjected. He shook his head. 'That's enough.' It was his master who turned to both sheriffs. He spread out his hands. 'The both of you know me. You have been told – or warned – by the previous sheriffs. And the sheriffs before that knew what we do to fill our tables. And the ones before that. *And* before that. It is no secret what I do . . . what *we* do for a living, my lords. And if Jack is found – among the company of others – examining a corpse, then you should know that he does so with the authority of the Tracker. We find thieves, criminals, and murderers. It's what we do, for good or ill. I'd like to think it's for the good of London. Now. There is no question that I am guilty as the First Finder for failing to call the hue and cry, for allowing someone else to find the corpse. I have given my reasons for not doing so. We are now standing in the midst of my reasons.'

Tremayne examined his nails. 'Sheriff Walcote, do you wish to make charges against Jack Tucker for murder?'

Jack's breath caught. His eyes fastened on the sheriff, scowling as if his supper had been snatched from his plate. After a long pause the sheriff finally shook his head, mouth clamped tightly.

Tremayne cracked his neck. 'Right. And so. This other matter of women strangled. My lords?' He looked at each sheriff in turn.

'We have no information on them yet, Lord Recorder,' said Loveney.

'Do you think it may have to do with the murder of which Master Guest is accused?'

Loveney, again, shook his head. 'We do not know, my lord.'

Tremayne paced, hands pressed behind his back. Master

Crispin watched him mildly. 'I tell you, gentlemen, I am not pleased by this. All the evidence must be presented to the jury prior to coming to court. It is the custom since King Henry III's day. Yet now we have new witnesses, new information. It's what comes of holding the trial at a *breakneck pace*, gentlemen.' He stopped and speared Jack with his sharp eyes. 'And you! You came into my court most impolitely, Master Tucker.'

'I am heartily sorry for that, my lord, and I beg your mercy. My only thought was for the deliverance of my master.'

Tremayne's narrowed gaze did not leave Jack. 'Such a loyal apprentice,' he muttered. He elbowed Master Crispin. 'I hope you are properly humbled.'

'You have no idea,' said Master Crispin, gazing at Jack fondly.

Jack's face flushed.

'Very well,' said Tremayne with a deep sigh. 'We will call in new witnesses – that Peverel woman and those Noreys brothers—'

Sheriff Loveney cleared his throat.

'You have something to say, my lord?'

'Yes. It's just that . . . one of the brothers recently died by misadventure.'

'By Saint Cuthbert! What is happening to this city? Deaths everywhere you look!'

'He was attempting to assail . . . er . . . the prisoner, when the prisoner threw . . . him out the window.'

Tremayne glared, mouth agape, at Master Crispin. Jack's master stared at his own shuffling feet. 'It was self-defense,' he said quietly.

'My God. There is no respite from this, is there? Was Master Guest charged with this murder, too?'

'It was a clear case of self-defense, my lord,' said Loveney.

'Thank Christ for that,' he muttered. He blinked and then looked up at the assembly. 'Well. What are you standing around here for? Get that relic as evidence, send this prisoner back to Newgate, and gather your new witnesses. Court will convene again on Monday. Thank God for Sunday.'

The sheriffs moved toward Master Crispin, but he raised a hand and asked if he could speak to Jack for a moment. Seeing Tremayne of a mind to let him, they backed off, talking quietly together.

Jack hastened to his master's side since those heavy irons still encircled the man's ankles.

'You've been busy, Jack.'

'Aye, master. I've been trying me best.'

'And a good job, too. What else have you learned?'

'I went to the Widow Peverel and something about that curse or *gift* or whatever you'd call what that relic does . . .'

'Yes?'

'Whatever Madam Peverel said, it don't seem to do it.'

'Explain.'

'I talked to the steward. He said he'd been there since the relic came to the household and he never felt naught for no one because of it.'

'So the story that Elizabeth le Porter left because of this relic . . . is false?'

'That's my thinking.'

'Then why *did* she leave? I've been doing my own thinking, Jack. I'm thinking that it was me that the mysterious stranger intended to hire after all. He *wanted* me to go to Elizabeth. He knew I would relay the message but do her no harm. And, further, she knew it, too. She knew who it was that had sent her that warning. And that it was merely a threat. And it might have been a threat from those Noreys boys. They hired her to steal the Tears, she didn't, and now they wanted to force her hand.'

'Did they kill her after all, master?'

'I don't think so. Especially in light of these other murders.'

'When I questioned Master Noreys and his son . . .'

'God's blood, Jack! You didn't! How on earth did you? They're a house in mourning.'

Jack adjusted his coat. 'Took a page out of your book, sir. I told them I was a clerk from the sheriff's office.'

He laughed. 'Well done!'

It felt good to see his master smile, see him cheered. Jack smiled back. But he sobered again on relating his information. 'Master William Noreys said that they are in dire straits. Poverty is creeping upon them. They wanted the relic to sell. And I don't think he approved of his sons' plan. It was a surprise to him as well as the murder.'

'And what of Walter Noreys?'

'Oh, he hired her right enough. But he seemed surprised at her death. And he still thinks you got the relic.'

'Hmm.' Master Crispin folded his arms over his chest. 'This all may be coincidence. It seems as if we are looking at a killer of many women. Perhaps now that the sheriff is not after you, you might enquire as to the details. Find out also if there have been more women in the past that were strangled, the killer unfound.'

'Aye, master. I'm . . . I'm sorry you must spend another two nights in gaol. It's not right, sir. They know you're not guilty.'

'All the better for me, for now there is doubt. But it doesn't mean you have time to rest.'

'I shall never rest, sir, until I find the knave what done it.'

'That's the spirit.' He slapped Jack's back. 'The sheriffs are eyeing us most carefully. Confer with Cobmartin. And . . . thank you for finding *him*.'

'Aye, sir. I didn't think we could do this alone.'

'I'm not alone. I have you.'

Jack beamed. 'Right, sir . . . Blind me, here they come.'

Sheriff Walcote approached and sneered at Jack. 'Time to return to your cell, Guest.'

'Very well, Lord Sheriff. I would thank you for your hospitality but . . . well . . .'

He shoved Master Crispin forward. 'Be still or be struck.' His master turned back once to offer a nod before he was ushered out of the chamber, manacles clanking.

'You're free to go, Tucker,' said Loveney down the length of his nose. His arms were crossed tightly over his chest.

'Yes, my lord. Thank you, sir.' Jack straightened his coat again and hurried out.

Nigellus was waiting for him.

'Master Tucker, we must talk.'

'I will meet you outside, Master Nigellus. Staying within . . .' he looked back and caught Loveney eyeing him again, 'isn't good for me health.'

Jack breathed deep as he left the confines of the Guildhall. He hated such places, especially crowds that meant to hang his master. He shook out his cloak as if shaking the gloom of the proceedings from his heart. He already felt lighter.

'You're the Tracker's apprentice,' said a gruff voice behind him. He turned and saw the eel monger's round face. Hugh Buckton was his name, he recalled.

'Aye.'

He thumbed back toward the Guildhall. 'I didn't know the man I saw was the Tracker. I never would have said naught had I known.'

'You saw what you saw. It's the truth, isn't it?'

'Aye. I saw him go in. Didn't see him go out.'

Jack smiled, nodded, then turned away.

Buckton seemed reluctant to leave him. He fidgeted with the hem of his coat. 'I wouldn't have said naught. The Tracker's done a lot of good in London.'

'Aye,' said Jack, keeping a polite expression on his face.

'I'd like to help make it right.'

'How could you do that?'

'I dunno. You tell me.'

'I won't have you lie. Even for my master's life. He would forbid it.'

'But suppose I help you. With something else.'

'Well then, let me ask you this. Did you ever see them Noreys men come to le Porter's rooms?'

'I . . . I don't know the men by name.'

'But you said you seen men come and go.'

'Aye. She was a friendly thing. She borrowed money from me. To keep her till she found another situation. I don't suppose there is any getting that back?'

'Er . . . no. Why did she entertain so many men, Master Buckton?'

He shrugged. 'It's not what you think. At least, I don't think it is. She had women visitors, too.'

Jack considered. 'Master Buckton, if you'd truly like to help, may I call upon you to bring you around to identify various people? There may be some that are useful to prove my master innocent.'

He smiled. 'I'd be happy to do that, Master Apprentice.'

'It's Tucker. Jack Tucker. And I'll be by on Sunday, if that will suit.'

'Oh. Is that proper on a Sunday?'

'I don't think the Lord will mind our clearing my master's name on His day.'

'Oh. Right then.' He saluted and lumbered away.

Jack watched him go, curious about what Buckton might be able to tell him.

Once Nigellus joined him, Jack and the lawyer reached Gutter Lane and wove their way through the townsfolk with their burdens and their carts until they reached the Boar's Tusk. They settled in, and Jack found himself absently searching for Isabel. He hoped she had gotten back all right without Gilbert knowing. She was a clever girl. He was certain she could do it.

'Master Jack, you have given new life to this case,' said the lawyer. 'Only a few brief hours ago it looked mighty bad.'

'What that coroner said.' Jack shook his head. 'And to think about all the help my master gave him.'

'Well, men of position don't like to lose it. And I'm afraid Master Guest is a constant reminder of just how much a man can lose.'

Jack couldn't disagree. He took a sip of ale and set his horn cup down.

'What are your plans now, Jack?' asked the lawyer, taking his own sip.

'Well, Nigellus, I don't mind saying it is an uphill battle. I must find this third witness who seems to have eluded everyone. Either the man gave a false name or the clerk misheard. Either is possible. But I worry over the former. And then there is this knave who is out there, strangling women.'

'Yes. A horrible crime. And yet, I am of two minds on it. One, I cringe as any good Christian must. But on the other, to find him is to free my client.'

'Just so, Nigellus. That man is the key to opening my master's cell door. I am also seeking the help of Hugh Buckton, the eel monger. He has promised to help identify some of the men who visited Elizabeth le Porter. I suspect he will identify Walter Noreys.'

'Ah yes. Quite an interesting turn, there. You and your master, *magnis animis similiter cogitent*.'

'Well, I've been taught to think like my master, certainly.' Jack drummed his fingers against his cup. He stood and ran his hand over his face. 'I need to clean m'self up. Time to get home and make sure all is well before I head out again.'

'I will go with you. I have property on the Shambles that I must look over.' They walked out together. 'Indeed. Property my father owned. A poulterer's shop that now lies empty. I am afraid I am not the business man my father was.'

Jack never had cause to think on it. Business was business. It always looked thriving in London. At least it seemed so in the Boar's Tusk. But hadn't he and his master encountered many a man whose business seemed to dwindle? Like the Noreys household. Ill-management and over-spending all contributed. 'Was your father a poulterer?'

Nigellus looked at him aghast. 'Oh no, no, no! He certainly could not have sent me to study law if he were. No, my father was a trader in property. He was not a wealthy man, but he died enjoying his trade. He did not see me fulfill my ambitions as a lawyer and that I regret.'

'I'm sorry. My parents died a long time ago.'

'And I am sorry, too. But it is the way of it. The old make way for the young. And on and on. Here it is. And a disreputable place, as you see.'

Jack looked up at the two-story structure, a building he passed every day but seldom noticed. Its shutters had always been boarded up as long as he could remember. Its lime-washed daub was gray and dingy from smoke and mud.

'It isn't much, is it?' Jack admitted. 'Still, you can rent it out to . . . well. Another poulterer?'

'It needs fixing and my income as a lawyer has yet to meet that expectation.'

They both looked up at it silently for a moment. 'Well, Nigellus. This is where I leave you. I must see to my master's well-being.'

'Fare you well, Master Jack. He is in good hands.'

They bowed to one another and moved off in their separate ways.

Jack hurried to his lodgings. It smelled musty and unused within, but he scanned the room with its two beds, coffer, table, chair, and stool. It wasn't much, he supposed, but it was home. More home than he had had in a long time. There was water in the bucket, and he poured some into the basin, rolled up his sleeves, and did his best to wash.

Feeling better, he closed and barred the shutters, locked the door, and tromped down the stairs. Almost immediately he spotted a man selling roasted meat on sticks. He exchanged a ha'penny for two skewers and wolfed them down as he walked toward Watling, tossing the sticks into the mud and wiping his hands on the thighs of his stockings.

Fortified, he felt a new purpose swell in his heart. He was close. Close to saving his master. A sense of pride overwhelmed him for a moment before he tamped it down. He had a job ahead of him and he needed to get to it.

But after more wasted time trying to find Thomas Tateham, Jack considered. Perhaps he was going about this in the wrong way. Perhaps instead of the name of Thomas Tateham – which Hamo Eckington might have gotten wrong – he should go by a description of him.

It was back to Newgate.

He slid his glance toward the shadows and slanted light of the sun peeking through the clouds. It was getting late. The business day was drawing to a close. It must be around six of the clock. He hurried his steps and arrived at the prison in no time, slipped by the gruff serjeants on the watch, and made his way up the stairs. He supposed it might be easier to break *into* Newgate than out of it.

He spared a thought for his master sitting alone in a cell and sent up a prayer for him.

When he got to the sheriffs' chamber, he peered around the corner. 'Psst!'

Eckington was bent over his never-ending pile of parchments. He raised his head, looked about, but then turned back to them.

'Psst!' said Jack louder. This time the man turned around.

'Why do you make that sound at me, Tucker? What do you want?'

'Master Eckington. I am having the devil's own time finding that third witness, that Thomas Tateham on Mercery Lane. Might you be able to give me a description of the man instead?'

Eckington's brows converged over his eyes. 'Well then . . . he . . . he was a man of some middling height – shorter than you,

Master Tucker, but I must say, you are exceptionally tall. He wore a hood and kept it close – bless me. Do you suppose he *was* trying to conceal who he was?'

'I have no doubt of it, Master Hamo. Why do you suppose he would be doing that? Why would he even stay to give testimony to the sheriffs?'

'If he were trying to hide himself, then running away would draw attention to him. Better to send the sheriffs on the well-worn path than to offer them an opportunity to give chase.'

'Then which is more likely wrong? His name, his address . . . or both?'

'His name is most certainly false. It takes a man most devious to think of another address on the spot as well.'

'I'll have to hope that he does live on Mercery, for if he does not, there is no hope of my finding him. Please, Master Hamo. Go on with your description.'

Eckington seemed of a better humor to comply. Their mutual curiosity was surely their united cause. 'He wore a beard, brown, close-cropped to his face. His nose was hawk-like – hooked so.' He demonstrated with a gesture. 'With brown eyes, brown hair to his shoulders that I could see in his hood. His teeth are small. His accent is like the sheriffs', so I must conclude he is a merchant of higher trade. I know that is not much to go on, Master Tucker . . .'

'It is a great deal more than I had before, Master Hamo. I thank you.' After bowing, he turned hastily to go when Eckington stopped him.

'Tucker, I . . . I wish you God's blessing. Master Guest . . . everyone knows he is not guilty. Let us hope your evidence will prove it so.'

Jack hurried out. 'I hope so, too,' he muttered.

FOURTEEN

Saturday, 17 October

The shadows were lengthening, and Jack hurried. He did not want doors slammed in his face. How he wished for Ned's help again. Or perhaps even Isabel's.

Isabel. Such a pretty, young thing. And she seemed to like Jack. He liked her, too. Her cheerful eyes that he could see even now in his mind's eye. Her kittenish smile.

He pulled himself up short with a shiver. No! He hadn't time to think of her. And besides, what would Master Gilbert say? He was getting ahead of himself. Once Master Crispin was freed from gaol and only then would he consider . . . consider . . . 'Blind me. What *am* I considering?'

He shook himself again. Nothing. He was considering nothing. Not while his master's life was still at stake.

He came to the first door on Mercery, screwed up his courage, and knocked.

A woman answered the door and looked down at Jack. 'Didn't I talk to you the other day, lad?'

'Oh, aye. It's possible. For you see I am looking for a man . . .'

'And I told you I did not know him.'

'And right you did, but I have since discovered that he is using a false name. If I told you what he looked like, might you be able to tell me then?'

'Oh, I see. Well then?'

Jack gave the description and the woman listened, her eyes shifting heavenward in thought. 'That does sound familiar. But I cannot put a name to that face.'

'But have you seen that man on Mercery?'

'I'm almost certain I have. Almost certain, mind. I don't want no trouble with the law.'

'Oh, no, madam. No trouble at all. I thank you.' He backed

away with a curt bow and trotted to the next shop. Encouraged, he climbed the stair and knocked.

But after a few more houses, it became apparent that though the description seemed to sound familiar to the folk on the street, no name or address was forthcoming.

As the sun glided past the rooftops, he had to conclude that he had been wrong. He would not find the witness this way. At least not today. With a heavy heart, he trudged back up Mercery to Milk Street and thence to Catte. This was the murder Nigellus had told him of, and he set about to find some witnesses, those that might have known the woman. He came first to a female shopkeeper, carefully stacking the thick wheels of cheese up under her arm to bring inside for the end of the day.

'I beg your mercy, demoiselle,' Jack said with a bow. The woman, thin and pale with her cotehardie laced up tight to her throat, stopped. Her linen kerchief hid her face so well that only her cheeks, chin, and eyes were visible.

'Eh?' she said.

'I understand you knew the woman who died the other day.'

She frowned, burling her chin. 'And who's asking?'

'Jack Tucker, the Tracker's apprentice.'

Her brows – or what he could see of them – flew up her forehead. 'Tracker? By the Mass. But . . . the sheriff's men already came round . . .'

'As you might also know, me and my master are not with the sheriff.'

She nodded. 'And so. What can I do for the Tracker's apprentice?'

'You can tell me about the woman.'

'Avice Weedon. Well. One shouldn't speak ill of the dead . . .' She crossed herself. 'But we all knew the sort of woman she was.'

'And . . . what sort was that?'

'The sort what lay with men . . . for coin. That was a stew, after all.'

'Oh. And . . . this was well known?'

'Oh aye. We all knew it. And though many scorned it, they didn't bother no one. The girls even went to church regular. To think they couldn't find decent work. Or didn't want to.'

She ticked her head. 'She was a right sweet lass, too. Often gave over charity to those in need. Sweet lass. Oh, I know the stews belong in Southwark, and now that the sheriff's discovered it they will be turned out, but they were good neighbors. Surprisingly quiet. Ah, what will they do now? I suppose it's off to Southwark for them. And who knows who will rent the place after. If the law would only leave well enough alone . . .'

Jack bit his lip. 'Then . . . did you or anyone see a man go up to her, er . . . lodgings Thursday last?'

'Which one? There were many she'd bring up there.'

'I imagine the *last* one.'

She squinted at him. 'You're cheeky for an apprentice.' She sighed. 'Who can say? Some men don't care if they are seen with a whore. Some do care. She had regulars, too. They'd meet her on the street or at the stew.'

From Nigellus's information, Jack knew the woman had been killed Thursday evening. Could have been before or after Elizabeth le Porter was dispatched. But why run from one woman to the next, killing them?

'Did she have any regulars Thursday night?'

'A few.'

'How would you know the difference between the other customers and hers?'

'Because she would always see them off at the step. Little wonder they came back to her. She had a good head for business.'

'Any you know by name?'

She laughed. 'Are you going to go round their houses and ask them? With their wives present?'

Jack felt his face flush. He certainly knew the mechanics of it. Hadn't he heard enough rutting from Master Crispin and seen more in taverns. Jack himself, though bestirred as the best of men, had no taste for whores. He was as yet untried, and he wasn't certain how he felt about that.

'If I must,' he said. 'Can you . . . *will* you give me their names?'

She sobered. 'Aye. If it will help. If one of them is responsible . . .'

Jack took out the parchment and ink that he still had in his scrip and took down the names. Perhaps being a clerk was a handy thing at that.

'It's a shame about Joan Keighley.'

Jack looked up, his quill stopped short. 'Eh?' Joan Keighley was the woman Jack had found along with Sheriff Walcote. 'Did you know her, too?'

'Oh, aye. She used to work in the stew . . . until she went out on her own.'

'You wouldn't know her clients, would you?'

'No. Only Avice said her farewells to the men on the threshold.'

'I see.' He folded his parchment and slipped it back into his scrip. 'I thank you, madam.'

'Find her killer.' She rubbed at her neck. 'It makes us all a bit . . . shivery . . . thinking about it.'

'Make sure you bar your windows and doors at night,' he admonished before he walked away and headed toward Watling. If Avice and Joan Keighley knew one another, they might even have some of the same clients. But would Joan's neighbors know *their* names?

He soon discovered that though Joan's neighbors called her quiet and charitable, they, too, knew what she was up to. One nearby shopkeeper said he did not know the name of her clients but that a neighbor woman did, but she was not at home. Jack thanked him and vowed to return.

With thoughts rambling around in his head, Jack wandered back toward that private stair near the roper and eel monger. He paid a call to the roper, who was exasperated at being bothered again.

'She's more trouble dead than alive, isn't she?' He crossed himself. 'Forgive me,' he grumbled, 'but she tried keeping to herself and now I've heard more about her than I have in the fortnight she lived here. She was a vixen, to be sure, but quiet, like I said. Though she wasn't above using her wiles to wheedle money from me . . . and others. Always borrowing, that one. Now no one's getting their money back, I suppose.'

'I've heard that before,' said Jack. 'But sir, if she had no money, how could she afford such lodgings? Two rooms? That's fine accommodations.'

The roper shrugged. 'I suppose. Her lodgings were paid for in full. As for income to live day to day, I know not. Lived on borrowing. But I don't mind saying I always felt as if . . . well, as if it were all temporary. As if she was only in those rooms for a short while and intended on moving on.'

'What makes you think so?'

'All sorts of things. Things she'd say. "Wait till next month, Master Roper." Or "But you'll miss me." Strange things like that.'

Jack scratched at his curly mop of hair. 'Do you know if she were betrothed?'

'She said not a thing about it. Seems one would.'

'It seems.'

'I didn't mean to rail at you, Master Tucker,' said Croydone. 'If you need any help from me, any at all, I'd be glad to offer my hand.'

He thanked the roper and stepped outside. If le Porter had secured these lodgings only temporarily, where had she intended to go? Was she getting married? Was it to the man who had strangled her?

Jack turned and started when Hugh Buckton suddenly appeared behind him. 'Blind me, Master Buckton, but you gave me a fright.'

'Sorry, Master Tucker. I just saw you there and wondered if you had gotten any further in your investigating.'

'Not as far as I would have liked, sir. You said that Elizabeth le Porter owed you money?'

'Aye. Is there any getting it back?'

'Not according to what I hear of her. Looks like she borrowed from a lot of men.'

Buckton scowled and looked away.

'I know it's a hard thing . . .'

'It's just . . . you haven't found the man what killed her. What if it was . . . well, they arrested the Tracker . . .'

'That's my master you're talking about!' He hadn't meant to shout, but others along the street had turned to look, some straining their necks to peer above the crowds.

Jack chastened but faced Buckton squarely. 'It isn't my master,' he said quieter, 'and I am doing the best that I can. But these things take time. Be assured, Master Buckton, that I *will* find the culprit and I'll make certain he hangs from the highest tree.' He calmed himself, straightened his cotehardie, and took a breath.

'And so, Master Buckton, would you be willing to come with me now to identify those I mentioned before?'

The man shook his head. 'No. I have to get back to my work. You told me Sunday.'

'That I did. I only thought that if you had the time now . . .'

'No. Sunday.' He turned abruptly away and shambled back to his shop.

Jack ran his hand up over his face. Not what he expected from the murdered women, no help about the third witness, and Buckton was putting him off. Could this day get any worse?

He gave it up, and with his apologies sent toward Newgate to his master, he set out toward home.

But he hadn't gotten more than a few streets and down an alley when a man in a dark cloak accosted him. Jack spun, knife drawn, and leapt back from his attacker. It turned out to be a good tactic. Walter Noreys, teeth bared, glowered.

'What do *you* want?' Jack wished fervently that Buckton had agreed to accompany him for here was the first of many he wanted the man to identify.

'I want that which is mine. I know who you really are and I know that Crispin Guest has the Virgin's Tears. I *know* he has it! It is known he traffics in relics. There are countless tales of such. He must have it, and you know where it is.' He pulled a long blade and crouched as if to fight.

Jack backed away. 'Master Noreys, I am warning you now. Stand down. My master hasn't the Tears. I saw the relic myself just yesterday at the house of the widow Peverel. And your father knows about your antics. Isn't it bad enough that it got your brother killed?'

'Don't you speak about my brother!'

'But it is true. You know it is. Give this up, Master Noreys.'

'Here! What's this?'

A man came into the alley and cried the alarm. Others came running and stood around them.

'You see, Master Noreys,' Jack urged. 'You cannot win this. Go home. See to your family. It's over and done.'

Noreys swept the crowd with a sneer and slammed his knife back in its sheath. 'It's *not* over, Tucker. While I live and breathe it's not over. You just watch your back.' He spun, his cloak whirling after him.

Jack slowed his breathing and carefully sheathed his dagger. The crowd watched him, while some stepped back out of the alley and followed Noreys' retreat.

'Are you all right, son?' asked an older man, hand on Jack's shoulder.

'Thanks to you and your friends, sir. No harm done. Just an excitable fellow is he.'

'Well I'd take his advice. To watch your back.'

'And so I shall, sir. Thanks to you all.' Jack saluted them and hurried on. But instead of heading home, he decided to stop by the Boar's Tusk.

Blind me, I'm taking on my master's habits, he admonished. No wonder Master Crispin drank. A little wine, a little ale went a long way to relaxing a man's tensed shoulders.

He ducked inside the darker interior and found a place with a clear view of the room.

Gilbert arrived shortly thereafter and brought a jug and two cups. He sat opposite, not saying a word, and poured, scooting one cup toward Jack. He set the jug down and drank.

Jack cautiously took the cup and drank it down. It was enough to cleanse the day from his throat but a second dose helped his disposition. He set that cup down and wiped his mouth. 'Thank you, Gilbert. That was needed.'

'Any more word on the case, Jack? Are you any closer . . .'

He shook his head. 'The more I dig, the more muddled it becomes. I tell you true, Gilbert, I never done a case on me own. And I surely never wanted that first one to be so grave a chore as to save my master's life. It is harder work than I ever dreamed. I'd watch Master Crispin at it and he always seemed so calm, so precise. I feel like a bumbling, stumbling fool. At least his lawyer is confident that there is enough doubt not to convict. Is that so, Gilbert? Do you think there is a chance?'

Gilbert filled his cup again and set the jug down. 'Well, as I've heard it – and there have been many at the Guildhall this day – there are some that hold fast to the witnesses, saying it could be none but Crispin, but there are still others who took your testimony to heart. They are not keen to convict, but they don't know if they can acquit either.'

'Damn!' Jack stared sourly at the table. 'I must try again tomorrow. Sunday or no, there is no rest while my master languishes in gaol.'

Gilbert patted his arm. 'You're a good lad, Jack. And so . . . I wish to ask you something of great import.'

Jack drank another dose of ale and set his cup down, waiting for Gilbert to speak.

'Jack, my lad. It has come to my attention that . . . well, that Isabel might have been in your company the other day when she went missing.'

Jack straightened to his full height. He swallowed hard. 'Now, Gilbert . . . there was nothing amiss. The lass wanted to help me in my cause. And once she did, I sent her back right quick. I did try to send her back right away but . . . she's a bit . . . headstrong.'

Gilbert sagged, nodding. 'Aye. That she is. Then . . . no harm done I suppose . . .'

'Master Gilbert.' Jack cleared his throat again when it suddenly thickened. 'Master Gilbert, I was wondering. If a lad, such as m'self, someone who hasn't quite got great prospects, should . . .' He suddenly grew shy and couldn't raise his eyes to the man. Instead, he drew circles in the rings left by his cup. 'Should, say, want to . . . woo her. What would you say?'

The tavern keeper looked around and then hunkered down over the table, keeping their talk private. 'Well now, Jack. A man like me must take into consideration that he'd want the best for his ward. He'd look for a man with a proper house and vocation. Someone who could support her and her children. I'd be a poor uncle indeed if I considered any less for her.'

Jack's shoulders fell. He frowned and stared at the drawings he had made with the spilled ale. All nonsense. 'I see. Aye, I should do no less for my own kin. One would have to be a fool to . . . to . . .' He swallowed again and kicked the bench back as he rose. 'Maybe I should be getting back home . . .'

Gilbert reached over and grasped Jack's arm. 'Sit you down, lad. I wasn't done talking.'

Jack sat reluctantly, feeling like the biggest fool. His face felt burned like it was afire, burnished red and warm. He should have talked to Master Crispin first. He should have pled his case, and then his master would have talked him down, eased his mind with his clever words and sage advice. Maybe the two of them were meant for a solitary life like two monks in a cell.

'But . . .' Gilbert began, 'I would also be a fool if I didn't take into consideration the measure of the man. For a man could have all the gold in the world and be a villain. What sort of match would that be if my kin were soured and trodden? Her babes would be sickly, and if they lived would turn out to be scoundrels and shrews. No, it's a fine responsibility being a guardian, for parent I am not, but I do love her like a child of my own. A fine upstanding man would be my choice for her. Even if he did make a meager living. For one day, this tavern and all that is in it, she would inherit, so it isn't as if she would be left with nothing if this lad – whoever he is – didn't make the living he should. He would be honest and true to her, and keep his oaths. That is the gold no man can keep in a money pouch.'

Jack flicked his gaze over Gilbert's kind, round face. 'Sir?'

Gilbert smiled. 'If the lass is willing . . . I'll . . . give my consent.'

Blinking Jack rose again. 'Y-you . . . you will?'

Gilbert stood, leaned over the table, and slapped the boy's shoulder. 'Jack Tucker, did you ever doubt it?' He laughed out loud, grabbed the jug, and made his way through the customers toward the back of the tavern.

Jack watched him go, his open mouth growing into a smile, and his chest swelling with pride. 'God blind me! Did you ever!'

He headed toward the door, body straight and tall with expectation . . . until he shuddered to a halt. *If the lass is willing*, Gilbert had said. And what if she weren't?

Jack swung around, eyes searching for Isabel, horror on his face. He'd only just met her. How presumptuous of him to assume, with so little acquaintance, that she might think him a good prospect. For what was he? An apprentice and servant to a man who had no prospects of his own. And that was fine for the two of them, but add a wife into the mix and babes, it was a sour thing indeed. He had little to offer, earning only a farthing for each job he and Master Crispin took on. How was a wife to put that away for their retirement? Or a dowry should they have a girl!

But then his gaze fell on Isabel as she carried in the wood for the fire. She happened to look up in that instant and caught Jack's gaze. A smile, all dimples and mischief, tore across her face, and her eyes shone with the brilliance of a spring day.

Jack's heart melted. *She* does *like me*, he consoled himself. He gave her a shy little wave that she tried to return, though her arms were burdened. Instinctively, he moved toward her to help. And then a man burst through the door of the tavern, yelling, 'Where's Crispin Guest?'

Jack swiveled to look, and the man caught sight of him. He pushed his way forward – since the tavern customers began moving to discover what the matter was – and stood before Jack. 'You must come quickly! Your house is on fire.'

'What?' Jack shoved him and cast open the doors. He ran and heard the footfalls of others following. Above the rooftops toward the Shambles, Jack saw angry black curls of smoke rising. 'No!' He ran harder, skidded around the corner, and saw the flames leaping from the tinker shop. He stopped before it, assessing. Red and gold flickered within the now black-rimmed windows. He peered inside, but hands grabbed him from behind, and he beheld the tinker and his family cowering in sooty clothes.

'We're all right, Jack. We worried over you.'

'Then you are all well?' His eyes tracked over Matilda, the tinker's pig-faced daughter, and Alice, Martin's shrewish wife. She did not seem to have anything to say today. Instead she wept and held her daughter.

The fire licked upward, quickly reaching the rafters; *Master Crispin's lodgings!*

Jack made for the stairs, but some of the citizens of the Shambles held him back. 'You can't go up there, boy!' cried the poulterer from next door. 'The fire will be there in no time.'

Jack's desperate search of the street saw men running forward with buckets of water, and soon a line formed. They tossed the water through the burned opening of the tinker shop, passed the empty bucket back, and got a newly filled bucket.

But all Jack could think of was their goods – Master Crispin's sword! The man couldn't lose it a second time. Not while Jack lived and breathed. He tore away from the gripping hands and shouts of the others and leapt upon the stairs, skipping every other one. He wasted no time with a key but kicked the door hard, once, twice. The third time broke the jam and he pushed inside. It was full of smoke. He raised his tunic over his face, went to the peg by the door, and grabbed the sword in its scabbard, hoisting it over his shoulder. He was turning to leave when he thought of their cache. Jack's retirement of gems and coins, and Master Crispin's family ring.

Coughing, he dug into the floor, hot already from the flames just inches beneath his feet, and pried up the boards. He reached in for the tightly bound bags. They were smoldering, but he quickly stuffed them into his scrip. He looked around. The Aristotle! His master prized it so. He threw open the coffer, gagged on the smoke and coughed until his eyes watered, before he reached in and grabbed the precious little book. There was no more room in his scrip, but his hands touched on the chess set from Abbot de Litlyngton.

And here he thought they owned nothing.

He scooped that up, too, under his arm, and made ready to leave when he thought at the last minute about the small portrait of his master's lost love, Philippa Walcote.

Jack turned. Flames now burst up through the floorboards, and Jack nearly fell over from surprise. The heat was terrific and the smoke blinding. He slid on his knees before his master's bed, shoved his arm under the mattress, and felt for the small frame. *Where the sarding hell is it?* Just when he was about to give up, his fingers closed on it and he pulled it free.

But when he turned toward the door, it was engulfed in flames like the gates of Hell itself. Everywhere he turned there was fire and smoke . . . and no exit.

You're in for it now, Jack. Oh vanity! Why had he stopped to gather all these goods? They would all perish in the fire now, with him clutching them all.

His desperate search snagged on a vertical line of light through the smoke. The back window! He rushed toward it, barking his shin on the corner of his bed. *Aw, my bed!* That, too, was for the flames, and he'd only had it for a year.

Clutching the sword to his chest, the chess set under his arm, and the book and the portrait in his left hand, Jack closed his watering eyes and leading with his shoulder, he ran hard for the shutters and burst through them. Into the air he sailed, without the sweet earth beneath his feet. And still leading with his shoulder, he curled, and waited for the feel of the tiles of the roof on the shop behind them that slanted just outside their back window. Yet just as he was beginning to think he had miscalculated and was heading for the stony courtyard below, he landed hard on the roof, rolling and rolling, snapping the clay roof tiles as he went. Slipping farther, he slammed his foot down into the roughened tiles and stopped his progress over the side. His body came to a halt on the edge, his goods still wrapped tight in his arms and fingers.

He looked back, and a roar of fire burst from the window he had left only seconds before.

And though his shoulder ached, his lungs heaved from the smoke, and his hand was beginning to feel the heat of the burns he had received, all he could think was, *What on earth will Master Crispin say?*

FIFTEEN

Sunday, 18 October

Jack awoke the next morning to the sounds of church bells tolling all over the city. Sunday. The day of rest. The day to atone and to be refreshed in the blood and flesh of Christ.

But today was a day of mourning, as far as he was concerned.

After the fire had destroyed most of the tinker shop's building, the citizens of the Shambles and surrounds had managed to stop the fire from going farther. There was nothing as fearsome as a fire in a city, for there was almost no stopping such an inferno when it hungrily devoured. But all sang the praises of the sooty men who had helped, who had worked hard into the evening and had declared the fire out by Compline.

The men of the Boar's Tusk had lent a hand, and exhausted, Gilbert led them all back and offered them a round, free of charge. Jack, heartsore and injured, never had to ask for the charity he needed. Eleanor took him under her wing and set him up in a bed with Ned by the fire. She and Isabel saw to his burned hand with ointment and a clean bit of cloth wrapped tight around it, and sent him to sleep. The things he had rescued were stored beneath his cot, except the sword. No matter how they pleaded he would not relinquish it, and lay on the straw-stuffed mattress, clutching the sword to his chest all night long.

And now he stared up at the rafters. Ned was already at his duties, but Jack was still stunned by events. He'd been homeless before. For years after his mother died he had abandoned their master and taken to the streets. But this was different. He had become a civilized man. He had accustomed himself to a fire and a roof and even the comforts of a bed. What were he and his master to do? They had nothing, save what Jack had rescued. And only the clothes on their backs. Master Crispin's writing things were gone. Their extra clothes – linen chemise, stockings, braies. All burned. True, he had saved what little money they had . . . and a few baubles Master Crispin held dear. But . . . all the rest . . .

And of course, there was still the problem of setting his master free.

Jack felt the tears at his eyes, the lump warming his throat. It was all too much.

And then suddenly, Eleanor was there. 'Now lamb. You mustn't fret. You'll have a place with us for as long as you need it. And Crispin, too.'

He sat up, set the sword aside, and turned away to wipe at his eyes. What sort of spectacle was he making of himself, weeping like a maiden? He'd had troubles before, and he hadn't wept at them. Why succumb now?

'I'm all right, Eleanor,' he muttered. His bandaged hand throbbed with pain, and his throat was dry, his mouth still tasting of smoke. He rose and his gaze met hers. 'I still have work to do.'

'Eat first, Jack.'

'Eleanor . . .'

'Jack Tucker, you *will* eat. What would Crispin say if I let you go on an empty stomach?' And then her own eyes teared up and she daubed at them with the hem of her apron.

He slid his arm in hers and leaned against her. 'Of course, Eleanor. I need me strength, don't I?'

He sat down to a meal with Ned, Gilbert, and Isabel, while Eleanor fussed over him. He wanted to gaze at Isabel, thinking it might cheer him, but he was filled with so many dark thoughts, so much loss, he couldn't bear to raise his head. He certainly did not relish seeing pity in her eyes.

He ate as much as he could under Eleanor's watchful gaze, asked Gilbert to secure his things in a safe location, and left hurriedly before anyone – especially Isabel – could approach him alone.

He had to go to Newgate first. He had to tell his master what had happened.

He made the turn at the Shambles. The acrid smell of burnt timbers and cloth still lingered. He tried not to but couldn't help flicking his eyes toward the charred beams and fallen walls. There was nothing left but a black skeleton and a sooty foundation. The bitter smell was strongest when standing before it. Passersby ticked their heads, and some even approached and rested their hands condolingly on his arm.

There was nothing left of the top floor, their lodgings. It had fallen in to the floor below and burnt to a crisp. Nothing to salvage, yet he moved forward anyway. The outside stairs were gone. Only a charred pile of rubble and ash was left of that. He climbed up over the stone sill to the tinker shop and carefully made his way over the smoldering remains. He could just about tell where the walls had been that separated shop from bedchambers. The forge was still there, blackened, and its stone base cracked from the heat, but it was there, along with the hearth.

He looked up not into rafters, but into the gray sky.

Long ago he and his mother shared a pile of straw under a leaky roof at their harsh master's shop. That was all he had known until she died and he struck out on his own at eight years old. He had made his way in the shelter of a church doorway or an abandoned storehouse. There was a brief stint in the boy's stew, but he had shut that from his mind long ago. He had liked the open. Seemed safer sometimes. But in the winter he had had to find some place to keep him from freezing to death. A church was barely warm enough but it sufficed. He had eaten what he could find or steal, but six years ago when Master Crispin saved him from the sheriff, he decided he would serve that recalcitrant man . . . whether he had wanted a servant or not. Mostly he had not. But Jack had found a way to worm himself into these lodgings and not just for the shelter and meager warmth they provided. Master Crispin was a man worth serving in more ways than Jack ever could have imagined.

He shuffled through, kicking at charred cooking pots and tools that the tinker had been fixing or creating to sell. They were all too burned from the fire to do anyone any good now.

He bent down and picked up a knife, or what had been a knife. The wooden handle had burned away, leaving the blackened tang, naked and alone. The thin curved blade was strange in shape, unlike any he had seen before. He turned it in his hands, but it left black marks on his palms and fingers and he let it fall with the other detritus. He wiped his hands on his cotehardie and sighed.

Climbing out the window, he met Martin Kemp, his erstwhile landlord, looking just as woebegone.

The man was muttering into his clenched hands. 'What are we to do?'

'How are you faring, Master Kemp? Have you gotten your family situated?'

'Yes, we are living with my in-laws.' He wore a drooping expression that Jack could well appreciate if the rest of Alice's relatives were like her. 'But I can't understand what happened.'

Jack shrugged. 'With a forge there is always the possibility of a coal getting loose, one you never noticed, even with the forge outside as it was. It's not your fault, sir.'

'But that's impossible. The forge has been cold for days. I was making repairs to it. Some of the mortar has been cracked over the years. And the hearth was banked before we retired.' He shook his head. 'But it *might* be as you said. A coal could have escaped the hearth . . .' His voice trailed off as he frowned, looking at the building he had called home for far longer than Jack had.

But Jack ruminated and turned to the tinker. 'The forge was cold?'

'Oh yes. For days. And with so much work ahead of me. I don't suppose I can do it now. All those repairs ruined! What will become of us? I do not know if I can afford to rebuild.'

Jack's thoughts couldn't be spared for what might happen to Kemp and his family, or even Master Crispin and himself. But he focused instead on Martin's words about his forge. The man was precise in his work, and always conscious of his forge and the danger. He had his family to consider, naturally. But if he *had* been careful and the hearth was banked as he claimed – and Jack had no reason to suspect otherwise – then what had started the fire?

Or even more disquieting, *who*?

He sucked in a breath. Walter Noreys had threatened him. And that family had already tried to do his master harm. Everyone knew where they lived. It was a matter of course. If no one knew where they were then how would clients find them? Walter Noreys had said that he would get his revenge. Had it been him?

He turned to tell that to Martin . . . but shut his lips again. It would not help the man or his loud and shrewish wife to know that the fire that had left them all homeless had been deliberately set. Surely Alice Kemp would sue them for damages, for funds they did not possess, and he would be damned if he allowed Master Crispin to be beholden to Alice Kemp for the rest of their lives.

He offered a few absent well wishes to Master Kemp and finally took his leave, watching the man carefully climb through the sill and pick his way delicately through the sooty maw.

Giving the burnt shell of his home one last look, Jack trudged onward toward Newgate prison. When he reached the arch, the serjeant Wendell Smythe, leaning on his pike, looked Jack over. 'I suppose you want to speak to your murdering master.'

Jack was too weary to take the bait. 'Aye. May I pass?'

Wendell cocked a brow at him, and sensing no sport out of Jack today, only gestured with his head to go on.

Jack took the stairs slowly, measuring what he was going to say. He traveled down the long passages, skipping the sheriffs all together, and heading toward Melvyn, the head gaoler. He would either let Jack in to speak to his master or he would not.

When he reached the open arched chamber with the large brazier, Melvyn spotted him first.

'And there is Young Master Jack. How goes it, Tucker? How does it feel to live in a live coal?'

'Oh. You heard, eh?'

'Who hasn't on the Shambles?'

'Then . . . does *he* know?'

Melvyn grinned a crenelated smile. 'I was the one what told him.'

Jack sighed. Of course. No dignity was to be left either of them. 'Can I see him?'

Melvyn folded his arms in a mockery of consideration. He licked his lips. 'Maybe. For a coin.'

'Ah, man. I just lost everything in the world and you want a coin?'

The other gaolers muttered, and if conscience Melvyn had, it was bruised by their mockery. He sneered, unfolded his arms, and trudged forward. 'Come on, then!' he groused.

Jack followed quickly into the darker passage. The man unhooked the chatelaine of keys from his belt, chose one, and unlocked the door. 'No more than five minutes.'

Jack moved forward eagerly, but cringed when the door

slammed and locked behind him. He certainly hoped Melvyn intended on letting him out again.

And there was his master, sitting on his pallet bed, feet shackled with heavy iron manacles with a strong chain between them, leaning back against the wall with – of all things – a black and white cat on his stomach. Absently he stroked, looking distantly at nothing at all.

'Master . . .' said Jack quietly.

The man's head immediately shot upward. 'Jack!' He dislodged the cat as he rose. He took three shuffling steps and enclosed Jack in an embrace. 'Thank God you are well. I feared the worst but no one knew, no one would say.'

'I am well, master. But our lodgings . . .'

'Well . . .' He stood back and shrugged with a deep sigh. 'Nothing lasts forever.'

It was true that his master had had his fair share of sorrows and bad luck. And anyone else might be surprised by the seeming glibness of his response. But Jack knew him. Knew what was meant by the tautness of his jaw, the burling of his brows over his eyes. 'But I did manage to salvage our few belongings.' He stepped forward and said reverently, 'I saved your sword, sir. I couldn't let it burn.'

'Jack!' The tight gnarl of muscle at his jaw unwound all at once and his eyes widened with astonishment. The grateful brightness in his eyes was worth the pain of Jack's burned hand.

Jack stared at his shoes. 'And your chess set. And here.' He reached into his scrip and pulled out the book. 'I brung you your Aristotle, sir.'

His master took it reverently, turning it over in his hands as if he hadn't seen it before, as if he hadn't spent every brief moment of leisure poring over the thing.

'I'd have rather brought you a prayer book, but seeings that we don't have one . . .'

He chuckled. 'Ah, Jack. A poor son of the Church am I when the words of a pagan offer me more comfort than the words of God. But I know God watches over me and my ways. He made the pagans as well as the Christians.' He lifted the small book. 'I do thank you for this. You don't know how much I appreciate it to fill the long and lonely hours.'

Jack slouched, for the thought of it always made him uncomfortable. 'And I also saved the . . . the little portrait.'

His master looked up from his scrutiny of his book. 'Jack,' he whispered. Master Crispin approached again. Soft at first, he took Jack's shoulders, until his fingers dug in, tightening with emotion. 'What made you do such a foolish, dangerous thing?'

Jack gazed at the face of his master, his savior more times than he could count. There were lines at his forehead, lines etched down from his nostrils nearly to his chin, lines at the creases of his gray eyes. He was thirty-five years old but he looked forty-five.

'For *you*, sir.'

His master's face, as lined and as wind-burned as it was, lay naked, open. So raw was the emotion in his eyes that Jack had to look away.

Master Crispin shook his head, eyes now puzzled, wet. He turned away from Jack and hobbled toward the window, gazing up at it, bathing himself in the gray light. 'No one . . . has ever done such a thing . . . for me.'

'Always for you, sir. Because I'm grateful.'

'It's a miracle you got out alive at all. So many burdens.'

'I know,' he said, wiping at his eyes. 'I was beginning to think what a fool thing it was when the smoke filled the room. But you know me.' He chuckled even though he didn't feel it. 'I just barreled through. Right out the back window and along the roof. Burnt me hand a little.' He looked down at the bandaged hand, turning it this way and that. Suddenly a pair of callused hands gently held it, turning it to examine it for himself.

'My poor apprentice. You've earned your fee today, there's no doubt about it. And I would pay you . . . if only I could.'

Jack nodded, all words done.

Master Crispin stood looking at Jack for only a moment more. He slowly returned to his place on his cot. The cat returned, too, and settled on his stomach as if he had never risen.

'You've made a friend,' said Jack.

'Yes. God knows where he came from. He keeps returning. I call him Gyb.'

'Original,' muttered Jack.

Master Crispin stroked the cat. 'I was thinking of calling him "Lancaster" . . .' Jack snorted. 'But it was only a fleeting thought.

Well, what's the news? I hope it is better than the last I received so gleefully from Melvyn last night about our lodgings.'

'About that, sir. Master Kemp said he was assiduous with his hearth and that his forge has been cold for the last two days.'

Master Crispin slowly looked up from his attention to the cat. 'Are you saying that *someone* set our house on fire?'

'Aye, sir. And I have reason to believe it was Walter Noreys.'

'The devil you say!' He jolted to his feet, and this time the cat made his displeasure known at being so abused, yowling and scrambling toward the corner.

'A vile devil it is, sir. He still believes you have the Tears of the Virgin and are hiding it. He accosted me on the street with a knife and, without the help of my fellow townsfolk, I might have been laid low. And then he swore his revenge.'

'The cur. Should we bring charges?'

'I don't know, sir. I'd not have Alice Kemp turn on us with a suit for damages.'

'I see your point. Martin's family is well?'

'Aye, sir. No one was hurt.'

'That is a blessing, then.'

'Aye. A blessing. Today I will steal the eel monger, and we will be stealthy so he may identify Walter Noreys. At least it is my hope. That he was one of many men who paid Elizabeth le Porter a call.'

'Ah. Good thinking, Jack.'

'And I have also begun my investigation of the two women who were strangled. They were both whores, sir. One in a stew right there in the Bread Street Ward, and the other plying her trade on her own.'

'You don't say.'

'I do. And since their patrons were well known by their neighbors, I am making a list to see if any match. Surely a client might have done the deed.'

'Good, good,' said Master Crispin, thinking.

Jack felt reassured by his master's acknowledgment.

But then his throat dried up with his next thought. Could he burden his master with this?

He swallowed and licked his lips. 'And . . . there is one more thing. Er . . . Master Gilbert . . .'

Master Crispin looked up expectantly.

Jack bit his lip and, conscious that he was mangling his cote-hardie hem, made his hands rest at his sides. 'H-he has a niece and she's come to live with him on account of her father. Well, he died. Gilbert is raising her as his ward. And so . . . she, that is, Isabel, works in the tavern. And she stands to inherit all, you see. And . . . and . . . But it isn't just for that. Not at all.'

'Jack.' Master Crispin's tone softened and he cocked his head. 'What are you saying?'

'Er . . . It's about . . . Isabel.'

'Oh, I see. Do you . . . fancy her?'

He knew his master would understand. 'Aye, sir. I do. I know I haven't much to offer a lass, but . . .'

'You mustn't do a thing until you ask Gilbert's permission. You haven't, have you?'

'Oh no, sir! Never would I. And Gilbert did talk to me. And he's granted it. Permission, I mean.' Jack shook his head, still stunned by the wonder of it all.

'He did? What were his reasons? Forgive me, Jack. But as you said, our prospects – especially now – are thin.'

'He said that I was a man who would keep his oaths, and he said that was more important that a man with riches and no soul.'

'God's blood,' he said under his breath. The grin formed on his master's face and he approached again, and again enclosed Jack in an embrace. 'Well . . . bless me. And God's grace on you, Jack. Look at you. You think yourself a man, do you?'

Jack stood tall. 'I am, sir.'

'And so you have proved yourself to be. Is the lady willing?'

'I think so, sir. Though I have not yet talked to her. She's still a young thing. All of fifteen.'

'Well, not as young as you think. Though give it some time. Let the fruit of your venture ripen in its proper course.' He rocked on his heels. 'If she has turned *your* head, she must be pretty . . .'

Jack felt his cheeks burn and he nodded.

'And clever . . .'

He nodded again.

'Then well done.' His grin soon faded. 'I suppose this means . . . you will leave me.'

'Sir?'

'When a man marries he must see to his family. And right now . . . there is no place for me to live, let alone you and a wife.'

'But sir! I would never leave you!'

'There comes a time, Jack . . .'

'No! I will not. And there will be no further talk on it. You and I, we have an understanding. Do you not remember the vow we made to one another in Canterbury?'

The lopsided grin was back on his master's face. 'I did not think you remembered.'

''Course I did! You said to me "there are to be no lies, no secrets between us. My *yes* means *yes* and my *no* means *no*. And thus it will always be between you and me." I took you at your word, sir.'

'And I took you at yours. Very well, Jack. Woo your lady, with my blessing. And we will work out the rest. As long as I can get out of this damned prison alive.'

'You will, sir. If *I* have anything to say about it.'

Master Crispin said no more. He merely gazed at Jack with a mild expression that seemed to say much. When Melvyn came to the door, Jack was ready to leave.

He headed to Watling and came up to the eel monger's door. The smell of salt and fish was strong around it and the stone portico seemed to be perpetually wet from those sloshing barrels. He knocked smartly on the door and waited, hoping the man had not headed yet to church.

Buckton opened the door and blinked. 'Oh. Er . . . you're here.'

'As I said I would be, sir. Are you ready to oblige me with your company?'

He seemed to consider, but with a reluctant shrug, the man donned his cloak, locked his door, and followed Jack out.

Jack admitted to some distraction of his own. His mind lighted on burning timbers, on the lined face of his master, of the good fortune of a future with Isabel to whom he had not yet spoken, and to . . . so many other things. *Keep your mind on it, Jack.*

He hurried Buckton to Lombard Street and hovered in the shadows across the way from the Noreys household. He had no wish to run into Walter Noreys. His anger at the man bubbled like a pot full of stew over the fire. How dare he! How dare he destroy Jack's home? He wanted to take his blade to him but knew he mustn't. Instead, he concentrated on what Buckton would see *if* he could identify him. The eel monger was uniquely situated to observe the comings and goings of Mistress le Porter's guests and this would be the proof of it to bring to the court.

They waited. The shadows wended their way across the lane. Church bells rang, skipping from church to church, parish to parish. And still they waited.

Buckton fidgeted. 'How long must we wait?'

Jack clenched his arms over his chest and leaned back against the rough daub of the shop wall. 'I don't know,' he grumbled.

'Must we spend all of the Lord's day here?'

'You practically begged me to help. Why this sudden change of heart? And besides, what better way to spend a Sunday? We are doing God's work, helping to free my master.'

'I do wish to help you, Master Tucker. As I have said. But this waiting . . .'

'Shush!'

The Noreyses' door finally opened, and out stepped the man himself. Jack tensed. He was joined by his father William and his mother Madlyn. They stood in the street for a moment, accompanied by a maid and a male servant, before setting out.

Jack turned eagerly to Buckton. 'Well? The younger man. Have you seen him before?'

Buckton slowly nodded. 'Aye. I seen him go up to Mistress le Porter several times in the last few days. There was many a time she barred him from coming.'

'Aha! There's a devil in him to be sure. I thank you, Master Buckton. You've done well.'

'And the other, too.'

'Eh?' Jack turned to look over the Noreys party again as they moved up the lane, away from them. 'Who?'

'That older woman. She came a few times as well.'

'Are you certain?'

'Aye. I saw her. She crept in, stealthy like. Didn't want no one to notice. But I saw.'

Madlyn Noreys? Jack watched them disappear around a corner. What in heavens did she have to do with it?

SIXTEEN

Sunday, 18 October

Crispin lay back on his cot and listened as the church bells pealed from parish to parish, each tone different from the one before. Having little else to do, he tried to guess which church bell it was by the sound. He could identify St Paul's easily enough by the deep resonance of the many bells pealing, and he thought he could detect the sound of St Martin's, a tinny discordant bell, most unpleasant, unlike Christ Church Greyfriars' bells that had a roundness to their sound that was agreeable to the ear.

He gave up after a while once they all began to blend together. He cast a glance around his familiar surroundings: hearth, whose fuel was too little; wobbly table; decrepit chair. And Gyb the cat, sitting on the hearth and licking his paw after another rat supper.

'You're a dangerous creature,' he told the cat, who flicked only one ear in his direction before ignoring him. 'You're far more dangerous than I am. You've killed more than me, surely. And yet I rot in here while you are free to come and go.'

Foosteps. He knew he was the only prisoner at this end of the tower so they must be coming for him. On a Sunday? *God's blood, what now?*

Keys jangled in the lock and the door whined open. Melvyn. He held a dagger – Crispin's dagger. Crispin tensed.

'What is this?' he demanded. Was he to be dispatched and by his own blade? Was he too much trouble for this trial to continue?

Melvyn tossed the dagger to the table. It clanged on the wood. 'You're to come with me to the sheriff. And there's your property.'

Crispin squinted at him. 'What did you say?'

'You're to come with me,' grumbled the gaoler.

Crispin didn't move. 'Do you jest with me?'

'Get off your arse now, Guest, or I will lock this door on you again.'

Crispin jolted to his feet. 'You don't have to tell me twice.'

Melvyn looked as if he was gathering himself to strike when Crispin slid the dagger from the table and shuffled backward into the corridor, dragging the chains with him. They glared at one another for a moment before Melvyn pushed Crispin forward.

Crispin walked thoughtfully down the corridor to the hall where the gaolers stood over their brazier. They barely noted his passing. It occurred to him that he now had his dagger – and why had that happened? – but that he could turn it on Melvyn and make his escape. Except that he wouldn't get far. Not with these manacles on his ankles. No, his only alternative was to see what the sheriffs wanted and consider from there.

At the entry to the sheriffs' chamber, Melvyn suddenly knelt at Crispin's feet and brandished a key. He unlocked each manacle, letting them fall with a clatter to the stone floor. He scooped them up by the chain and sneered as he stood to face Crispin again. 'Good luck,' he muttered cryptically.

Feeling suddenly lighter, Crispin nevertheless stood frozen, sensing a trap at every turn. Slowly, he moved forward, his hand resting on his knife hilt. He peered around the corner, and both sheriffs were there. Straightening, he cleared his throat and sauntered in as they looked up.

He bowed. 'My lords.'

'Guest,' said Loveney. 'We want to talk to you.'

'I am your servant.'

Walcote snorted. 'Indeed. Guest, you are the bane of this office. There is not a sheriff that has sat in this chair that wasn't glad to see the back of you. And here we are in the enviable position of helping you up the steps to the gallows. I can hear the cheers from here.'

Crispin quirked a brow but said nothing.

'The fact of the matter is,' said Loveney, taking up the speech, 'that you are a great deal of trouble.'

Walcote nearly charged over his desk. 'You make us look like fools!'

'I bring in the guilty. Is that not what the office of the Lord Sheriff should be doing? Should I be vilified for doing the job you set out to do?'

'For your fee,' he snarled.

'Yes, for a fee! Why not? I work for it. What else am I to do to earn my keep?'

Both sheriffs fell silent and merely stared. Crispin ran his palm over the worn leather covering the hilt of his dagger. 'Why have you . . . why have I been given my dagger?'

'All in good time, Guest,' said Walcote. 'I want to know what you know about these women who were strangled.'

He spread out his hands. 'Only what you have heard in court from my apprentice. As you well know, *I* have been in one of your cells.'

'But surely you know!'

'My lords, I would tell you if I knew anything. For I've no doubt it would free me.'

Walcote exchanged glances with Loveney. He walked to a sideboard, and for a moment, Crispin thought they might be bringing him wine. But no. Walcote took a key from his belt and unlocked the cupboard. Carefully he removed an object. Crispin saw only the glimpse of gold before Walcote hid it in his cradled hands. He walked to the center of the room in front of Crispin and held it up. 'Have you seen this before?'

It was the monstrance that held the Tears of the Virgin. 'How did you get that?'

'Have you seen this before?' Walcote asked again impatiently.

'Yes. It is the relic owned by the Widow Peverel, the Tears of the Virgin Mary. Why do you have it?'

'Because Madam Peverel feared for its safekeeping. Just this morning someone tried to steal it. And, coincidentally, we need it for evidence. It appears your trial may hinge on this matter.'

'May I see it?'

Walcote gave a glance toward Loveney and, not seeing the man say otherwise, took the two steps toward Crispin and gently handed it over.

Crispin held it in his hands, studying the liquid inside the crystal. The phial felt loose in its monstrance and he was careful not to dislodge it. Letting it crash to the floor now in *his* hands would certainly not endear him to the sheriffs.

'Such a small thing,' he said, 'to cause so much pain. Have you arrested Walter Noreys?'

'No,' said Loveney. 'What for?'

'For burning down my lodgings.'

'Oh yes. We heard about that.' There was the tiniest twinkle in Loveney's eye.

'And for trying to steal this.'

'We have no proof.'

'You'll get it.'

Walcote reached over and snatched the monstrance from Crispin's hand, shoving it quickly back into the cupboard, and locking it smartly.

'That's partly what we wish to talk to you about,' said Loveney. 'If you were temporarily freed, what would you do?'

'Temporarily freed? What do you mean?'

'What he means is,' said Walcote, 'if we were to release you, what would you do? Would you run?'

They both stared at him. He narrowed his eyes. Would he? He'd have to leave England. There would be no going back. He could sail to France, he supposed. Better than being an outlaw in England. But France! England's enemy? How could he? What would Jack say? Oh, he'd tell Crispin to run for it and what had England ever done for him? But still. He expected to lay his bones in English soil. His family was buried here. His soul sprouted from English roots, and he could not leave it. But worse. He could not leave the task undone. If he left, with the shade of dishonor over his head . . . *Not again.* Once in a lifetime was enough. He could not dishonor himself a second time. Even if it did not go his way.

'No, Lord Sheriff. I would not run. I have a trial from which to be exonerated, for one. And for another, it is a matter of honor to find the true culprit and bring him to justice.'

Walcote shook his head. 'That's what I thought you'd say. Then you are free to go.'

'What?'

Loveney gestured vaguely. 'As he said, Guest. You are free to go. But remember, you must return Monday to continue the trial. Bring all the evidence you find to us first.'

Crispin blinked. This was unheard of. Unprecedented. 'You're . . . releasing me?'

'Temporarily,' snarled Loveney. 'You must return Monday. Do you understand, Guest? If we get wind of the slightest stepping out of line, of trying to flee the city, we will be upon you like a boar on a hunter.'

'Don't you mean a hunter on a boar?'

'Guest!'

'Of course, Lord Sheriff. But . . . I thought, according to the Statute of Westminster, that a felon accused of murder could not be bailed.'

Walcote slammed his hand on the table. 'Are you now a lawyer, Guest? What do *you* care? You are being so bailed.'

'By whom?'

'By God, Guest! Just get out and thank the Almighty for this unexpected boon!'

Crispin studied them both, but they would not look at him. 'I . . . I might have to go to Westminster. But I shall be back forthwith.'

Loveney shrugged. 'Very well. I don't care to know the details of your travels. Just be sure to be back to the Guildhall on Monday.'

Crispin checked them both carefully once more for any sign of deceit. He didn't fancy stepping out of Newgate only to be brought down by an arrow or a pike for escaping. 'I must take you at your word, then.'

They said nothing more, so he decided to make a hasty exit. He bowed curtly, pivoted, and marched out the door.

Down the wooden steps he went, and down into the stone archway. Wendell Smythe and the other serjeant, Tom Merton, merely looked his way but made no other move toward him. They must have been told. He hoped so. Crispin bore no writ, no letter of safe passage. He had only the sheriffs' word, and he still wasn't certain he could trust it.

Hurrying down the street, Crispin looked back only once before he threw his hood up over his head, secured his scrip, and pulled his dark cloak around him.

He needed to get to Westminster, but first, as much as he hated to see it, he had to go to his lodgings and take a look around. He hurried down Newgate Market, keeping his cloak tight about his body and his hood low until Newgate gave way to the Shambles.

Good Christ! There it was. A burned shell, like a beached

whale, ribs heaving skyward. Except they weren't ribs but the charred remains of the beams and uprights that had made up the tinker's shop. There was nothing left of Crispin's lodgings. How the hell had Jack gotten their goods out of that inferno? The boy was blessed, to be sure.

He stood before it, surveying the carnage. Yes, it was very much like after a battle, especially a besieged town, ravaged by troops ready to pillage all they could and destroy whatever was left. He had been part of many a rout. But he never expected to be the recipient of such damage. He had lived there nine years. He winced, feeling the sting of loss, of violation and destruction so complete that he suddenly felt set adrift. And he hadn't experienced that feeling since he had been exiled from court.

He stepped over what had been the lintel and was startled by the wiry tinker Martin Kemp when he suddenly sprang upward from a pile of rubble.

'Who is it?' cried the man, brandishing a burnt meat hook. 'Crispin! Bless my soul. What are you doing here? I thought . . . I thought . . .'

'Hush, Martin. I have been given a reprieve of sorts. Freed to do my own investigating. But, er . . . I would like to keep that information quiet for now.'

'I understand.' Martin glanced about the street and pulled Crispin in. 'I've been looking to see if I can salvage anything.'

'Have you . . . talked to my apprentice of late?'

'No. But that boy. He ran right up those stairs to save what he could. Stairs that no longer exist. When he didn't come out I feared the worst.'

'Jack is a resourceful lad.'

'That he is.'

'But I dread that I must share an unpleasant truth with you.'

'Oh? More unpleasant than . . .' He gestured to the blackened room. 'This?'

'I'm afraid so.'

Martin lifted a cooking pot, crusted with soot and dented from heat. 'Well then?'

'Jack seemed to think – and I am inclined to trust his judgment – that this fire was deliberately set.'

Martin's brows juggled over his puzzled eyes. 'I don't understand.'

Crispin sighed. 'Martin, you know I have garnered my own legion of enemies over the years. I fear it has culminated in this disaster.'

Understanding blossomed in his eyes and fear, too. He crossed himself. 'Bless me, all the saints. Someone tried to . . . kill you?'

'Or Jack.'

'But . . . my family, Crispin. You put my family in harm's way.'

'I never meant to do so, Martin. I am heartily sorry for all this and I thank God that no one was injured.'

'Injured? Aye, that is a mercy. But . . . my business. My livelihood. Crispin . . .'

'I know, Martin. I . . . I would make good for you . . . if only I could.'

He patted Crispin's arm absently. 'Yes. Yes, I know. What's to be done?'

'I don't know. I am currently . . . without shelter. But I shall find something.'

'Ah me. What a world, eh? What is this city coming to when people start fires and women are strangled?'

'I know, Martin. But it is the world we are born into. It is my task to find those responsible and make them pay.'

'Well . . . you are good at that, at least. Look at these, Crispin. Just look.' Another pot, burned down to a dented brittle thing. It flaked off in Martin's blackened hands. 'And this. And this . . . What's here?' He bent to retrieve a knife, blade and tang only. It was long and curved. 'This isn't mine.'

'A repair, perhaps?'

Martin shook his head. 'No. I never treated a knife like this. Do you suppose the fire changed it? So slender and curved a blade.'

'Let me see that.' Crispin took it and turned it over in his hands. Despite its treatment in the fire, it did not appear nicked or old or in need of repair. 'Are you certain this is not yours? Either your wife's cooking knife or one a customer brought in?'

'Aye, I'm certain of that. I know my inventory.'

Crispin narrowed his eyes at it. What sort of knife was this? But more importantly, to whom did it belong, for surely it might have been dropped by the arsonist?

'May I keep this?' he asked the tinker.

Martin shrugged. 'If you find it useful.'

'Thank you, Martin. God's blessing on you and yours.'

'And to you, too, Crispin. Give my prayers to your Young Jack. God grant that he stay out of trouble.'

'Amen to that.' Crispin gave the shelter one last look before he turned up the Shambles. He stuffed the knife blade into his scrip as far as it would go, leaving the blackened end sticking out. His first thought was to go to the Boar's Tusk, but just because the sheriffs might have made an error by letting him free didn't mean he had to advertise where he was. No. He stopped and looked up St Martin's Lane. Gray's Inn was a better choice. Best to entreat his lawyer for lodgings. They could surely plot their next move at any rate. And Crispin needed the legal help to prove he intended to return to his trial. For he did. At least . . . for now.

But first, he had to get to Westminster. To the abbey and to the abbot, William de Colchester.

SEVENTEEN

Sunday, 18 October

A quarter hour later Crispin found himself outside the grand church. People poured from its western door after Mass. Crispin felt only a short pang of regret that he hadn't made use of his time in church, but he had so little time to spare, he was certain the Almighty might be in a vein to forgive him.

He went around to the abbey side and rang the bell at the gate. He was glad to see Brother Eric open for him. 'Master Crispin! How . . . unexpected.'

He offered a lopsided grin. 'An understatement, I'm sure.'

'You wish to see the abbot? He is breaking his fast in his chamber.'

'Should I wait?'

'No. I think he will be pleased to see you.'

Crispin followed Brother Eric, though he well knew the way. He had been longtime friends with the late abbot, Nicholas de Litlyngton, but his no-nonsense replacement had been less than approachable. It was only last year, when Crispin had solved the crime of the Coronation Chair, that William de Colchester had finally warmed to him. Crispin found him to be a quiet and studious man of intellect. More often than not, they had discovered many mutual interests and though he did not keep his company as he had with Abbot Nicholas, he did make use of their burgeoning relationship by the occasional sociable visit. Though today was far from sociable.

When they arrived at the abbot's lodgings, they met Brother John just bringing in a tray. 'Oh! Master Crispin. What . . . what are you doing here?'

'It's good to see you, too, Brother John. I've come to see the abbot.'

'W-well . . .'

'I assure you, I am not a fugitive.'

'No, of course not . . .' he said doubtfully. 'Please. Follow me.'

Brother Eric left them to it and receded into the corridor's shadows, while Crispin followed on the heels of Brother John.

The monk opened the door to the abbot's lodgings and peered around the door. 'Father Abbot, you have a visitor.'

The abbot sat facing the fire. His tonsured head laid back against the chair and, as far as Crispin could see, his eyes were closed, his wrists loose and hanging over the chair arms. In the anteroom, the abbot's desk was messy with parchment rolls and open accounting books.

'A visitor? Really, Brother John.' His voice was muffled from the crackling fire. Brother John set the tray down on the small table near the abbot. 'I am exhausted from singing the Mass,' Colchester went on, 'and need my sustenance. I don't have time or vigor for a visitor.'

John poured his ale and offered the full cup to his abbot. 'Even for . . . Crispin Guest?'

Abbot Colchester sat up. 'Crispin Guest? Here?'

'In the flesh,' said Crispin, unable to resist.

The abbot twisted round to look. 'By Saint Peter. It is you.' He stood. The abbot was a man who didn't seem to want to appear flustered, and he stood by his chair, ruffled but smoothing out his expression and cassock. He had what Crispin always described as a workman's face, solid and square. Those blue, dusky eyes were always sharp, always tracking, and his features, though firm, were usually set in a stoic posture. Except now there was a brightness to his eyes and the wisp of a smile on his lips.

'Are you seeking sanctuary?'

Crispin coughed a laugh. 'No, Lord Abbot. I was lawfully released by the sheriffs. To what purpose . . .' He crossed to the fire and stood before it, warming his hands and face. 'Who can say?'

The abbot seemed relieved at those tidings and sat again. 'Brother John, bring Master Crispin a cup. He can share my tray if he hungers.'

'I am well, Lord Abbot. But I thank you.'

'Then to what do I owe the pleasure?'

'I come to you as I used to come to our dear late Abbot Nicholas, to ask about the nature of relics.'

'Ah.' Colchester cut a slice of cheese and placed it on a torn piece bread. He ate them together and chewed thoughtfully. 'Might you be speaking of the Tears of the Virgin?'

'Yes. It does seem to be at the heart of these matters . . . as you obviously already know.'

'News travels fast. Especially news of this kind. The famed Tracker of London on trial for murder? How could it not have reached Westminster with lightning speed?' He tore a piece of meat from the bone and nibbled delicately on it. 'Well, what can one say? There are many such relics sprinkled about, all over the continent.'

'Are they truly the tears of the Holy Mother?'

'Impossible to know. When a church or monastery acquires a relic, there is provenance. When a private party has such in their possession it is difficult to know exactly where it came from.'

Brother John handed Crispin a full cup of ale. He sipped. Small beer, then. He took a heartier sample and then set the cup aside. 'It is said to heal . . .'

'As most relics do.'

'Indeed, but also to confer on those around it a sort of empathy for others. One feels the pain of one's fellow man.'

'Curious. I have never heard of this aspect of a relic.'

'Nor have I.'

'And you have a great deal of experience with them.'

'Too much,' Crispin said into his shoulder.

'*Gratia Lachrymarum*, the Gift of Tears,' said the abbot thoughtfully. 'It might be so, this empathy. A saint weeps for mankind, and our Holy Mother, the mother of us all, surely weeps the most. Her tears might easily grant others this "gift" of love for one's fellow man. A most interesting prospect. I must study it further.'

They sat in collegial silence, sipping their beer, until the abbot spoke again.

'Since you are free . . .'

'Temporarily.'

'Temporarily, what do you intend to do?'

'Find the true murderer, of course. I must be fully exonerated. It won't do to have the scent of such about me.'

'I'm certain treason holds its own strong scent.'

Crispin forgot how blunt the man could be, and so he only grimaced as he put the cup to his lips. 'Yes. My treason is a stain on my character that no amount of hot water will clean away. That is enough for any lifetime.'

'I imagine so. If you've come to me for advice, I will gladly give it. You are innocent, yes?'

Crispin tamped down his affront. 'Yes. Very.'

'In that case, my advice to you . . .' He set down his cup and shifted to the edge of his seat. 'My advice, Master Crispin, is to run.'

'What? My Lord Abbot!'

'We have not known each other long, it is true. My predecessor knew you for a much longer time. And though I at first dismissed his glowing accounts of your character as the ramblings of an old man . . .'

Much thanks for that, Crispin mused.

'. . . I have gotten to know well your character for myself. The evidence would seem to be against you. Ordinarily I would never flout the law, for I do serve the king, but I serve God first. "Render unto Caesar what is Caesar's and render unto God what is God's." But it is not fitting to martyr yourself when the great good you do can go on. Run, Crispin. It is the only sensible thing to do.'

When he finally closed his jaw at the surprise the abbot's words engendered, Crispin sat back. 'I . . . I do not intend to martyr myself. I intend to clear myself. And I shall not run. That is not the honorable course.'

'I see.' The abbot, too, sat back and took up his cup. He turned the silver goblet and stared at the intricate designs etched on its shiny surface before he drank. He firmed his lips and set the goblet's base on his thigh. 'You think you have a chance?'

'I sincerely hope I do. If I can get enough time. There are new witnesses, new testimony to be gained. And I intend to find even more. If the proceedings had not been so rushed . . .'

'Yes, we all wondered at that. No doubt the sheriffs . . . or even at the king's urging . . . Well, it is best not to speculate too deeply. But I'm certain those sheriffs are betting good coin you will not return. Perhaps hoping for it. To hang you now, after you've proved your worth to the people of the city. Well, there might be an uprising. I'm almost certain that they released you so that you would flee and prevent that which they hope to avoid.'

Crispin cradled the goblet against his chest and chuckled. 'They'll lose that bet.'

'But will you?'

He raised his brows. 'Pray God I do not. But look here. There is something else I would discuss with you.'

After Crispin talked at length to the abbot, he was satisfied, and finally with a bow, withdrew from the abbot's chamber, saying his farewells.

He needed no escort out of the cloister, but there was a porter waiting for him at the locked gate, and he used his key to release Crispin – twice in one day, he mused. Once outside the confines of Westminster, he turned on the lane, and headed back toward the outskirts of London to Gray's Inn.

He reached the courtyard to the inn, scanned the surroundings, and spotted a portico that seemed to be the entrance. He headed there and was greeted by the porter, an old man with wispy white hair and a stooped shoulder. 'Good day, good master,' said Crispin, sweeping down to a graceful bow. The porter seemed amused by this. 'I am looking for a lawyer—'

'And you've come to the right place.'

Crispin smiled. 'Well, yes. One lawyer in particular. Nigellus Cobmartin.'

'Oh indeed. A most accomplished and affable fellow. Though . . . he lost his first case. God have mercy.' He crossed himself and shook his head. 'I fear for the fellow who struggles for his life in his current trial. What was the name of the prisoner . . .?'

'Crispin Guest . . .'

'Oh yes! That's it. Being tried for murder. Cobmartin's second murder trial. Dear me. Hope it doesn't end as the first did. Not always the lawyer's fault, you know. Sometimes . . . well, sometimes the prisoner *is* guilty. I'll take you to his lodgings. What did you say your name was?'

'Crispin Guest.'

The man looked back sharply, mouth open. 'God's teeth! I . . . I . . .'

Sighing, Crispin reassured with a congenial expression. 'And sometimes the prisoner may not be guilty but is under onerous circumstances.'

'Forgive me, Master Guest. I have been at this too long and my tongue flies away from me at times. But here. What are you doing free if your trial continues?'

'That is a very good question. One I should like to put to my lawyer.'

'Oh! Indeed. Let us go then.'

'Let's.'

The old man led Crispin through a passage and into a great hall. Men milled. Each seemed to be discussing great matters with deep frowns, wild gesticulations, and loud voices. Some looked to be no older than Jack, while others were Crispin's age and some far older. A mix, then, of apprentice, student, and tutor.

Out of the great hall they went, leaving behind the subtle fragrance of meals cleared away. The scent reminded Crispin that he had eaten little today and food would be in order soon, especially after his walk to and from Westminster. If he hadn't been in such haste he might have partaken when the abbot offered.

Up a staircase and then the old man stopped. He pointed even farther up the stairwell. 'Master Cobmartin resides up in the attic room. He may be there now. And . . . do forgive me again for my wayward tongue, Master Guest. I do hope for the full acquittal of your trial.'

'As do I, sir.'

The man scurried away while Crispin climbed. He got to a door and knocked, little expecting it to be answered. But when it was yanked open and Cobmartin stood in the entry, staring at Crispin in incredulity, Crispin felt a measure of relief. 'May I come in?'

'Master Crispin! What are you doing here?'

'Can we not discuss it inside rather than out?'

'Of course, of course. Come in.' He stepped aside and allowed Crispin passage.

Crispin ducked inside and looked around the cluttered space, with its cramped and slanted ceiling, full shelves, and table covered in parchments.

'May I offer you refreshment?'

'I am hungry, Master Nigellus. If it isn't too much trouble . . .'

'Not at all.' The lawyer grabbed a wide wooden bowl that had the leavings of his meal in it – a haunch of coney, a quarter of a meat pie, some roasted vegetables – and shoved it into Crispin's hand. He scooped up the parchment rolls from a chair and deposited it on his bed, already cluttered with rolls, and bid him sit. He cleared a space at the table and cleared another chair and sat, pondering his client as he ate.

A jug on the table held ale, and he poured a cup and slid it forward.

'Much thanks,' Crispin said between mouthfuls.

Nigellus watched him eat for as long as he could, wriggling and resettling himself in his chair. Crispin took pity. He swallowed a dose of ale and wiped his fingers on the tablecloth. 'It seems the sheriffs released me.'

'From the trial?'

'They said nothing of that. They said only that I was to be released but I was to return Monday for the trial.'

'Well, I must say, it is more than a surprise to see you here, Master Crispin.'

'Not as surprised as I am to be here. What might be the reason I was freed prior to the completion of my trial?'

'I know of no reason, sir. No point of law that would see you freed before trial's end. It is most unusual.'

'Hmm. And I have another difficulty. I don't appear to have lodgings any longer.'

'I had heard there was a fire on the Shambles. It was your residence?'

'Yes. And not only that. It was deliberately set by a person having to do with this trial.'

Nigellus gasped. 'Blessed Saint Ives! Why?'

'Because they believe I am in possession of the thing on which this trial hinges. The Tears of the Virgin.'

Nigellus shook his head. 'Dear, dear. I understand the sheriffs have confiscated it for the trial, so it is safe at Newgate.'

'Yes, I've seen it.'

Nigellus rose and paced as Crispin ate. 'I tell you, Master Crispin, I do not understand the reasons for the sheriffs letting you go. I have never seen the like.'

'I try not to question good fortune when it comes my way.

But I had wondered if there wasn't some sinister intent behind it.' He continued eating, but when he felt the man's eyes upon him he looked up. 'What?'

'Master Crispin . . . why didn't you make your escape?' He moved toward him and slowly sat opposite. 'Any other man would have left the city, never to return. The shadow of the gallows still falls upon you. The jury could still easily convict. Why did you not go?'

And so he asks it, too. He sopped up the last of the scraps and sauce with a torn piece of bread. 'I am not like other men,' he said softly. 'At least . . . well. It . . . would have been dishonorable to simply run. How could I live with myself if this conviction were hanging over my head?'

'Forgive me, Master Crispin, but how could you live? You still might die if you stay.'

Crispin pushed the empty plate away and wiped his lips. 'I have given you my answer.'

Nigellus looked as if he might reply but changed his mind. Instead, he stared at the table, at the empty plate, and finally at his ink-stained fingers. 'I will do my best for you, Crispin. But you must know, that my last trial . . .'

'So I've been told. That was your last trial. This is your current and best. Your advice has been sound. It will be through no fault of yours if the jury convicts me. But I am free and I will fight the Devil himself to make certain I grab all the facts so that they will have no alternative but to declare me free of guilt. But, er . . .' He cast a glance toward the window, whose shutter lay open. 'I have no shelter for the night. Might I . . . might I impose upon you . . .?'

'Oh of course! You must be my guest, Crispin. I can . . .' He whipped around, looking for a suitable place amongst the detritus of his law books and scrolls.

'Never fear, Nigellus. I have slept on the floor before. If I can find the floor.'

'Forgive me. My accommodations here are small, and I am not the tidiest of persons. Do make yourself at home as much as you can.'

'I suppose I should send word to my apprentice. But I have much to do before that.'

'I will see to it that he knows your whereabouts. But why keep it a secret?'

'A man burned down my lodgings. I shouldn't like it to happen again. I think it likely that Jack is staying at the Boar's Tusk. I will return later this evening, Master Nigellus, with your indulgence.'

'Investigate away, Master Crispin. Would you like me to accompany you?'

'No, Nigellus. I work best alone. I thank you.'

'Don't thank me yet. But by the Mass, this is all most interesting. I might someday write a poem!'

Crispin said nothing, only smiled as he made his way from the lawyer's humble lodgings.

EIGHTEEN

Sunday, 18 October

Jack was making his way back to the Boar's Tusk when a hulking shadow crossed his path. 'Noreys!' He yanked his dagger from its sheath to face him . . . and faltered when he saw the bewildered countenance of Hugh Buckton instead.

'Master Buckton!' He breathed with relief and sheathed his blade. 'I didn't know it was you, sir.'

'I come to see if I could help you any further. Maybe there's another man you would have me identify. For there are all sorts of scoundrels on the streets. I see them all.'

'I'll wager you do. But I have naught at the moment.'

'Oh. Then maybe we should look around Mistress le Porter's lodgings. Just to see.'

'See what?'

'What might have been left behind.'

'The sheriffs went through it, Master Buckton. If it's your money you're looking for, well, they would have been sure to snatch it up already.'

'Oh, I see.'

They stood in thoughtful silence for a time. Until Buckton heaved a sigh. 'Well, then. If there's nothing else I'll be off.'

'God keep you, master.'

The man said nothing as he reluctantly trudged away. He stole glances over his shoulder at Jack, but Jack urged him on with a nod of his head. He watched a long time until the eel monger finally disappeared. Shaking his head at man's folly, Jack turned away toward Gutter Lane and reached the Boar's Tusk at last. He kept to the rear of the tavern, hoping to remain inconspicuous. He needed time to think.

He tried to keep all the facts fresh in his mind, but as he saw it, he had two main concerns: He had to identify the possible murdering client or clients of the strangled women, and he had to find that third witness. Why was the man in hiding? Why keep his identity a secret? It was a fine puzzle, but also a frustrating one.

It was also frustrating that Isabel was so busy that she couldn't spare him a moment. He wanted desperately to talk to her. But she was either consumed with the heavy work of the tavern or that slattern Ned was trying to worm his way into her good graces. She gave Ned her smiles, too. Had Jack misread them? Had she simply given every man she met her charming smile and attention? It was driving him mad.

As he considered Isabel and his vexing problems, he also kept half an eye on the door. He didn't necessarily want it known that he was there at the Boar's Tusk, just in case the sheriffs got it into their heads to nab him.

And then the door opened and he nearly slipped off his seat from shock.

'I beg your mercy,' said the woman to someone at a table near the door. 'Do you know where I can speak with Crispin Guest? I was told . . . his lodgings . . . I was told he often came here.'

He did not hear the reply but he did see the man rise and point directly at Jack. So much for his own stealth. He stood as Helewise Peverel made her way improbably toward him through the Boar's Tusk.

He wiped his face and straightened his shoulders.

'Master Tucker,' she said. She appeared nervous, twisting her fingers. 'I must speak to Crispin Guest. Can you get a message to him?'

'I am afraid, madam, that currently he is beyond my reaching him. But if *I* can help you . . .'

She searched around the tavern, no doubt taking in the rough faces and accents of those surrounding them. The low laughter, the dangerous arguments. But Jack had nowhere else to go. 'Won't you . . . sit down, Madam Peverel? May I get you ale . . . or wine?'

'No, thank you.' Gingerly she sat on a bench, drawing her cloak in around her so that she would not touch anyone or anything unseemly.

Jack sat opposite and leaned in, folding his hands together on the table before him, as if he did business with rich and important clients all the time in the Boar's Tusk. 'Now. Won't you tell me why you've come?'

'Oh, Master Tucker. I fear . . . I fear . . . that much must be explained.'

She looked far different from the proud and wealthy patron she had appeared to be in her own residence with her pet squirrel and her retainers. And Jack could see no retainers nearby at all. That was always troubling.

'Tell me,' he said.

'All is not as it appears to be, Master Tucker. Far from it. I weary of it all. The lies, the deceptions. Times have been rough for the last few years. Investments have dried up. Crops have been bad. Livestock, sick. My finances . . . We all thought my dear husband had left me in good stead, and in many ways it was the truth. But in many other ways . . .' She sighed. Jack poured ale from a jug into his cup and slid it toward her. She took it and downed it, setting it aside with a grimace.

'My family relic.'

Jack breathed. He knew he was about to hear something vital and it was about time, too.

'Jack!' Ned suddenly slid in beside him on the bench.

'Ned! What are you doing here?'

Ned scratched his ruffled hair. 'I work here.'

'I know that but I'm—'

'Look here, Jack. I think you've got your notions about Isabel and I got mine . . .'

'Ned!' he said between clenched teeth. 'Not now.' He gestured across the table toward a weeping Madam Peverel.

'Oh! I . . . sorry.' Ned rose from the bench, but before he left he leaned in to Jack's ear. 'No doubt she's rich, but she's a bit old, isn't she?' he hissed.

Jack gave him a sour look as Ned wended his way back through the tables, looking worriedly over his shoulder at Jack.

Jack settled himself on the bench again, face blazing with heat. He folded his hands before him and tried again to look like a professional. 'I apologize for that interruption, madam.'

She rose. 'If you are too busy, perhaps I should leave . . .'

'Oh no, madam.' Jack stood and with calming gestures, urged

her back down. 'You were saying—?' He dropped his voice to a quieter level. 'About your family relic . . .'

She nodded and smoothed out her gown. 'The Tears of the Virgin. How proud we were to have it.' But her words had an ironic lilt to it as she frowned and stared at the table. 'Recently, as recently as a fortnight ago, I was preparing to approach our rivals, the Noreyses.'

'Oh?' He tried to keep his tone neutral and official, much as the sheriffs did.

'Yes. I was preparing to . . . make them an offer.'

'You were going to sell it to them?'

'Yes. They've wanted it for years. They certainly made no secret of it.'

'They said it belonged to them.'

She crushed her hands into fists but just as quickly relaxed them. 'Yes. I know. Which was why I was preparing to sell it to them. But then those bedeviling Noreys boys tried to break into my home – my *home*, mind you – to *steal* it! I did not know what to do. Approach Master William or not? Sell it to him or lock it away? But . . . times are hard. It was time to sell it for a goodly sum. And even as I fended off his unruly sons, even as I tried to negotiate . . . I still couldn't do it.'

'The relic . . . it is a precious thing.'

'Not for that.' Tears filled her eyes and one small bead spilled over and ran down her cheek. Jack unfolded his hands and reached across the table to touch her hand . . . but stopped when he looked again at her face. Someone little better than a servant offering her comfort, *touching* her? He withdrew his hand, knowing it wasn't fitting.

'Our family possessed that relic for years. Years! But . . . my husband did not bring it from the holy land or acquire it by reverent means. My husband . . . won it in an unfair wager . . . from William Noreys, more than ten years ago.' She put her trembling hand to her mouth at the horror of it.

Jack realized that she had probably never uttered those words aloud to another living soul. His hands dropped to his lap and he blinked at her. Finally he recovered from his amazement and licked his lips. 'And so . . . the Noreyses' contention that it belonged to them all along is true.'

'Yes, yes! How many times must I say it? It is the humiliation of my family. To hold such a holy thing in so dubious a circumstance. But it is all moot now. I need the money to maintain my household. Although, that is not the worst of it, Master Tucker.'

'I'm listening.'

She leaned farther in and spoke in low tones to the table. 'A few years ago a dreadful accident happened. I was holding the Tears, as I was sometimes wont to do, praying, seeking guidance as to what to do with it. You see, I did not feel that we should keep it. It was acquired under such a dirty state of affairs – when I . . . dropped the phial. Oh holy saints! It shattered into a thousand pieces. The Tears. I did not know what to do. I cut myself trying to soak it up in my gown. But I finally surrendered to the disgraceful moment. After all, my prayers had been answered. The Holy Mother decided that no one should possess the Tears, for surely it was her hand that made my fingers slip.'

Jack listened rapt, mouth open, eyes huge. The rest of the noisy tavern fell away, and there was only the voice and snuffling of the woman before him.

'I gathered what pieces of the phial I could. I locked the chapel and allowed no one to enter. And then I secretly sought out a craftsman to make me a new phial to resemble the old. And when that was done . . . Oh God forgive me . . . I filled it with false tears. With oil. And I placed it back in its monstrance and behaved as if nothing had changed. It's monstrous! Monstrous what I did! And more! Oh my sins were not enough. No. For it was this phial, this false relic that I was attempting to sell to William Noreys. His own relic. And yet *not* his relic, but a fakery, a devil's own snare. How will I ever be forgiven?'

Jack wiped his hand down his face. 'So . . . what you are telling me is, the relic I saw and that my master saw in your chapel . . . was a fake?'

'Yes. All of it. Deception. Lies. And you knew it, didn't you, Master Tucker? That's why you asked me if the relic had been replaced. My sin was obvious even to you.'

Jack considered but then another thought occurred to him. 'Then . . . wait. If that were so, then the reason Elizabeth le Porter left was also false, for she could not have been overcome by the relic's power for it was not a true relic.'

She nodded. 'Yes. You see how far my sin treads. That, too, was a lie.'

'Then why did she leave?'

'I don't know. One day she came to me and told me she had to leave. I argued with her, I pleaded. For she was a dear, dear servant to me, though she had not been with us long. I felt that she was more than a servant. Kin, you see, and I didn't want her to depart. But she insisted. Apologized to me as if . . . I don't know. As if it were for more than her leaving.'

Jack frowned. 'Well! Madam Peverel. I don't know what to make of all that. It certainly doesn't change the fact that the Noreys boys wanted to steal the relic and went to great lengths to make their attempts.' *What madness!* Here the Noreyses wanted the relic to sell because of their dire circumstances while at the same time Madam Peverel wanted to sell it to them for the same reason. What cruelty! And now neither would be redeemed.

But it got him thinking about Madlyn Noreys, for Hugh Buckton had seen *her* visit le Porter as well. What was her business there? Was she too trying to get the maid to steal it? But no. Elizabeth le Porter was already gone from the widow's employ when she got her lodgings on Watling Street. It would have been too late. So why were the Noreys boys troubling her there as well?

Jack realized that he had been silently contemplating and suddenly looked up. Madam Peverel's face was tired with worry, but her confession seemed also to have lightened her soul. Her eyes were still wet but not weeping.

'How long had Elizabeth le Porter worked for you, madam?'

'Three months. She came highly recommended.'

'By who, may I ask?'

'Well . . . I don't know. My steward was in charge of that.'

'I thank you for this most interesting information, Madam Peverel. Is the relic . . . the Tears, I mean, still in your private chapel?'

'No. The sheriffs came yesterday to confiscate it as evidence for the trial of your master. They are keeping it safe at Newgate . . . for all the good it will do now.'

'That was announced at the trial, I think. For now, madam, I would not tell this tale to anyone. Unless or until you must at the trial. It is safe at Newgate and as long as it is there, *you* are safe.'

She nodded. After a moment, she pushed herself up from the table and stood. 'I thank you, Master Tucker. You have been most discreet. I pray your master is acquitted shortly.'

Jack bowed. 'Madam.' He watched her make her way out of the Boar's Tusk. Whistling low, he fell back into his seat. 'God blind me with a poker. That's the damnedest tale I ever heard.'

'What's the damnedest tale you ever heard?' asked Ned, taking up the empty jug.

'Never you mind. And by the way.' He poked Ned in the chest. 'You stay away from Isabel.'

'Eh? What's it to you, Tucker? I saw her first.'

'Well I saw her next. And . . . and . . .' Was he to tell this knave before he ever mentioned it to Isabel? What if he bragged about courting her and she turned him down flat? He'd never hear the end of it. He shut his lips and adjusted his belt and cloak. 'Just never you mind. I've got important business to attend to.'

Ned crossed his arms over his chest with a sneer. 'All right.'

'All right!' Jack yanked his hood up and swept away. And it would have been a proud exit, too, if he hadn't tripped over the bench and nearly spilled himself onto the floor. He righted and left hurriedly, red-faced, ears ringing with Ned's laughter.

He shucked his embarrassment to concentrate on what needed doing. Monday would be upon them sooner than he desired. But where to first? Mercery Lane or Watling?

Jack decided that the strangled women took precedence, so Watling it was. But as he traveled through the streets, edging past oxen hauling their carts, boys running without looking where they were going, a man with a prize porker tapping a stick on its back to urge it forward – and Jack got a pungent whiff of the creature as it passed him – he felt that strange tingle at the back of his neck, and he well knew what that meant.

Slyly, he maneuvered to the edge of the road where the ruts were fewer and slipped into a doorway so that he could look back.

He scanned the lane but no one looked out of the ordinary until . . . Yes, there was a man with his hood over his face, and he lingered by a shop selling pelts. *Who the sarding hell is that?*

Too big and husky to be a Noreys. Could be the sheriff's man but, if so, there was no reason for his stealth.

He got it in his head that it was the third witness. But why would he be following Jack? Did he think Jack would lead him to Master Crispin? And yet the question was still why?

Nothing for it but to keep going. He'd have to keep an eye on his shadow and make certain he didn't interfere with his investigations.

He cut up to the lane just off Watling Street to the neighbor woman who had known Joan Keighley. He knocked, hoping she had returned from church and would talk with him. Surreptitiously, Jack glanced behind him and found his 'shadow' still in place.

The door opened, and Jack bowed to the woman standing in the entry.

'Yes?'

'I beg your mercy on this Lord's Day, demoiselle, but perchance your neighbors alerted you that I would return to ask my questions. I am Jack Tucker, humble apprentice to the Tracker of London.'

'Oh! Yes, they told me you'd come back.' She eyed Jack a little too lingeringly. 'Tracker's apprentice, is it?'

Jack smiled uncomfortably. 'Er, aye. I was told you knew some of Mistress Keighley's . . . clients.'

Her flirting demeanor changed. Her downcast eyes wore nothing but sadness. 'Yes. And further. I think I know who killed her.'

'You do?' Jack took a hasty glance about them. No one on the busy street could hear, even the shadow man. 'Who then?'

She drew near and kept her voice low. 'She talked of him sometime. He had an odd . . . custom. She told me he liked to strangle the women he lay with. Not to death, mind. Just as . . . something he liked. He'd pay extra for it. But after a few times when she nearly blacked out she wouldn't do it no more. He'd come back occasionally to her, but he took other girls instead. But I think it was him. I think she let him come back and he killed her!' Great rolling tears streaked down her face. She wiped it away with the backs of her hands.

'Demoiselle, this is very important. Do you know the name of this man?'

'Richard . . . something.'

'Richard?' He scrambled for his scrip and pulled out the parchment with his notes from the stew on Catte. He scoured the list of names. 'Richard . . . Richard . . . Ah! Was it Richard Gernon?'

'Yes! Yes, that's the name!'

'Now we're getting somewhere. You don't happen to know the whereabouts of Richard Gernon? On what street he lives?'

She shook her head. 'No. I never knew that.'

'You've been of great help, demoiselle. More than you know.'

'I'm glad for that. I've heard of other girls he's nearly killed. Maybe he had in the past. I hope your master can do something right quick.'

'I'll see that he does, demoiselle. Much thanks.' Jack bowed and pivoted but then turned back. 'Oh demoiselle, can you give me description of the knave?'

'He has brown hair and a brown beard.'

'Bless me, that's nearly everyone in London.'

'True. But he also had a long nose. Like a beak.'

'Well, that helps. I thank you again, demoiselle. God's blessings on you.'

'And to you, Master Tucker.'

Jack hurried away, thinking, but keeping the edge of his eye on his foe. He'd lead him as Master Crispin often did, down alley after alley until he could corner the knave.

He listened to the steps behind him. 'Keep following, me lad. Keep following.'

Finally he turned down a narrow alley that had a slim outlet, barely a handspan between the houses that his husky shadow could not traverse but that Jack, in his slender frame, could. At least he hoped so.

He slipped none too easily through and used the tightness to climb, his back on one wall and his feet shuffling him higher on the other. Finally he reached the roof and pulled himself up, relieved he was free of the narrow passage. He crouched on the slant of the roof, waiting. Presently, the man appeared, stopped, and looked about perplexed.

Jack leapt.

The man fell and Jack was thrown clear. But the man quickly enough scrambled to his feet, hood still low and shading. When he pulled a knife, Jack froze.

He'd seen that long slender knife before, or at least one like it. Its twin had been burned black and had lain in the bottom of the remains of his lodgings.

'You! It was you what burned down my home!' Jack pulled his own knife, but the man saw this as his cue to flee.

He took off back down the alley and Jack gave chase. But as soon as Jack had gained the main road, he encountered a holy procession of monks carrying aloft the statue of the Virgin blocking the road. He made only a weak attempt to skirt past them, but he knew it was useless. He slumped, watching them pass, knowing his shadow man had made his escape. Who was that whoreson?

With a sigh, he spun and ran right into Isabel.

He pushed her back at arm's length. His emotions ran the gambit: Gladness at seeing her, anger at seeing her here, worry that she could have gotten hurt getting in the way. 'What are you doing here?' He dragged her to the edge of the road and shoved her against the wall.

She cried out, but silenced herself when those who had come to watch the procession shushed her.

She rubbed at her shoulder and raised her chin defiantly. 'I saw you leave the Boar's Tusk and I wanted to follow you, see what you were doing.'

Exasperated, Jack threw up his hands. 'Lass, you can't do that! I do dangerous things. Like what happened back there. You could have been hurt.'

'Who was that man? Why did he pull a knife on you?'

'Isabel! You've no business following me. And not only will you get yourself in trouble with your uncle but me as well. He'll think I put you up to it.'

'I'll tell him you didn't, for it is the truth.'

'That won't matter. All he will see is his ward in danger and that it was my fault.'

She bit her lip. He couldn't help but snatch a glance at the gesture. It threatened to undermine his scolding her. He girded himself and grabbed her arm, yanking her with him. 'We're going back.'

'Jack, I'm sorry.'

'Not as sorry as you're going to be.'

'But you lead such an exciting life. I liked helping you last time.'

'I told you that was a one-time situation.' He shook his head. 'I knew I shouldn't have done it. It's put bad ideas into your head.'

'I'm sorry.'

'And here I was, wanting to talk to you.'

'You did? I'm here now.'

She stumbled as he dragged her over the rutted road of Friday Street, fingers wrapped tight around her slender arm. 'I'm afraid it's all moot now. Gilbert will never let me . . . he'll never . . . And it's *your* fault! Bah! It's shown me what a fool idea it was anyway. You belong with someone who will live a nice quiet, peaceful life. Not someone who has to scrape to get by, who runs into trouble with a knife blade at his throat at every turn. Someone . . . with a past.'

'What are you talking about?'

'Never you mind,' he grumbled, seeing all his plans slip away. What right did he have to woo someone like her anyway? She was genteel. Raised by a merchant. True, she was in a tavern now, but it was a fairly clean one, and an honest one to be sure, and with enough customers to keep the place busy and in coins. There was always a warm fire and food, and wasn't that all anyone really needed? And here he was, the son of a scullion, a cutpurse by age eight . . . and worse.

He kept his lips tightly closed, angry that his chance had slipped away. Maybe she was too willful to woo. Who wanted a wife who took off at a moment's notice? How would such a creature ever care for children? They'd be wild, dirty, and unkempt. And isn't that what he deserved for leading the kind of life where danger lurked in every shadow?

They turned the corner at Gutter Lane but well before he could even see the ale stake of the Boar's Tusk, Jack whirled and slammed her against a wall again.

'You don't understand.' His voice shook, cracked. Her eyes were wide, lashes dark against her fair skin. 'I was going to ask you . . . ask you . . .'

'Ask me what?' Her demeanor softened. Her gaze darted from the scrappy beard on his chin to his amber eyes.

'I was going to ask you if you . . . if you would accept me. As a suitor. I already asked Gilbert and he told me aye. Now he'll take that back.'

'You were going to ask to woo me? You were going to ask . . . if I wanted you to?'

He stepped back, feeling like a spring fool. He flapped his arms in surrender and stared miserably at his muddy boots. 'Of course I was. Maybe you don't even like me.'

'I do,' she said hurriedly. She smiled to hide her own embarrassment. 'I do like you.'

Yet the sudden spike of warmth could not ignite the flame that had been doused within his chest. 'But I wager you like Ned, too.'

'Ned? From the Tusk? *No*.'

That small spark was back. 'You don't like Ned?'

'No. Oh, he's a fine lad and all. But he's coarse. He's not . . . like you. Handsome and all.' She dropped her gaze.

The ember in his breast burst into flame. 'You think I'm handsome?'

She rocked herself against the wall but didn't look up. 'Maybe.'

'And you like me? Then . . . shall I be your suitor? Shall I . . . Isabel?'

She said nothing for a long time. She merely rocked, her shoulders rolling along the wall. When she finally raised her head, she wore a tender expression. 'If you want. If you want a willful, disobedient girl as a wife.' A splinter of worry pulled her delicate brows downward. Jack drew closer.

'A willful disobedient wife. That's not much to recommend to a lad.'

'I know.' She bit her lip again, twisting it in her teeth so tightly that it reddened. Jack couldn't look away from it. He stood directly above her now. She came up to his shoulder and he had to crouch slightly to keep that rosy lip in his sight. He drew closer, for those lips called to him, made him brazen with longing. He wanted a taste of those lips. Just a taste. For he knew now they were his. He leaned in to take them.

'Are you Jack Tucker?'

Jack leapt back. 'God's blood, man! Can't you see I'm . . . I'm . . . occupied!'

The young page could see that very well, and he grinned. 'Sorry to interrupt.' He bowed to Isabel. 'Demoiselle.'

Jack stepped in front of her. 'What do you want?'

'I have a message for you.'

Jack snatched it out of the boy's hand. He wore livery, but Jack could not tell whose arms they were. 'A message from who?' He broke the wax seal and tore open the folded parchment.

> *Jack, much to my great surprise, the sheriffs saw fit to release me from gaol . . .*

'Master Crispin!' He read on.

> *. . . though I am not discharged from the trial. It seems I must return tomorrow and I shall. Make no mistake. I would not further the taint of my honor by becoming an outlaw. And so . . . I had to find a place to light just in case . . . well, in case I do not return to the trial quite as scheduled. Nigellus Cobmartin has shown extraordinary hospitality by offering me a place on his floor. I'm certain it will be attached to the bill. Continue whatever pursuits you were about . . .*

Jack glanced back at Isabel. Guilt at having forgotten the dire circumstances of his master served to cool that ardent fire that threatened to set him aflame. He read on.

> *. . . and I shall continue mine. By the way, the sheriffs are keeping the Tears so that Walter Noreys cannot get to them. Come tonight and we will exchange notes. Keep your mind to it, Jack. There is much I need to tell you.*

He did not sign it, but Jack well knew his master's hand. 'God blind me,' he muttered. The youth was still there, rocking on his heels. 'Well?' said Jack, stuffing the missive in his scrip. 'What are you waiting for?'

'A farthing maybe.'

'How about the sole of my boot.' Jack swung his leg back and the page stumbled backward.

'No need to be rude, my lad. Fare you well. With . . . your doings.' He offered Jack a salacious grin and a wink before he trotted away up the lane.

'Was that from Master Guest?' asked Isabel.

He'd almost forgotten her. 'Aye. I have to go. But please, Isabel. For my sake. If you care . . . and I think you do . . . don't follow me again. I can't be worrying about you while I pursue the knavery of London.'

She nodded soberly. 'Very well, Jack. I promise.'

He moved closer again and took her hand. 'Do you? Do you promise?'

'I do. And don't worry. Uncle Gilbert won't even know I was gone.' She smiled and tore away from the wall, skipping back to the Boar's Tusk, but instead of taking the front door, she went around the corner. Jack suspected she would either hop over the wall or gain entrance in some other stealthy way. A resourceful wench, he'd give her that.

So now. Pursue this Richard Gernon or the third witness? Though he had a feeling that somehow, he had met the latter already in that alley.

He was about to decide when he heard the thunder of hooves down Newgate Market. He was as surprised as anyone on Gutter Lane when the horses – the sheriffs, he suddenly saw – came hard around the corner and headed straight for him.

He backed himself against the wall and the horses roared forward, stopping just shy of trampling him. The stallions' hot breath snorted into his face. He could almost see his reflection in their polished bridles.

'Tucker!' snarled Sheriff Loveney. 'Where is it?'

Flattened against the wall with nowhere to go, Jack stared up at him. 'Where is what, my lord?'

'The damned Tears of the Virgin. And don't lie to me.'

For a moment, Jack was seized with a blankness of mind. He blinked. 'Begging your mercy, sir, but . . . don't *you* have it?'

'Of course I don't have it. That's why I'm asking you!'

'But I thought it was in safekeeping at Newgate.'

Walcote shuffled forward on his saddle. 'This is getting us nowhere. Get one of the serjeants to beat it out of him.'

'Here now!' cried Jack. 'I haven't got it. I swear by the Virgin herself. Why would I take it?'

'To delay the trial of your master, perhaps?'

Jack bit down on what he wanted to say. Wasn't that rather on the sheriffs now for releasing Master Crispin in the first place? What guarantee did they have but his master's word? And though Jack knew that word was law, there was always a twist that could angle the meaning just enough to suit Master Crispin.

'And just where is your master, Tucker?'

'I don't know, my lords. I thought he, too, was safe at Newgate.'

'He's not at the Boar's Tusk?'

'On me mother's grave, my lord, he is not.'

Walcote glared for a long uncomfortable moment until he glanced at his companion. 'What do you think?' he asked.

Loveney shrugged and glared heavenward. 'I think I want to go back to bed and forget this case ever crossed our paths.'

'Amen to that.' But Walcote wasn't done with Jack. 'What have you discovered, Tucker? Or have you been idle?'

Jack popped away from the wall, getting right up to the horses' muzzles. They shied, stamping and backing up. 'I have *not* been idle! I'd never shame my master so. But . . .' – he shook his head in frustration – 'when the Tracker investigates, only pieces of the puzzle come our way. And in the muddle, we don't always know what's important and what isn't. It'd be foolhardy to tell you all. Although . . . have you come across any other records of women having been strangled in Bread Street Ward?'

The sheriffs exchanged surreptitious glances.

'Have you, my lords?'

Walcote fiddled with his reins. 'Well . . . it seems . . . there were a few. But none like this, one atop the other. They were . . . spread out over a number of years.'

'And was anyone ever apprehended for the crime?'

'No. We looked into that,' said Loveney.

Jack considered, but in the end, three heads were better than one. 'Have you ever heard of the name Richard Gernon?'

'Richard Gernon?' said Loveney with a deeply suspicious tone to his voice. 'Why do you ask?'

'Well . . . because his name came up twice . . . on both client lists of the women who were murdered.'

Walcote was silent, simply eyeing Jack. Loveney found his saddle pommel unusually fascinating.

'What?' asked Jack eagerly. 'Do you know him?'

Quietly, Loveney said, 'Yes. We know that name well. It is the name of a man of our acquaintance, one of the most respected aldermen of the city of London.'

NINETEEN

Sunday, 18 October

Jack swallowed. *Well, that's done it*. 'I . . . I mean no disrespect to your compeer, my lords. But that is the name given to me.'

Walcote adjusted his gloves. 'There must be some mistake. You've obviously made an error, Tucker.'

'No, my lords. I didn't.'

Loveney leaned down over the withers of his mount. 'I don't think you heard him, Tucker. He said you made an error.'

'Oh.' Jack kept his own council. He knew how it was and there was no use fighting it. 'Yes, my lord. No doubt. I make . . . many such errors.'

'That's right.' Loveney sat back. 'Keep your nose clean, Tucker. And remember this, if your master does not return tomorrow for his trial, he'll be an outlaw. That means he's a dead man, trial or no trial.'

'Aye, my lord.'

They turned their mounts swiftly and rode up the lane, making the turn at West Cheap.

Jack breathed hard. Privilege of the rich. Of course. They would not condemn their own kind. Especially when the next year, the same man might be sheriff himself. And so it went. With his master at the bottom.

Jack's mind churned on the problem, stirring up notes and memories and words from one source and another and another until they came at him so fast like a hail of arrows that he had to slap his forehead. 'Jack Tucker, you are an idiot! You were told this. You asked the question, you heard them talk, but you did . . . not . . .' – and he punctuated his anger at himself with additional slaps to his head – 'listen to the reply!' What had Hamo Eckingtion told him about the third witness, the illusive Thomas Tateham? Middling height, a brown beard close-cropped to his face. With brown eyes, brown hair and his nose was hawk-like. And then what did the neighbor woman to Joan Keighley say? She described a man with brown hair and a brown beard, with a long nose like a beak.

'They're the same sarding man! Thomas Tateham indeed! A liar and a murderer! Well, I don't care if you are an alderman.'

He cast around. Anyone might know where this man lived. He'd find someone who knew and he'd follow him till he caught him in the act.

Mercery Lane. Nigellus had been right, that the man had had the presence of mind to come up with a false name but not a false street, too. Richard Gernon was a needle maker, encountering women with frequency. 'Diabolical is what it is,' Jack grumbled. Why did he strangle them? Why would he need to? The neighbor woman seemed to say that this was part of his, well, ritual for lack of a better word. He'd lay with them, but part of it was to strangle but not to kill. Then what had gone wrong? Had he gone too far? Unable to stop himself? 'Such a creature,' Jack hissed in disgust. And he had seen some things in London. Oh how he had seen! From the stews of his boyhood, to the depths of a damned soul. He well remembered the monster who had stalked the streets of London several years ago, killing young boys, when Jack himself had been caught in that horrific web. If it hadn't been for Master Crispin . . .

He owed that man his life seventy times seven and twice over that.

If Jack could do this for Master Crispin, it would do Jack's soul a good turn.

West Cheap became Mercery with a distinct change in the kind of shops. Mercers, traders in cloth, sprung up all along the lane. Wool merchants, thread makers . . . and needle makers. And there it was. He was told it was the two-story house with the stone archway. Ah yes. A fine place. But would the man venture out on a Sunday? Would he take the Lord's Day and use it for his foul purposes? Jack could not bring himself to hope it, but he now felt he was the hammer of the Lord, waiting to smite the evil-doer.

Though, thinking on it, he realized the man had already been out and about. He had been stalking Jack. Burning down his house. Threatening him with a knife. *Well, two can play at that game!* He would be the stalker now. All he needed was patience. He found himself a doorway to linger in, one nice and shaded, and he pulled his hood down low, wrapped his cloak about him, and commenced waiting.

He snorted awake. 'What . . .?' Jack cursed himself. How could he have fallen asleep? What a pitiful servant he was! He looked around, getting his bearings again. Across the way, the Gernon house. People on the street, but fewer of them, being a Sunday. The shops were closed, after all. But it was getting late. He had slept standing up, leaning against the alcove as he had done many a time as a lad on the street. Had Gernon returned and he had missed him?

'Think, Jack.' What would Master Crispin do? He'd survey. He'd take in details. And so Jack did. There were glass panes in the windows and so he could see inside, though the rooms were dark. Except for a higher floor. There were candles lit in those rooms. And smoke coming from the chimneys. And then the candles suddenly extinguished.

Jack fell back, trying to be as obscure as he could in the darkening shadows of the portico.

The door opened and a man emerged. His brown beard was clipped close along his jaw and his hair was cut to just under his ear. And his nose . . . Yes, he could see how it had been called hawk-like, or a beak. It was a honker, yet it was still elegant. He stepped off his threshold and into the street with the confidence of a man who knew where he was going. But as Jack watched him, he knew that this man was not the one who had earlier stalked him, for his frame was too slender. The man who had followed him and threatened him with a knife was a broader man. Damn! So it was someone else after Jack. Perhaps it had nothing to do with the doings of the trial, but it was too much of a coincidence if it wasn't. Who was that man, then?

He gave the man a lead of several paces before he, too, stepped into the street. Even if he hadn't met Gernon before, he had to follow him. The fact that this man had given evidence of having seen his master go into le Porter's lodgings meant that he had only done so to divert attention from himself. *It took ballocks, that.*

It was Sunday. Would the man actually go to a stew on a Sunday? But if he didn't mind killing, what would a Sunday matter to the likes of him?

Look at him. Everything in the world at his fingertips. Wealth, status, and he isn't happy with it. He can't live a decent life with a wife and leave off this whoring. It's a disgrace is what it is.

If a man had a good wife, there was no reason to stray. And those thoughts naturally led to Isabel. He couldn't help but smile. She *did* like him. She had given Jack permission to court her. He shook his head at it. Who would ever have thought that he, Jack Tucker, would have such good luck? He never imagined it. That someone as prosperous as Isabel would look his way! That he would have such a respected profession. God was smiling down upon him and he would not do anything that wouldn't make the Almighty proud. But whenever he thought of the face of God, more often than not, he wore the face of his master.

He followed Gernon all the way to Gracechurch Street as he headed toward the bridge. Was he heading toward Southwark? Of course he was. That's where most of the brothels were. But Jack didn't have a farthing for the toll, and he began to worry that he would have to sneak across the bridge by illegal means . . . and he sent a prayer heavenward in apology.

But the man slowed and instead turned toward East Cheap. He passed an ale stake and kept on going until he got to Love Lane and turned. There was a stew here that Jack knew about. It troubled him that some of the brothels were creeping over the Thames to situate themselves on this side of the river, but it was up to the Bishop of London to eradicate them and send them packing to Southwark. The law could do nothing.

Yes, the man was heading to a brothel. He looked both ways down the narrow lane little better than an alley, before he rapped on the door.

It opened, releasing music and light. The man at the door didn't seem to want to let him in, but Jack saw a coin being exchanged, and then all was well, and Gernon entered. The door shut. How was Jack to follow him now?

He stood outside and craned his neck, looking up the outside of the leaning building. It looked like it was being held up by the shops beside it, and it very well could have been. The frame had twisted, and the face of it seemed to swivel away toward the north while the level below faced west. They wouldn't likely let Jack in and anyway, he'd never been a customer of such a place and didn't quite know what to ask for.

Feeling helpless, he opted for merely sitting and surveying nearby. A brazier down the street glowed from its coals, and he trotted toward it. It had a view of the house and so he stood over the red embers, warming his hands.

Just as he settled in, a man suddenly blocked his view. Jack startled back, hand on dagger . . . and then expelled an exasperated breath. 'Master Buckton! What is it now?'

'I saw you on the street. Are you investigating?'

'Of course I am! So if you don't mind . . .'

'Oh. You don't want my help, then?'

Cursing to himself, Jack gave him a neutral demeanor. 'I know you are anxious to put away this killer. So am I. I'm watching him now.'

'Oh?' He seemed to brighten.

'Aye. So if you don't mind I'm supposed to be in hiding.'

'You want me out of the way?'

'If you wouldn't mind, good master.'

'I see.' The eel monger searched around, no doubt trying to discern who Jack was watching before he slowly backed away. He kept looking back over his shoulder at Jack, and Jack urged him on with an urgent gesture.

Blind me. As smart as his eels, that one. He hoped Buckton hadn't revealed his hiding place.

He hunkered down again and soon saw someone open the shutters from a window above. It was his man! Gernon left the window open as he returned to the softly glowing room.

Jack folded his arms, tucking his cold hands into his armpits. He tried not to think about what the man was doing because it made him think of Isabel and what he'd like to be doing with her, and *that* wasn't a very Christian thought, especially about a woman he was hoping to marry. Or was it? His master talked with him once a few years ago when Jack had had his first blush of the heart. It had been an inappropriate longing and it had ended badly but back then, Jack – as young as he had been – was only chastely devoted. Now that he was a man or nearly so, his thoughts naturally turned toward, well, manly pursuits.

He pulled his suddenly tight collar away from his throat and adjusted his braies. He shouldn't be thinking about it, but didn't all young men think about such things? They all talked about it in the taverns. Young men, old men in white whiskers, and every age of man in between. And here he was, as chaste as a spring lamb. But it didn't mean he didn't like to hear about it.

A scream. Jack tore away from the brazier. There was a commotion in the open window of the whore's room. She screamed again, the man shouted, and then a door slammed. Jack threw himself to the wall and climbed, gripping the half-timbers and scaling the structure till he reached the window and grabbed onto the sill. He pulled himself up and peered inside. The woman lay on the small bed, facedown. Fearing the worst, Jack swung himself up and landed hard in the room. Gernon was gone. He approached the bed and found the woman wearing just her thin shift, rucked up over her backside. Holding his breath, he reached out, hoping he'd find a pulse.

He barely touched her shoulder when she shot up, screaming again. Jack yelled and fell back on his bum on the floor.

'Who the hell are you?' she croaked.

'Are you all right, demoiselle?'

Her eyes looked around wildly and she reached for her throat. Dark bruising covered her neck. 'Where is he? Where is that knave? If I ever get my hands on him . . .'

Someone pounded on the door. 'Kate! Kate, what's the matter?' a woman called through the door.

Jack lunged for the window. A man beat a hasty retreat away from the brothel. Jack turned once to the woman, 'As long as you are well . . .'

She waved at him and staggered up, going to the door.

Jack hung out the window, bounced once against the wall, and then pushed away, landing on the street. He took off after the running man.

I've got you now, you whoreson! beat in his head as he pumped his legs hard. The man knew these streets as well as Jack, but with so few on the road on this day and at so late an hour, it was easy to hear the solid thuds of his footfalls. But as Jack turned each corner, he seemed to miss the man just as he turned the corner ahead of him. Jack was beginning to think he'd never catch up when he found himself making a wrong turn down a blind alley. It dead ended and he swore. When he turned, the silhouette of a figure stood at the entrance, limned in the dying twilight, blocking his escape.

Jack pulled his dagger and gathered himself.

Then the figure spoke. 'Put down your weapon, boy.'

TWENTY

Sunday, 18 October

'Master Crispin!'

Crispin chuckled. The lad was dangerous, no doubt about it. 'Glad you recognized me before attacking.' He moved to the center of the alley as Jack approached him.

'Master, what are you doing here? I thought I was to meet you later.'

'I had to do a bit of investigating on my own. It just so happened that I saw you earlier and decided to bide my time, see what transpired. That was quite a leap from that second story window. You should be more careful.'

'I didn't catch him anyway.'

'That little matters if we know who it is.'

'And that's even worse.' He related to Crispin all he had learned, and Crispin scowled.

'The sheriffs will surely never arrest their own.'

'That's what they told me,' said Jack wearily. 'And if they don't arrest him, that puts you on very unsure footing.'

'It puts me squarely on the gibbet.' Crispin stuffed his arms under his cloak. The alley stank like piss and he motioned Jack to follow. They walked together down East Cheap toward Candlewick.

'Are you truly going to appear at the trial tomorrow, master? I will sail with you anywhere you wish to go.'

'You don't have confidence in my lawyer's skills? He has yet to examine witnesses.'

'Why take the chance, master? Let's go!'

'And what of you and the young lady? Love blooms, does it not, Tucker?'

He watched Jack squirm, but he was still touched by the boy's offer.

'Women come and go,' he said sagely. 'But . . . you taught me everything. I will not abandon you.'

'Even if I commanded you to?'

Jack raised his chin. 'Even then.'

He smiled and slapped the lad's back. 'Ah, Jack. It does my heart good to hear you. But we need not abjure the realm quite yet.'

'What have you got planned, master?'

'A trap. And then my lawyer to call this witness and force him before the judge.'

'What sort of trap?'

'It's not yet formed, Jack. I'm thinking about it.'

'Well, while you're thinking we should talk to Madlyn Noreys, for she knows something's afoot as well. There's a witness what puts her to see Elizabeth le Porter at her lodgings.'

'Indeed. It might be worth talking to her. Perhaps she even knows this alderman as well.'

They talked and found themselves heading toward the Shambles when Crispin stopped. 'Good Christ. Look where I've led us.'

Jack stared at the blackened ruin of their home. 'Blind me. I forgot, too.'

They looked at one another. 'Are you safe at the Boar's Tusk, Jack?'

'Aye. As safe as anywhere, I suppose.'

'Come back with me to Gray's Inn and we'll talk about strategy.'

'Shouldn't we talk with Madlyn Noreys first?'

'I will have Cobmartin send her a missive. Perhaps she will meet us there tonight.'

'Why would she do that?'

'If I word the missive just right, I might strike the correct note. In other words, I could make it sound like . . . extortion.'

'Master Crispin!'

'I said it would *sound* that way, not that it would *be* that way.'

They hurried to Gray's Inn, outside London's walls, and together went up to the lawyer's eyrie. Nigellus was surprised to see Jack but took his hand in greeting. Crispin sat at the table – which had managed to clutter again – and made room to pen a quick note. 'There. Nigellus, if one of the inn's pages could take this note to the Noreys household on Lombard Street and offer to escort the lady here, we might get somewhere.'

'Interesting that you should mention that particular household,' said Nigellus. 'For they have sued the sheriffs to arrest *you* for the murder of their son.'

'Truly,' said Crispin wearily, 'this is getting old.'

'What do you hope to gain by talking to Madlyn Noreys?'

'She knows something. She was seen visiting Elizabeth le Porter. Either to propose she steal the relic or to beg her silence for her son's indiscretion on the matter. Either way, she will have much to say and it can only help my cause. Well, one of them, anyway.'

Nigellus said nothing more. He called for a page, and soon a boy in livery arrived and took the note with instructions to escort Madlyn Noreys back and only Madlyn Noreys.

They waited. Tucker fussed over Crispin and served him wine. He had to admit, he had missed Jack's care of him. Of any servant, for that matter. How quickly he had become accustomed to it in the last six years when the twelve years before he had been alone and too poor for such luxuries.

But Jack was more than a servant. Much more. Crispin rested his chin on his hand and watched under droopy lids as Jack moved about the room, trying to tidy.

'Jack, why don't you tell me about . . . Isabel.'

The boy stopped dead and whipped his head around. His face was pale. The freckles adorning it stood out particularly dark on the whiteness of his cheek. 'Oh. Well.' He toyed with a roll of parchment. Now the pale cheek reddened with a bloom of pink. Amused, Crispin sat back, hands folded together on his stomach. 'She's, er . . . she's willing.'

'That is good news.'

'Aye. But . . . now what, sir?' He pulled up a stool and scraped it across the floor as he slid it against the table. 'I mean . . . other men . . . they . . . they . . . and *you*! You're always bringing some lass home and then you . . . but I don't think . . . at any rate, she's young and . . .'

'Jack, is there a question somewhere in there?'

'Master, it's just that . . . I don't know what I'm to do next.'

'Why Jack Tucker. Are you by chance telling me that you are . . . inexperienced?'

'Yes, sir. I try to live by the saints and do as our Lord would wish me. Being chaste.'

Crispin felt a sudden wash of tenderness in his heart for his apprentice, as godly a thief as he had ever met. 'Oh. Then you must think me a very sinful man.'

'We-e-e-ll, sir . . . I . . .'

'Never mind. And I do atone. I shrive myself often. For all the good it will do me in the end.'

'Oh but, sir. You're different from me. I mean, you've been out in the world, haven't you? You've been to the Holy Land. You've sailed across oceans. You've been to *France*!'

Crispin dropped his chin to his chest to hide his smile. 'Men are much the same everywhere, Jack. And our needs . . . are the same. I have not lived as chaste a life as I should have, but I consider it just compensation for my . . . circumstances.'

'And I understand that, sir. That's what I meant. But as for me. Well, I can wait.'

Crispin gauged him anew. 'Then you do intend to marry this girl?'

'Aye, sir. She . . . she likes me. And I favor her very much. She's beautiful and . . . and . . . different. She likes what I do . . . what *we* do. I don't think I will get bored with her around.'

'Be careful, Jack. Neither do you want a woman who gets it in her head to stray. Too much freedom in a wife is intolerable. What will happen to your household, your children if she feels the need to roam?'

'What about that widow from Bath that you fancied in Canterbury? She seemed of much the same temperament as Isabel Langton,' he said primly.

Crispin smiled remembering her. Alyson was headstrong and independent. He had been surprised that this was appealing to him. But then again, Philippa Walcote had been cut from the same cloth . . .

'Ultimately, Jack, it is up to you. Better you than me.'

'I don't believe that, sir. Surely there might be a woman for you . . .'

He frowned. 'That time has passed.'

He was saved more platitudes from his servant by the knock on the door.

Nigellus, who had been studying his books, suddenly looked up and padded over. He opened it to a woman. Crispin and Jack stood to greet her.

She was in her middle years, with graying hair at her temples, though the rest was covered with a linen kerchief. She wore a modest cotehardie, laced in the front with an ornamented belt. Her amber eyes took in the surroundings, saw Jack and recognized him, and finally looked up at Crispin with a frown. 'You must be Crispin Guest.'

'Madam Noreys. I greatly appreciate your coming.'

'You have your nerve. After you killed my boy, to come asking me for favors . . .'

'Madam. These are grievous circumstances. And I . . . I am sorry for them.'

'Why should I help you?'

And yet he noticed she had come alone as he had requested. Why would she have done that? He gestured for her to sit but she declined. 'Let's get this over with.'

'Very well.' Crispin took a moment to collect his thoughts. 'You see, it has come to our attention that you were seen at the home of Elizabeth le Porter, the murdered woman.' He let it sit there, curious as to what, if anything, she might say.

She swayed slightly, and he feared she might faint. He stepped toward her and took her arm. 'Perhaps you should sit.'

'You are gracious . . . for a murderer.'

'I assure you, I am no such thing.'

She sank to the chair, releasing all her strength. 'So I have heard such of you. And yet, my boy . . . my John . . .'

'Tried to kill me. I'm sorry, but it's true. I merely defended myself. I did not know that he would . . . that he would be killed.'

She pulled a kerchief from her sleeve and dabbed at her eyes. 'He was always so willful. And Walter. Walter was always spurring him on. He has too much blood in him, does Walter. John always followed Walter about like a pup. He wanted so to be like him. Now he is . . . he is gone.'

'Madam, why did you visit Elizabeth le Porter?'

'It doesn't matter now.'

'It very much matters to me.'

Jack pressed his hands to the table and canted toward her. 'Have you ever heard of Richard Gernon?'

'Steady there, Master Jack,' Nigellus cautioned.

Crispin gave his apprentice a harsh look of admonishment, but Madlyn Noreys gasped. 'Richard Gernon. Richard *Gernon*? What has *he* to do with this? Oh Lord! Oh my precious Lord!' She pressed the kerchief to her face and wept into it. 'It was him, wasn't it? Oh, I should have known.'

Nigellus knelt down on one knee to her. 'My very dear Madam Noreys. If you understand well the character of Richard Gernon, would you be willing to testify to that at the trial of Crispin Guest on the morrow?'

Her face was blotchy and red and her eyes blinked rapidly from her tears. She glanced from Nigellus to Crispin. 'Should I spare you? Be the cause of your release from the gallows?'

'Madam,' said Crispin, 'if only to soothe your soul. For you know now that I did not kill that woman.'

'What about my son?'

'If another trial there must be then you will hear the truth in that one as well. If you know me, if you have heard of me, then you must have heard that Crispin Guest may be many things, but certainly no murderer.'

'I don't want to help you . . .'

'My dear lady,' said Nigellus in soothing tones. He handed her a full cup. 'The law must be fed. And its meat is truth. Justice – the justice of God on earth – cannot be served unless we feed it truth. I beg of you, madam, that you tell what you know in court. For our Lord despises a lie. And a sin of omission is still a sin.'

'I hear what you say, Master Cobmartin,' she said tearfully, 'but how will my boy obtain *his* justice?'

'Ah. Well. Some justice is reserved for God alone. For in the case of self-defense – and come now, you cannot deny that this is surely the case, for you admitted yourself how young Walter could spur on your John with little provocation – proof can sometimes be difficult, especially in such a dire situation. And in this case, it can be the word of one against the other. And if one is lying for a means to an end, then an innocent man goes to the gallows. What will you say when *you* are brought before the Almighty on that Judgment Day we must all face?'

She wept into her kerchief, finally wiped her eyes and nose, and lifted her face. 'I know in my heart that you were not at fault, Master Guest, but I suffer, and I wish for . . . someone to suffer as I have. And yet, I cannot let you die if you are innocent. I will speak at your trial. And I will ask my husband to remove the claim in the death of my son.'

Crispin breathed with relief. 'I thank you, madam.'

'And so do I,' said Cobmartin, 'in the name of the king's justice and that of the Almighty's. Now, perhaps we should hear what you have to say.'

'No.' She rose, gathering herself again. 'No. When I see you at the Guildhall tomorrow. I don't wish to talk about it now.'

Cobmartin followed her to the door. 'But, madam . . .'

She didn't look back but stopped on the threshold. 'I will be at your trial, Master Guest. And when all this is over, I hope to never see you again.'

Though she never turned around, Crispin bowed to her anyway.

On Monday morning, when the recorder and both sheriffs gathered at the guildhall with the nine jurymen, Crispin enjoyed the look of utter amazement on Loveney and Walcote's faces when he walked in. It almost looked like disappointment. Perhaps they *had* hoped he would leave England, never to return.

He strode forward and took his place before the bar, hands before him, gently crossed. Jack took his place by Nigellus and the clerk. The other witnesses were there: Hugh Buckton, Alison Keylmarsh. Even Helewise Peverel was there, biting her lip and looking worried. Jack had told him what the widow had related to him about the relic. And though unanticipated, Crispin was not particularly surprised by the turn of events.

The recorder was reading a parchment and when he noticed Crispin he lowered it to his lap. 'Very well. Guest is here. Your lawyer wishes to examine some of the witnesses and I have no objections to his doing so. I see we have a new witness . . . a Madlyn Noreys. Is she present?'

'I am here, my lord.'

Everyone in the room turned to look at the nervous woman

at the edge of the crowd. Her silken kerchief softened her lined features. She was accompanied by an older man. Crispin assumed by the sneer he directed toward Crispin that he was William Noreys, the patriarch.

'I do not see why my wife must be subjected to this,' he said.

'This is a court of the Common Pleas, Master Noreys,' said Tremayne impatiently. 'Unless you are called as a witness, kindly keep your comments to yourself. Madam, please step forward.'

Crispin moved aside so that he wouldn't crowd her.

'Master Guest, your lawyer has requested to question the witness. Are you agreed?'

'I am, my lord.'

'Well then, proceed, Master Cobmartin.'

Nigellus stood and preened like a barnyard cockerel. Crispin supposed that this is what the man lived for, this display of his lawyerly prowess.

'Now, Madam Noreys, why have you come today of your own volition to testify for Crispin Guest?'

'Because I know who the true culprit is, and my conscience and my soul will not allow me to be silent.'

The sheriffs leaned forward. Crispin watched them but also kept an eye on the rest of the crowd. He wondered why Walter Noreys wasn't present. Cobmartin had requested questioning him as well.

'Who, then, madam? The court is anxious to hear and leave Crispin Guest blameless.'

'This man is known in London for his vile treatment of women. For nearly strangling them. He *has* done it. He *has* killed. And the sheriffs turn a blind eye!'

Both sheriffs jerked to their feet. Walcote spoke first. 'This woman is a liar. She knows not whereof she speaks.'

'My Lord Recorder,' said Loveney. 'We cannot allow the perversion of justice to continue. She cannot be allowed to speak.'

The crowd burst into chatter and shouts of, 'Let her speak!'

Sheriff Walcote leapt off the dais toward her and William Noreys flung himself from the crowd to protect his wife. The serjeants didn't seem to know whom to guard. Crispin moved instinctively in front of her to protect her, but the sheriff merely shoved him aside.

'Confound it, give me order!' cried Tremayne. He gestured toward the guards, but again, they were confused as to who their commands were directed to. 'Protect that woman!' snarled the recorder. 'Sheriff Walcote, Sheriff Loveney, sit down and be still. This is the king's court and I will have order!' He waved to the crowd of men shouting. 'You there. If I have to clear this room I will begin with all of you.' The guards pushed the crowd back and threatened with their cudgels and swords. The sheriffs reluctantly returned to the dais and sat, looking at one another with grim expressions.

Crispin resisted the urge to grin.

John Tremayne resettled on his seat. 'Now then. Madam Noreys, you were about to say . . .?'

'Madlyn!' hissed her husband.

'I will not be silent, William! Too much. Too much has happened. I must speak.'

'Let her speak,' said Tremayne in a dull voice.

She pressed a hand to her mouth before raising her face again. 'It is not unknown that this man has a . . . proclivity of nearly strangling the women he . . . he comports with. All of London knows it. At least all in the Bread Street Ward do. He likes to pretend to strangle them. And he knew Elizabeth le Porter. It is Richard Gernon, alderman for the city of London.'

The crowd erupted again. Tremayne stood and turned a glare on the sheriffs, but they were busy either hiding their faces or staring heavenward.

Crispin found the antics more than amusing. *The cat is now out of the bag. You should have known it would scratch you once released.*

There was no getting order. Tremayne motioned to the guards, and they moved toward the crowd, bashing heads and shoving the men back against one another.

It took a while, but the rabble finally settled down. The recorder scanned the crowd when his gaze settled on Crispin who tried to keep his face as passive as possible. It was no use. The recorder blamed him. He stepped off the dais and approached. Once he stood right before Crispin with only the bar between them, he spoke in low tones so that his words would not be heard above the continued noise of the hall. 'Did you know?'

'I discovered it yesterday.'

'We will not bring the alderman into court,' he hissed.

'Then you would hang an innocent man.'

He paused to suck in a breath between his teeth. 'Damn you, Guest. I would be pleased to see you hang. To see you endure the punishment denied you all those years ago. I do not suffer traitors. It would only be your just deserts.'

'And then a murderer would continue his foul practices on London's citizens. How else can he be stopped?'

They were nearly nose to nose when the recorder suddenly pulled away and stomped back to his dais.

'Quiet!' he cried. 'I will have order!'

The crowd quieted again, grumbling their protests. Some nursed bloody noses and bruised heads. But they stayed, thirsty for the entertainment.

Fixing his demeanor into something as neutral as he could, the recorder leaned toward Madlyn Noreys. 'Surely this is only hearsay, madam. You must have proof. Witnesses.'

'And so I do. For Elizabeth le Porter told me herself that she had had trysts with the gentleman in question. He gave her coins and trinkets. She behaved as his mistress, and she was jealous of his other exploits. She sought to stop them and resorted to extortion.'

'Wait. Madam, you say Mistress le Porter told you this?'

Cobmartin raised his hand. 'My lord, before I proceed to that question, may I ask a question of one other witness?'

'Go on,' drawled Tremayne.

'Master Buckton!' Nigellus turned toward the eel monger.

The nervous man jerked his head. Plainly he had not expected to be called upon.

'Do you testify that you saw Madam Noreys here going into the lodgings of Elizabeth le Porter not once but several times?'

Buckton nodded his head. 'Aye, my lord.'

'Thank you, Master Buckton. So you see, my lord, she was acquainted with Elizabeth le Porter, as this witness says.'

'But how is this so?' insisted Tremayne. 'She was the maid of Helewise Peverel, was she not? How do you know her?'

'My lord,' said Cobmartin. 'I have another witness to call forth. Walter Noreys, the son of our lady witness here.'

'Good Christ, Cobmartin. Have we not made a circus of this already?'

'Justice must be served, my lord. Would you not extend every path to make certain an innocent man were not destroyed due to our negligence?'

Tremayne clasped his chin, mouth open in astonishment. He said nothing. Cobmartin must have taken that for assent, for he turned to the crowd. 'Will Walter Noreys be brought forth!'

There was a commotion at the door. Crispin craned his neck and saw Walter Noreys being dragged in with a serjeant on each arm. They pushed through the crowd and shoved him forward. He stumbled before righting himself and stood meekly next to his mother.

'Yes,' said Cobmartin. 'Master Noreys, did you know Elizabeth le Porter?'

'No!' he said sourly.

'Come, come, man. I have a witness that saw you at her lodgings many a time. Do I bring back my witness to counter your testimony?'

'All right! Yes, I knew her! This is ridiculous.'

'And how did you know her, Master Noreys?'

Walter made a scowling grimace and nearly charged the lawyer. 'That's none of your business.'

Tremayne stomped his foot. 'It is the court's business. You will answer.'

Tremayne's words seemed to frighten him at last. And though he gritted his teeth, he replied, 'Because I . . . I wanted to pay her.'

There were oohs and aahs from the crowd before the lawyer raised his hand to them. 'Pay her for what, Master Noreys?'

He kept shaking his head, looking at the floor. Madam Noreys touched his shoulder. 'Walter,' she said softly, though her face showed her anguish. 'Pay her for what?' Plainly she had not heard this before. Crispin glanced toward Noreys's father and the man covered his face with his hand.

'Master Noreys,' urged Nigellus.

'Very well,' he said tightly. 'I wanted to pay her to steal a relic . . . from that woman!' He pointed straight-armed at the Widow Peverel. The woman looked on unsurprised, chin raised proudly. 'To steal it back. It belonged to us. To my family. And now my brother is dead because of that man' – and he swiveled his arm toward Crispin – 'and you bring my mother into this sorry mess. I wish to God I had never heard of the Tears of the Virgin!'

Madam Noreys hugged her child, dropping her head to his shoulder and weeping.

Tremayne shook his head. 'What does this have to do with anything?'

Nigellus pressed his hands together and faced the recorder. 'My lord, these circumstances seem to surround this relic, the Tears of the Virgin that was in the care of Helewise Peverel, which is why I exhorted the sheriffs to take it into their possession for safekeeping.'

'And where is that damned relic?' said the exasperated recorder. 'Wasn't it supposed to be brought to court?'

The sheriffs sat uneasily. Walcote spoke. 'My lord . . . there was a problem. The, er, relic . . . was stolen.'

'What? God in Heaven! When? When had this trial gotten away from me? It's stolen. Do you know its whereabouts?'

Loveney shook his head. 'No, my lord.'

'God forgive me for what I am thinking,' Tremayne muttered.

'May I go on, my lord?' asked Nigellus.

Tremayne looked up. 'Truly? You wish to go on? You mean there is more?'

'Oh yes, my lord.' He swiveled back toward Walter. 'You tried to pay her to steal the relic. What did she do?'

Walter gently pushed his mother back and pulled his cloak taut. 'She refused.'

Madam Peverel made a loud noise, and Crispin saw her bury her face in a kerchief.

'How many times did she refuse?'

'What difference does it make, you tiresome man? She refused. But I think she was lying. I think she gave it to Guest for safekeeping.'

Crispin couldn't help himself. 'And so you burned down my house in retribution!'

'Burned down your house? I never!'

Crispin reached for his dagger but Nigellus lurched toward

him and stayed his hand. 'Pray silence, Master Crispin,' he whispered. 'Now is not the time.' Running his hand down his dark gown, Nigellus returned to the center of the floor. 'Let us put that aside for now. As you've heard, the sheriffs confiscated the relic while Master Guest was incarcerated. And in the same instance, the relic was stolen. Obviously, Master Guest has naught to do with it. Did you take it, Master Noreys?'

His eyes widened. 'I did not!'

'Are you certain? Perjury is a very serious charge.'

'I . . . did . . . *not*!'

But Crispin was studying Walter hard, seemingly for the first time. He stalked toward him, and the man took a startled step back, shielding himself behind Cobmartin.

'I have a question for the witness,' said Crispin tightly.

Cobmartin pondered him with raised brows.

'I promise to behave myself,' Crispin said softly.

Nigellus nodded and stepped aside.

Crispin faced Walter. Though he cowered at first, Walter raised himself and stared down his nose. 'Well?'

'Do you know who I am?'

He chuffed a laugh and looked around the hall as if to say, *This man is an idiot.* 'Of course I know who you are,' he said witheringly.

'*When* did you know?'

'What sort of question is that?'

'A pointed one. When had you heard of me? Last week?'

He shook his head and frowned. 'No. Earlier than that. I cannot tell when. Everyone knows who you are.'

'And so, presumably, you also knew my character, for one follows the other.'

'Yes, yes. What of it?'

'So you knew that, among other things, I find lost objects, that I am trustworthy, that I would never kill without a good reason.'

Walter rolled his shoulders uncomfortably. 'I suppose.'

'And you knew all that on Wednesday, fourteenth October.'

He wiped at his mouth. 'Yes. For God's sake.'

'Why then did you go to the Boar's Tusk with the express intention of hiring me to kill Elizabeth le Porter?'

'I . . . I . . .'

'There's no more reason to deny it. You gave me a pouch of coins with instructions to kill her. But you knew who I was all along. You knew I would not in fact kill her but warn her. You wanted only to frighten her, didn't you?'

'I . . . I did no such thing. My Lord Recorder, must I—'

'Yes,' growled Tremayne. 'You must. Now answer the question. Did you go to Master Guest with a pouch of coins and hire him to kill Elizabeth le Porter?'

'But he wasn't *going* to kill her . . .'

'By Christ's toes, man! *Did* you hire Master Guest?'

'Oh for . . . yes. It was a stupid, foolish thing to do. But I knew no harm would come to her.'

'Although,' put in Walcote, 'everyone also knows that Crispin Guest is in sore need of funds. A little murder for so many coins. And who would know?'

Crispin turned his glare on him. Damn the man and his perversity.

Cobmartin took the opening. 'But we have proved, even with this contrary witness, that he knew that Master Guest would cause no harm. Walter Noreys was in fact the catalyst for all these events to transpire.'

Tremayne leaned forward, his arm on his thigh. 'I don't understand. You accuse the alderman Richard Gernon of the murder and yet you bring in all these other facts and witnesses that have little to do with it. Madam,' – he turned to Madlyn Noreys – 'I ask again, how did you know this maid of Madam Peverel's? What had you to do with all this?'

Madlyn Noreys leaned away from the recorder so far she looked likely to fall. But instead of her son helping, Crispin moved in and took her elbow. Walter finally noticed and pushed Crispin back, taking her arm for himself.

'Madam?' asked the recorder. 'I am waiting for an answer.'

She cleared her throat. 'Because . . . because she is . . . was . . . my cousin, and *I* sent her to the Peverel household to spy upon them in order to . . . to . . . steal the relic.'

TWENTY-ONE

Monday, 19 October

Crispin watched the room dissolve into chaos. There was Nigellus, who hadn't expected to hear those tidings. Tremayne, who looked completely befuddled and frustrated. The sheriffs, with equal parts shock and indignation. And Jack, though surprised, seemed to be forming his thoughts into something orderly. *Good, Jack, good. Now we know why Mistress le Porter left Madam Peverel's employ and why she had her own temporary lodgings.*

One thing was clear. This was a distraction from the obvious. Richard Gernon was guilty, but Tremayne didn't want to bring him in. But if he didn't, Crispin couldn't depend on the confusion of the jury to acquit. The sheriffs wouldn't help in that regard – *and thank you, Sheriff Walcote, for your hearty endorsement*, he thought sourly. He needed that man. And he knew just how to trap him. He'd need a delay. Another day at least. He hoped that either he or Nigellus could accomplish that.

He was about to speak when the lawyer beat him to it.

'My lord,' he said loudly above the noise of the crowd. 'It is very clear to me that we need another day to discover this suspect, the man known as Richard Gernon. He must be found and questioned. If he is responsible for the deaths of the women in the ward then it is our Christian duty to find him and bring him forth. And if not, then it is also our duty to exonerate him and restore his good name.'

Crispin could tell that there was nothing of Christian duty on Tremayne's face. The man seemed to have something else in mind, but he held his tongue.

'By God!' grumbled the recorder. 'I see no alternative but to adjourn for the day. However, if you have gotten it into your head somehow to arrest Richard Gernon' – and Crispin noted that he was addressing Crispin rather than the sheriffs – 'excise it at once. I saw no evidence to indict any more than there will be to convict. Bring me a witness and I shall consider it.'

'Convenient, when all his witnesses are dead,' muttered Crispin under his breath, but not quietly enough that the recorder did not hear.

He frowned. 'I'm warning you, Guest. I need hard evidence. And someone find that damned relic! Get out, all of you!'

Crispin waited for the serjeants or the sheriffs to retrieve him, but when it looked as if they had no intention of doing so, he wondered again at his miraculous release.

Soon the hall was cleared, leaving only Jack, Nigellus, and the clerk who paid them no heed as he collected his parchment and rolls.

'This is certainly a disagreeable situation,' said Nigellus.

'You have a talent for understatement, Master Cobmartin,' Crispin sighed.

'Dear me, forgive me, Master Crispin. This has all been very disagreeable for you, I fear.' He looked around at their solitary condition. 'But I am still confused as to why you are free from your fetters.'

'It is a puzzle. But we must take advantage of it . . . while it lasts.'

Jack rubbed his fuzzed chin. 'I could go back to them stews. See if any of them whores will testify.'

'I have a better plan,' said Crispin. 'Shall we?' He strode forward toward the empty doorway, and it only took a moment more for the perplexed lawyer and Jack to follow.

Crispin headed toward Candlewick, and he wondered when or if his clever apprentice would catch on. He hadn't long to wait once they turned at the street.

'Oi, master! I see!'

'Do you, Jack? How quick of you.'

Cobmartin stared from one to the other. 'I don't. What mischief are we perpetrating, Master Crispin?'

Jack laughed. 'Just you wait and see, Nigellus.'

They arrived at the wick maker's shop and Crispin went first to the ladder and began to climb. Jack followed, and Cobmartin, tutting and muttering, followed in the rear.

Crispin reached the top and knocked upon the shutter. He couldn't be certain if his friend would be home, but then the shutter opened. John Rykener was dressed in men's clothes, but only barely. His chemise was loose about his neck and came down only to his thighs. His stockings were tied to his braies, but he wore no shoes.

'Crispin! Praise God! Then you are free. When did this happen?'

'Greetings, John. News of my freedom is still premature. May I . . . we . . . come in?'

John peered over the sill. 'Jack Tucker. And . . . a friend? That's quite a retinue for my humble lodgings. If you'll wait but a moment, I have a . . . guest . . . who is leaving.'

There was a rustle of the bedding, of clothing, and then a man, hastily dressing appeared at the window. 'It's a procession,' he complained. But he stepped aside so that those entering could leave the ladder first.

The man dropped a coin in Rykener's hand, kissed his cheek, and scrambled out the window and down the ladder.

'It's busy this morn,' John muttered and dropped his coin into a jar on a shelf, that clinked with many more coins. 'I think I have some wine, but not enough cups. If you don't mind sharing . . .'

'Don't bother, John. I have a proposal for you and it might be dangerous.'

'Oh?' He turned to his coffer and pulled out a cotehardie and laid it on the bed. 'Sounds interesting.'

'Pray, Master Crispin,' said Cobmartin, 'but who is this gentleman?'

'Aren't you kind,' said John with a grin. 'I'm hardly a gentleman.' He reached forward with his hand. 'John Rykener. Erm . . . embroider-er.'

'I am Nigellus Cobmartin. Lawyer.'

John let his hand go. 'I'm not being sued, am I?'

'Not at all.'

'Well then, you won't mind if I dress?'

'Hold, John,' said Crispin. 'We might need you to dress in your . . . other clothes.'

With his hand on his hip and his eyes narrowed, he gazed

at Crispin sidelong. 'And just what does *that* mean, Master Guest?'

'Well, there is a man who is murdering women. Whores, for the most part. He, er, he strangles them. As I understand it, he does not mean to kill, but enjoys sometimes going too far when he is engaged in his . . . doings.'

'Oh,' said John quietly. 'I've heard of him. I know those women. Some who will never allow his patronage again. They were frightened out of their wits. But I've also heard of . . . the others. They were not so fortunate.'

'Yes. And it is this man who murdered the woman I am accused of killing. But he is an alderman, and the sheriffs are reluctant to arrest him without ironclad evidence.'

'I see. And?'

'Well. John, with your unique talents and your unique attire, we were hoping you might be persuaded to . . . entice him into a trap.'

'Risk my neck for yours?' His tapered fingers covered his neck, and it was a long moment until his face broke into a smile. 'But of course I'll do it. You need only ask, Crispin. You've always done me a good turn.'

The lawyer still seemed perplexed. 'I don't understand, Master Crispin. How can this gentleman help?'

'Master Rykener is more than an embroiderer. Actually, he's an embroider*ess*. I have seldom seen him attired as a man, for he much prefers his "Eleanor" persona.'

Cobmartin blinked. Jack leaned toward him and whispered rather loudly in his ear, 'He dresses as a woman and plays the whore.'

'Thank you for that clarification, Jack,' said Rykener with a smirk. He knelt by his coffer and sorted through it, finally dragging out a gown. 'Crispin, if you will help me.'

Crispin scowled. Wasn't that just like Rykener to make a contest of it? His constant flirting wore on him, but Crispin supposed the man was doing him a great favor and putting himself in danger.

'Very well,' he grumbled. 'But this is the *only* time.'

John chuckled. 'I'll wager you've never helped a woman *on* with her gown.'

'John,' he warned.

Rykener was silent as he donned his clothing, allowing Crispin to lace him up the back. 'There!' Crispin stood back while Rykener handily arranged his hair into a coif.

'Such a transformation!' Cobmartin seemed impressed.

John turned toward him and curtseyed. 'Do you think it good enough to trap an alderman?'

Crispin helped him on with his cloak. 'John, I sincerely hope so.'

But now was the problem of finding the man and luring him to their web. They traveled to the stews they knew he patronized, but there was no word of him there. Yet word had traveled about what had been revealed at Crispin's trial. Not that it wasn't already well known on London's streets. But it might have made Gernon less likely to venture forth. And just as Crispin suspected, the women refused to testify, for there were many alderman as their patrons, and their silence was bought just as their time was.

Crispin made a sound low in his throat.

Rykener glanced at him. 'Did you just growl? I must say, it was very appealing.'

'Stop it, John. We need to find this man.'

'Has anyone tried his house?'

They all looked at him. It was growing later and later, and they had gone everywhere but the needle maker's shop.

'What do you plan on doing?' said Jack with a skeptical tone. 'Knock on his door and ask for a tumble?' Crispin well knew Jack had a difficult time accepting John as a friend though John had been one of Crispin's first true friends on the Shambles.

John glanced at him sidelong. 'No, Young Jack. I intend a far more subtle approach. After all, he does sell needles. I am an embroideress.'

'Oh.' Jack deflated and knitted his brows.

They found the shop, and Crispin and company held back across the lane in the shadows of an alley. Before John left them he said, 'If I am successful, I will signal you by opening a window. Since I am unsure which window that will be, I suggest you surround the house as best you can. Young Jack, perhaps you will scale the wall since your master is getting on in years.'

'I beg your pardon!'

John smiled, but the smile soon faded. 'Forgive me, Crispin. It is only my nervousness that makes me jest so.'

'Don't worry, John. I won't let anything happen to you. You are brave to do this for me. I shall not forget it.'

'Please,' he said touching his throat again. 'That sounds too much like an epitaph.' He took a deep breath. 'Well, into the snake pit I go!'

Rykener crossed the lane, skirting carts and people with their animals and packages. If Crispin did not know who it was, he would imagine the person in the gown to be a woman.

'Jack,' said Crispin, 'make your way round the house to the other side.'

'Aye, master. Will you be here?'

'Close by.'

'This will never work,' said Nigellus as Jack trotted away. 'Surely Gernon will know he is a man.'

Crispin sighed and leaned back against the alley wall. The daub smelled of mildew and was rough, pulling at the weave of his woolen cloak. 'There are men, my dear Nigellus, who care not whether they lay with a woman or a man as long as they get their satisfaction.'

'Dear me. And this man is a friend of yours?'

'Though I little understand this aspect of his character, there is no more loyal man or caring friend than John Rykener . . . unless he be named Jack Tucker.'

Nigellus studied him with a thoughtful expression. 'You do surround yourself with . . . interesting people, Master Crispin.'

'I have to say,' he said, measuring the street and the best place to watch the house, 'that my associates are far more interesting now than they ever were in my former life. Whether that is a compliment or not is left to the observer. Look.' He pointed. John entered the shop and appeared to be greeted by Gernon himself. Crispin's hand went to his dagger instinctively. And then John disappeared within. 'Now we wait. I suggest you stay here, Nigellus. I shall explore the area.'

Crispin trotted across the lane and examined the two-story structure. A simple shop below, household above. Servants. Exterior kitchens. Extensive back garden. Several chimneys. A merchant's home of some wealth. It still struck him as strange – even after all these years – that he should now be envious of a merchant!

He waited, wondering if perchance he should find a way inside. Or at least into the shop . . . when he heard, 'Psst!' from around the corner. He saw just the tips of Jack's red hair and made his way over. Jack pointed to a second story window. 'I saw Master Rykener open yon shutters.'

'I'll be damned. He did it.'

Jack shook his head. 'I been on the streets a long time, master; seen a lot. But I'm still surprised every day.'

'I know you don't particularly like him, but he has served me well over the years. He was charitable to me when others were not.'

Sheepishly, Jack lowered his face. 'I know it, sir. He and I have come to an . . . er . . . understanding. He did right by both of us just last year. And I even borrowed writing things from him only a few days ago that I have yet to return. I . . . I admire him greatly, sir.'

Taken aback, Crispin warmed. It appeared much had transpired in his absence. 'I am heartened to hear that, Jack.'

The boy said nothing more. He tilted his face upward toward the window, and Crispin watched it too for an agonizingly long while.

'Jack,' said Crispin, breaking the stillness that had fallen between them. 'Why don't you climb up there to see what's going on?'

That tore the boy from his musings. 'Me?' He grimaced. 'Master, what if . . . what if . . .'

'What if Master Rykener is already strangled to death and we did nothing?'

'Aye. You have the right of it.' He turned and immediately leapt up to the stone foundation and grabbed on. Then, like a rat, he scaled the wall, holding onto god-knew-what till he reached the stone sill. He grasped the edge of it and slowly pulled himself up enough so that only his eyes could peer over. He seemed to hang by one hand as he wildly gestured for Crispin.

Crispin trotted over and didn't wait. He climbed, and when he gained the sill he got the same eyeful as Jack. There was white naked buttocks and rutting, but more importantly, the man had his hands around John's throat and seemed to be squeezing so tightly that John could make no sound. John began thrashing about, and that was enough for Crispin.

He swung up over the window and landed squarely into the room. 'Let that man go!' he cried, brandishing his knife.

Gernon startled back, his braies hanging around his knees. He fumbled, trying to draw them up. 'What the devil . . . oh. It's you, Guest.'

Crispin saw Jack minister to a choking John, but was glad to see his friend was all right. Jack even helped to right his skirts.

'Caught at last, Gernon. How many women have you similarly caused harm? How many have you killed? It stops now.'

'You're making a huge mistake, Guest. The sheriffs will never arrest me.'

'Oh but they will. And it will be you on the gibbet, not me.'

'They'll never arrest me. What do I care for your little murder? Come now, Guest. You can surely admit to me that you did it. I above all men can understand the inclination.' He stepped closer and smiled an oily grin. 'Your hands around those white throats. The bruises, the marks left behind. Like rose petals on a white sheet.'

Crispin sneered. 'Shut it . . . or I'll make you.'

'You want to fit me into your little murder plot. I must say, it was amusing accusing you to the sheriffs, for I did see you as I was passing through, quite innocently, I assure you. But I tell you I never killed the bitch. Oh, I am glad she is dead, for her extortion plots are now dead, too. But I didn't kill her. After that last night with her, she wouldn't let me near her. And her neighbors seemed to guard her well.'

'Why lie about it now? As my lawyer would say, you have been caught in *flagrante delicto*. With more dead women to condemn you in your wake.'

'I tell you they will not arrest me. There is nothing you can do.'

John stood unsteadily with Jack offering him a hand. 'Give me a moment, Jack.' He stepped away from Jack and walked on wobbly legs toward Gernon. When he stood before him Gernon sneered.

'What do you want, wench? Your silver? Here.' He reached

into his scrip, took out a coin and flung it to the floor. It clinked and rolled away under an ambry.

Rykener merely flicked a glance at it before turning his attention back to the man.

Gernon huffed a breath. 'Very well. I suppose I owe you more for your trouble.' He took out two more coins and dropped them at John's feet. John looked down.

'You don't think the sheriff will arrest you?' John rasped hoarsely, neck red, voice as loud as he could get it. Crispin cringed at what had been inflicted upon his friend.

'No. So you'd all best be out of my sight before I call in the law to arrest *you* for trespassing.'

John nodded. 'That's what I was afraid of.' He took a moment longer to stare at the unrepentant man before he cocked back his arm and punched Gernon square in the face. Blood gushed from his nose, and the man went down like a sack of turnips.

TWENTY-TWO

Monday, 19 October

Bound and gagged, an enraged Richard Gernon was shoved down the lane by Crispin, John Rykener, Jack Tucker, and Nigellus Cobmartin. His bloody nose soaked the rag covering his mouth, and though it was an unusual sight, by virtue of Crispin's presence no one seemed inclined to stop them. Crispin was surprised, in fact, by the show of support when the townspeople even waved at him.

He had no time to consider it. They were in a hurry to secret Gernon at Grays Inn, but Crispin was wondering at the wisdom of it when the inn was yet so far away.

He pressed them to cut down a narrow lane to an inn on Old Fish. He reckoned no one would bother them, especially at the disreputable inn he was thinking of.

Old Fish was busy today. Yet as he suspected, no one paid them any heed. The fish mongers were busy selling their wares, and Crispin caught a snatch of one such fish seller's swiftly moving hands with the deft slice of his blade as he fileted. Crispin stopped. The others stopped with him.

'No,' he told them. 'Don't wait for me. Jack, you make certain to get a room for our guest. I'll be there anon. We'll have a long night ahead of us, keeping watch of him before the morn.'

Jack looked back quizzically at his master, and Crispin was surprised Jack did not voice his curiosity aloud, but perhaps the boy was used to Crispin's ways.

Crispin watched the workers in their shops for a good long time when it clicked into place like the pins in a lock once the key is turned. *Of all the damned things . . .*

He took a deep breath before he hurried to catch up to his companions and prayed that tomorrow would come swiftly.

*   *   *

Still bound and gagged, Gernon was marched into the Guildhall the next morning behind Crispin and John Rykener, who was attired for the occasion in his men's clothes.

Jack had a determined look on his face. 'Soon, master. Soon you'll be free. We've got the churl at last!' He shook the rope tied to Gernon in emphasis.

Crispin leaned over toward Jack and whispered in his ear, 'Unfortunately, he didn't do it.'

Jack pulled back. '*What?* Master Crispin . . .'

'No time to explain now, Jack.'

Crispin pulled the rope away from Jack. The boy froze, staring at him with lips parted. Someone behind the boy shoved him, and stumbling, Jack had no choice but to make his way toward the clerks with Cobmartin, questions stuck fast to his lips, while Crispin yanked his prisoner forth.

When Tremayne saw who it was, he nearly choked on his wine. He leapt from his seat, cast his goblet to the ground, and stormed down the dais.

'Guest, I thought I told you . . .'

'And so you did, my lord. But a funny thing happened yesterday. We caught him in the act. And my lawyer suggested I question him in court.'

Tremayne blinked, mouth open impotently. But in the end, he could do nothing but stomp back up the dais and take his place. The sheriffs were equally dumbfounded, though it was soon giving way to rage.

Crispin shoved Gernon into the bar, where he bounced off it and spun ungainly before righting himself.

Tremayne tensed back against the bench. 'The third god-dammed day of the trial of Crispin Guest commences,' he snarled. 'Untie and ungag that man at once, Guest!'

Crispin drew his dagger and swiftly cut Gernon's bonds. He took his time sawing the gag from his mouth.

Gernon grabbed the gag in his fist and heaved it to the floor where he proceeded to spit. 'My lords!' he cried. 'Is this how an alderman of the city is treated! I was abducted, snatched out of my own home, and kept against my will in the hands of Crispin Guest until forcibly brought here today. I ask you. Where is the justice for London's honored citizens?'

'Where indeed,' Crispin answered. 'I told you, my Lord Recorder that there were witnesses who told me and my apprentice in confidence about the deadly doings of Richard Gernon. And you further told me that unless I had hard, irrefutable evidence against him, that he may not be detained. Well, my lord, I do have that evidence. May I proceed?'

Tremayne was staring at Rykener and finally tore his gaze away. 'I . . . very well.' He slumped back against the bench and snatched the goblet that a clerk retrieved for him, newly filled with wine. He drank a long, deep draught.

'First, my lord,' said Crispin, eyes sweeping over his beaming lawyer, 'I should like for the witness John Rykener to testify.'

The recorder watched John move from his place in the crowd to the bar. He squinted at him, and when John began to speak, he shrank back.

'Your name is John Rykener,' said Crispin.

He cleared his throat. And with a still slightly raspy voice replied, 'Yes.'

'And your occupation?'

'Well, that is a little more complicated. You see, I sometimes serve as an embroiderer. But I am also a, well . . . a harlot.'

The crowd murmured. The sheriffs shifted to the edge of the bench.

Crispin looked at him sternly. 'How can you, a man, be a harlot?'

'Because I wear the clothes of a woman when I am plying that trade. I use the name Eleanor . . .'

Tremayne coughed, choking on his wine. He hacked for several moments. Sheriff Walcote slapped him on the back until he recovered. He sat back in his chair, red-faced and staring at John anew.

John turned to the sheriffs. 'I know it is wrong to do so, my lords. But a man has to make a living. And embroidering is slow work with an even slower pay day.'

'What happened yesterday?' Crispin looked on gently but spared an eye for an ever nervous John Tremayne.

'I was dressed as Eleanor,' said Rykener. 'And I sought some new needles, for my trade, you see, as an embroideress. And there I met Richard Gernon in his shop. He's a needle maker.

Oh there were some fine needles there. Metal, bone, and lovely cases for them, too. Master Gernon was most solicitous to me, him thinking I was a woman. You see, my lords,' he said, addressing those on the dais, 'most men don't know I'm not a woman. Even when we . . . well . . .' He paused to scan the room and the fascinated faces of the crowd. He edged closer to the dais right up against the bar. 'Even when I ply my trade as a whore. There are tricks one can do, you see.' He gestured vaguely. 'And so. It didn't matter what manner of man I encountered. If they found me pleasing, we can get on with it. And Master Gernon was interested in more than my trade as an embroideress, if you get my meaning.'

'We get it,' Tremayne nearly barked. 'Make haste with your testimony, Master . . . Master Rykener.'

'Well, there I was. Making a purchase and minding my own business when Master Gernon propositioned me.'

'That's not true!' cried Gernon. '*She* propositioned *me*! I mean . . . *he* . . .'

Rykener waved his hand back and forth. '*He* propositioned, *I* propositioned . . . it matters little when there is the same result. In the end, he invited me up to his room. He proceeded to kiss me and make the noises men make when they are trying to soothe and cajole a woman; soft murmurings and promises of this silly thing or that. But then he asked me if I wouldn't play a game with him. He would see how hard he could squeeze my neck while we were, er . . . *captus in medio*. I didn't see the harm and I've had clients ask for stranger things, believe me. And so I agreed. He squeezed harder and harder. At first I could endure it. It seemed little enough to withstand for the promised silver. But it came to the point where he squeezed too tight, too tight for me to speak, to breathe. I could not stop him. I was falling into a faint. And if it weren't for the timely arrival of Master Guest and his apprentice Master Tucker, I should no doubt be dead.' He opened his cloak and showed the court the bruises on his neck, turning so that all could see.

The crowd gasped, as did Sheriff Loveney.

Tremayne raised his face to Gernon. 'What have you to say for yourself, Master Gernon?'

'I have nothing to say to this farce.'

'Do you admit taking this man . . . er . . . this, this . . .'

'Eleanor,' John supplied.

'*Him* to your rooms,' said Tremayne, studiously ignoring Rykener.

Gernon sniffed. 'I don't deny it.'

'And this game you play. Do you play it often?'

'It is merely a game. If the woman faints, I stop. It's simple. There's nothing wrong with it.'

Crispin eyed the jury. Plainly, they thought there *was* something wrong with it. However, Gernon was no judge of the crowd. He could not seem to see that they were not with him. Yet Tremayne seemed to know it.

'One plays a little game with a wench and offers them extra silver for their trouble,' said Gernon with a toss of his hand.

Loveney gripped the edge of the bench. 'Master Gernon, are you aware that three women were killed in the Bread Street Ward just this past sennight? And that the office of the sheriff has more records of deaths other than their rightful deaths of women similarly strangled?'

Gernon didn't bother looking at the sheriff as he brushed off the sleeves of his houppelande. 'I know nothing of that.'

The court fell into silence. Tremayne's brows danced over his eyes. He was plainly deciding and Crispin hoped that the final decision would be toward the cause of justice rather than a political one.

At last Tremayne spoke. 'Lord Sheriff, I implore you now to arrest this man for murder.'

Gernon's face snapped upward. 'What? You dare!'

'It is plain to me that more investigating in this matter – and in past situations – must be delved into more deeply. Master Guest, we thank you for bringing in this man for examination. It seems to me, though I am not a member of the jury, that this man is guilty of the murder of Elizabeth le Porter.'

Crispin stepped forward. 'Er . . . not quite, my lord.'

Tremayne's resigned expression mutated to sputtering rage. 'What the devil, Guest! Is that not why you dragged this man here against my express orders?'

'Well . . . yes, my lord. But upon examination of the facts, I do not think him guilty. At least not in this case. For the others he is abundantly so.'

Cobmartin was desperately trying to get Crispin's attention but he ignored the man.

'If I might clarify,' Crispin went on, 'by calling back another witness.'

Tremayne threw up his hands again. 'By all means, Guest. Take your time. It is your neck, after all. And these jurymen have all the patience in the world.'

Crispin glanced their way, and many did wear scowls. They had been away from their jobs for far too many days, far more than any other jury in his memory. He bowed to them. 'Masters, this will not take long.'

He waited as the serjeants hauled a struggling Richard Gernon away before he announced, 'Will Hugh Buckton please come forth to testify?'

Buckton seemed surprised to be mentioned, and he stood dumb for a moment before one of the men in the crowd tapped him on the shoulder. He seemed to awaken and walked slowly to the bar. He wore his rustic cotehardie, his hood and its long liripie, his belt, knife, and scrip. His eyes never left Crispin as Crispin walked around him.

'Master Buckton, you told us before that you knew Elizabeth le Porter.'

'Aye. She was a neighbor.'

'And a pretty thing.'

He flushed. 'Aye.'

'So pretty, in fact, that she cajoled you, as she had many men in the ward.'

He blinked stupidly and shook his head. 'I don't know your meaning.'

'She cajoled you into loaning her money. Money, I daresay, you could ill afford to lose. And now, of course, you'll never get it back.'

He ran his hands down his coat. 'It . . . it was charity. She needed it.'

'But so do you. Rent, bait for the eels. There is upkeep and whatnot. Expenses in any business.'

'It was a kindness,' he said in a harsher voice.

'You asked her for it back.'

'She couldn't pay.'

'But she had money. Her rent was paid, she had fine clothes, much finer than yours. And men. More men paying her way for her. Men like you. Silly, misled men.'

Buckton shifted but said nothing. He gnawed on his lip. Crispin decided on another tack. 'You sought to help my apprentice find the killer, did you not?'

The eel monger lifted his chin. 'Aye. It . . . it seemed the proper thing to do.'

'But you weren't helping, were you? You were trying to get information out of him. You were getting in his way.' Crispin reached carefully into his scrip and removed the burnt knife. 'I retrieved this from my former lodgings. I call it "former" because it was burned down by an arsonist.'

The crowd gasped. But Tremayne was losing patience. 'Good Christ, Guest. What does this have to do with aught?'

He sighed. 'If you will allow me to go on, my lord, you *will* see the relevance.'

Tremayne glanced at the window and the slant of the sun. 'Make it fast. I have more trials to sit through, you know.'

'The shop below me that belonged to my landlord was a tinker's shop,' said Crispin. 'All his goods were destroyed. But I found this in the rubble.' He lifted the knife so that all could see. 'My landlord, the tinker, did not recognize it. He repairs many goods on the Shambles; butchering hooks, knives of all stripes, cooking pots and kettles. But he did not recognize this. And it certainly didn't belong to me. It's unusual, isn't it?' He turned it, showing off the long slender blade, its curve like a scythe. 'And I wondered why it should be there. The only explanation was that it belonged to the arsonist.' He squared with the now sweating eel monger. 'Can we see your knife, Master Buckton?'

His hand slapped to his sheath. 'Why?'

'I should like to compare.'

Buckton turned to Tremayne, appealing to him. 'M-my lord, I was asked to give testimony and I did that. May I go now?'

'No. Give Guest your knife.'

His wild eyes lit from face to face. He made a half-hearted laugh as he reached for his own blade. Slowly he withdrew it. 'It's a common knife. Any fishmonger is bound to have one. It's for fileting.' When he pulled the blade free, all and sundry could see it matched the burned one in Crispin's hand.

'And yet this one is yours. You left it behind when your torched my home, hoping to kill or hurt Jack Tucker, my apprentice, because he was getting too close to the truth.'

'I never did!'

'You did. That knife in your hand is brand new. See how the handle is still smooth and oiled. The blade not nicked or even marked by much sharpening. You needed to replace the one you accidently left behind.'

'No, no. It . . . it just needed replacing, my old knife. My lord . . .'

Crispin tossed the burned knife to the floor. It clanged and startled Buckton. 'You went to Elizabeth le Porter's rooms that night. You thought I'd left. You went to her at night, pleading with her, demanding that she pay back the money she borrowed. Did she laugh at you, poor sorry fool that you are? Did she tell you to wait, always wait? Or did she tell you to get out? Whatever she said, it enraged you. You grabbed her by the throat and you throttled her. And perhaps you would have done something to dispose of the body, but you then happened to notice me, still there, dead to the world, but a witness nonetheless. You fled.'

'No! I did none of that. I don't know who killed her. That man that was just here.'

'Richard Gernon is a callus turd who strangles women for the thrill of it. He strangles whores whilst he swives them. But Elizabeth la Porter was not his victim. She was not playing the harlot for him that night. She already had someone abed with her. Me. What happened to Elizabeth le Porter was a random act by a desperate man. And while you strangled her to death, she fought. She fought so hard that bits of the skin and hair from her killer were still beneath her fingernails. And that surely left scars behind.'

He lunged for Buckton, grabbed that ubiquitous hood and snaking liripipe, and yanked it away. The eel monger's neck was covered in deep, reddened scratches, some so deep they had begun to fester.

Crispin turned to Tremayne. 'Hugh Buckton is your killer.

Not I.' He tossed down the hood. 'Will you arrest him and charge the jury to acquit me?'

Walcote surged forward, feet planted as he balanced on the edge of his seat. 'But what of the Tears of the Virgin? What of the Noreys household?'

'A distraction. A false path.'

'But the Tears were stolen. Did the Noreyses—'

'*I* stole the Tears,' said Crispin.

The crowd erupted. Tremayne stomped his foot, and the serjeants moved forward, threatening with their clubs.

Once they had quieted, Crispin went on. 'I stole the relic when you showed them to me in your chamber. I palmed the phial from the monstrance. And then I took it to the abbot of Westminster Abbey for safekeeping. But since they are false, there is no need to guard them any longer.'

'False?' asked Tremayne. He looked as if his head were spinning.

'Yes.' He bowed toward Helewise Peverel. There was nothing for it. He couldn't let the deception go on. 'The real relic was destroyed some years ago.'

The crowd still softly murmured in anxious susurrations while Tremayne absorbed it all. He glanced again at Rykener and seemed to come to a decision. 'Jurymen, I urge you all to acquit Crispin Guest from all wrongdoing. What will you decide?'

To a man, it was 'not guilty.'

TWENTY-THREE

Tuesday, 20 October

Jack Tucker ran to keep up with Crispin's hurried strides. 'Master Crispin, how did you know?'

'The knife. I saw the fish mongers on Old Fish Street using the very same style knife as they worked. That particular knife was too distinguishable. Martin never saw it before. And then I merely speculated about the fact that Buckton needed that money. He mentioned it a few times. And then there was his unusual habit of wrapping the liripipe of his hood around his neck to conceal his scars.'

Nigellus, parchment rolls bundled in his arms, chuckled. 'That was quite remarkable, Master Crispin. Quite good entertainment. When you whipped off that hood . . .'

'I was quite overcome,' said Rykener. 'But our Crispin does know what he's doing.'

'I got lucky,' he said. 'If we had not passed by a fishmonger on our way to the inn, it might never have occurred to me in time.'

Rykener laid a hand on his arm as they walked. 'But Gernon *is* guilty, is he not?'

'Oh yes. Of these other murders, I have no doubt. But as the plan to trap him went on, I began to speculate that it could not have been him. He had every reason to stay away from her. And of course, it was not him who hired me.'

Cobmartin shook his head, amazed. 'That was genius. Walter Noreys plainly hired you because he knew you *wouldn't* harm her. Pure genius.'

'And Mistress le Porter knew exactly who it was,' said Crispin. 'She scorned the notion of him, knew it was meant only as a threat without teeth. No doubt, if she hadn't been murdered, she would have given him a piece of her mind on the matter. For once it was truly revealed she was also his cousin, he would have to have backed off.'

'It don't matter,' said Jack cheerfully. 'You're free, sir. But how is it the sheriffs were compelled to free you on your own in the first place?'

'"Compelled" is correct.' Crispin slowed and the others slowed with him. They looked in the direction Crispin was looking. When they saw the man across the lane nonchalantly straightening his gauntlets, the others hung back as Crispin walked forward.

Crispin stopped only when he stood directly before him, and with a slight bow, he said, 'My Lord Derby.'

Henry Bolingbroke smiled. 'I was hoping we would meet.'

'It was you, Henry, wasn't it? Was it a letter or was it perhaps your secretary that took the order to the sheriffs?'

'A letter. A letter seems to look more official to the self-important, what with its seals and all.'

Crispin shook his head but couldn't contain his smile. 'Thank you.'

Henry's smile faded. 'I couldn't stand the thought of you in that place again. I wouldn't have let you hang, you know.'

'I don't know how you could have stopped it . . . hold. Did you think me guilty?'

'Of course not. But I know John Tremayne and the rest. If you hadn't a big enough bribe . . .'

'I hadn't a bribe at all.'

'Then you would have hanged for a certainty. Aren't you glad you didn't?'

He touched his neck lightly. 'Exceedingly.'

Henry glanced up to the sky. Two magpies chased each other across the clouds. 'My father will be home soon.'

'How is his grace of Lancaster?'

'Disheartened. He did not win his crown. A pity.' His gaze steadied on Crispin's. 'He would have worn a crown well, I think.'

Crispin nodded solemnly. 'I thought so, too. Once.'

'So you did.' Henry looked away again. 'But I keep you from your friends. Surely there is to be a celebration.'

'I suppose so.'

'And there is Young Jack!' He grinned and waved. Crispin looked back to see Jack's awed expression as he gingerly lifted his hand to return a feeble greeting.

'You mustn't tease him, Henry.'

'Tucker knows it's good-natured. Besides, I am glad that particular knave is your apprentice. He did good work for you.'

'Oh? Have you been following the trial?'

'Of course. All of court was most intrigued by it. Including my royal cousin.'

'King Richard knew about it?'

'Should not the king know all that transpires in his own realm?'

Crispin grunted a sound of affirmation.

'But here.' Henry reached into his scrip and pulled out a small kidskin pouch. 'Let me handle the fee for your lawyer.'

'Haven't you done enough for me?'

'A simple letter? I'd have done far more if I could have. Take it, Crispin.'

'I can pay my own way.'

'But I want to.'

'Henry, I can do it myself.'

'But . . .' Crispin's expression finally seemed to register with him. He shrugged and returned the pouch from whence it came. 'If you will have it so,' he said, disappointed.

Crispin laid his hand on the man's shoulder. 'It is enough that you offered. Now . . . surely there are duties for you to get back to. You know you mustn't be seen with me. Richard's spies are everywhere.'

'Why must you be so damned practical?'

'It keeps me alive.'

Henry grinned. 'So it does. Fare you well, Crispin. I heard about your lodgings. Where will you go now?'

'That is a very good question. But I'm certain that when I do find new lodgings, you will hear about it.'

Henry laughed. He rolled away from the wall and strode toward an alley, where Crispin could see a glimpse of the retainer holding Henry's horse.

Crispin returned to his companions and gathered them in. Just as he leaned in to speak to them, a familiar figure trotted forward.

'Crispin!' Martin Kemp, with the same knobby knees, the same flapping cap stopped before him. And though he also wore the same world-weary face, his whole demeanor was somewhat brighter. 'I hoped to catch you. Did you succeed? Are you a free man?'

'Yes, Martin. Praise God I am delivered. Thanks to these three.'

Martin's gaze took them in: Jack, of course; he frowned slightly upon recognizing John Rykener, then his eyes flitted over Cobmartin's unfamiliar features.

'I am gratified to hear it, Crispin. And I can share my own good news, too. I've got a new place, not too far from here, down Ivy Lane. Alice is even pleased with it and that's half the battle won.' He elbowed Crispin. 'Oh, it will take some clever moving of coins here and there but . . .' He rubbed his hands. 'I'll be back in business in no time.'

'I'm heartily happy to hear it.'

'Well.' He rocked on his heels. He seemed to have run out of conversation. Crispin took the opportunity to offer his hand. A little in awe, as Martin always seemed to be of Crispin, the tinker fit his hand in his.

'I want you to know that I am grateful to you, Martin, for taking me in all those years ago. And though I haven't been the best of tenants . . .'

'Say no more, Crispin. You always eventually paid me. And I don't mind saying . . .' He looked around. Crispin could only imagine he feared the sudden presence of his often cross wife. 'I don't mind saying that it was . . . *interesting* . . . being your landlord. Your doings and your clients. Never a dull moment.' He chuckled before sobering. 'I do pray for God's blessings on you, Crispin. May he watch over you and keep you.'

'And to you and your family, Martin.'

'If you ever need a pot mended . . .' Martin backed away, waving.

'I know where to go.' Crispin waved as he took his leave and was surprised to feel regret. Though the man's wife was a shrew and his daughter a horror at times, Martin himself was a kind-hearted and gracious man. Crispin would miss him.

But with Martin's departure his own predicament suddenly loomed large. 'Well, that's Martin sorted, but what's to become of Jack and me?'

'God blind me,' muttered Jack. 'I nearly forgot we got nowhere to go!'

Nigellus chuckled. 'That's not quite true. Come with me, gentlemen.' Crispin enquired of Jack with a mere look, but Jack shrugged his shoulders. They had no choice but to follow their swift-legged lawyer.

They found themselves on the Shambles again. 'Master Nigellus,' Crispin began. But when the lawyer took them up the road and stopped at an old poulterer's, Crispin frowned.

Nigellus gestured. 'You see! Master Crispin, this structure belonged to my family, but it has long stood unused. I would gladly rent it out to you.'

Eyes traveling upward over the building, Crispin slowly shook his head. He hated like hell to admit it aloud, but he knew he had to. 'I'd happily oblige you, Nigellus, but there is no hope of my ever being able to afford such a place. And we would be in need of furnishings . . . I'd have to rent that as well. It would come too dear.'

'But don't you see, I have this standing empty earning me nothing. Whatever you think is fair, I will take.'

'What I think is fair, Master Cobmartin, I still, regretfully cannot afford.'

'See here, Master Guest. There's no need to be stubborn about it. I am offering you a place to live at a much reduced cost. You get new lodgings, and I get a lodger I can trust. And if the rent is too dear, then pay what you paid before and when I need something investigated, why, I know I can rely on you to do it.'

'I see. But would you require me and my services in sufficient amounts to supplement what I cannot pay?'

Nigellus merely grinned. 'Let's go inside, shall we?' He took a key from his belt and unlocked the door. When he pushed it open, a veil of dust rained down. And a pigeon, who had made a home in the rafters, took flight. Apparently, there was a hole in the roof. Rain and snow had damaged the wooden planks beneath, and a mound of bird droppings was proof the pigeons lineage was prodigious.

'Oh my!' said Nigellus. 'I haven't been in here for nearly five years. Look what time and neglect have done to the place. I think that whatever rent you can pay, Master Guest, will be more than sufficient, given the circumstances.'

Crispin glanced around the ground floor room. It was a shop or had been. There were still discarded cages piled in one corner, dusty, broken, and the whole place still stank of the poulterer's, of pullet shit and old feathers. Dust motes soared freely with every shaft of light from the broken shutter to the hole in the roof.

A wobbly table of some length was covered in a layer of dust but seemed sturdy enough despite its quaver, and the few chairs also seemed of solid construction.

'Let me see,' said Nigellus. 'Jack, have you parchment and quill?'

'I do, sir.' He pulled it from his scrip before turning sheepishly toward Rykener. 'Oh. By rights, this is your property, Master Rykener.'

John waved him off. 'I have so little use for it these days. And you seemed to have the greater need. Consider it a gift, Young Jack.'

Jack bowed. 'I thank you, Master Rykener. You are kind indeed.' He set the ink on the table, dipped the quill, and poised it over the parchment. 'I am ready, Nigellus.'

'Take this down, Master Jack. One table, six pence. Four chairs . . . no three, one appears to be broken . . . at three pence each. A coffer, two shillings . . . And now the upstairs.'

Nigellus led the way up the stairs situated in the middle rear of the shop and they all climbed. Crispin saw that the upper floor was divided into two rooms with a narrow corridor in between. The one on the right opened to a large room with a bed with bed curtains.

'One bed with curtains,' continued Nigellus, 'six shillings. Another coffer, one shilling. A basin and ewer, two shillings eight pence. A disreputable towel . . . free. A small table, three pence.' The hearth was wide and made of carved stone but had not seen a fire for years. There were feathers on the hearth. Crispin was certain something nested in the chimney.

Nigellus sneezed from the dust and exited, pushing through to the other room. Jack scrambled after, ink pot in hand, quill in his teeth, and parchment in his other hand. He set the ink pot down on the nearest surface. Crispin was adding the sums in his head and cringed at the amount.

The room was smaller, no doubt for a worker, apprentice, or servant and held a smaller bed with curtains and one coffer. 'A small bed with curtains, three shillings, and a coffer, one shilling. There,' said Nigellus, running his hand distractedly through the layers of dust. 'Calculate that, Master Jack.'

'Very well.' Jack bit his tongue as he added the sums. 'I have it as three crowns, two shillings tuppence, sir.'

'And the rent two pounds a year,' said Nigellus.

Crispin shook his head. Never had he dreamed when he used to awake from his featherbed in those long ago mornings and look out his manor house window to the fields he owned and worker's cottages under his tenancy, that he would have imagined that a few dusty rooms with old, tired furniture would be a welcomed sight. But he understood now the reality. 'It simply cannot be done,' he offered quietly, tamping down his humiliation. No, those long ago days were gone. He didn't have the means of acquiring decent housing for him and his servant.

'I shall take five shillings now, and five quarterly, Master Guest. Due compensation for the work that must be done to make these rooms habitable.'

'Master Cobmartin, perhaps you didn't hear me. I cannot pay this sum. Even at half the rent.'

'Very well, three shillings, but you are getting a bargain, particularly since I will throw in the furnishings for . . . half. Paid when you can. Or in kind.'

'Master Nigellus . . .'

'Master Crispin!' Jack beckoned to him and Crispin walked over. Jack leaned in to his ear. 'Master Crispin, I have the rent. And in a year's time, if it is well with Gilbert and Isabel Langton, I shall gain a fine dowry. We can pay it.'

'I'll not have it! My servant will *not* be paying *my* way!' It was humiliating. He pushed his way from Jack and hurried down the stairs. He had to leave, had to breathe fresh air. Stomping across the dirty shop where dust kicked up in clouds, he yanked the door open and inhaled deeply of the rancid air of the Shambles. The same street, the same circumstances he had suffered for the last thirteen years. He knew he would die here in some ramshackle room. And he would die the pauper he was. But, by God, he would not take charity from his own damned servant!

Breathing hard, he stared at the mud. He had hoped for one spark of a moment that this *might* work. For there was a separate space for Jack who was a man in every sense of the word now and needed that privacy, especially if he was to have a wife. But it was the master who was to care for the servant, not the other way around. It seemed that Jack was in better stead than he. And he supposed in the long run this was a good thing since he had nothing to leave to the boy but his expertise. And what was that worth in coin these days?

Still, the boy had accomplished much on his own. He was becoming this invention of Crispin's, this 'Tracker' and with his own natural cleverness, he had managed to reason his way through the nearly impossible. He was proud of the lad, to be sure. He deserved a place such as this.

Crispin turned and ran his gaze over the structure, its sorry state of plaster, its rotted timbers, it's patched and broken tile roof. His gaze dropped to the ring on his finger. This one was his from all those years ago as a baron and part of the chivalry of the kingdom. But he also still had his father's ring in his keeping, and little good it did them in its hiding place . . . well, former hiding place. Jack kept it safe somewhere. Probably the Boar's Tusk.

The thought rippled the skin of his spine. If he sold it . . .

What would his father have said, the man he hadn't truly known and little remembered? The ring had no value as it was, hidden, stored away, forgotten. Wouldn't it be more practical if sold? He could get five pounds at least for it.

He looked up again at the old poulterer's place and suddenly envisioned the possibilities. They'd have to do the work themselves. Or maybe he could barter his services to a carpenter. If not 'tracking' then do the books or write out documents. He'd done it before for a living.

It would be good to have a separate parlor for clients. True, it would also have to serve as their kitchen, but that was manageable with maybe a curtain. Someday.

Was he talking himself into it?

A dark shape suddenly appeared over the top of the roof and minced delicately along its spine before trotting down till it landed on the sill of the window that would serve as Crispin's chamber.

'Gyb? Is that you?'

The cat, with its black mask and white blaze down its nose and muzzle, gazed down at him with bored yellow eyes, meowed once, and made himself at home on the sill, hunkering down and wrapping his tail about his plumped body.

Crispin smiled. He supposed that settled the question as much as anything else.

AFTERWORD

As you have seen throughout the Crispin Guest series, sometimes the relic is forefront and sometimes it's only a McGuffin, the thing that propels the plot forward. In this instance, it was definitely in the McGuffin category. In the next book, however, it comes to the forefront. A blood relic – Jesus's blood in particular – was the holiest and most prized. And so Crispin must pursue an old nemesis, acquire yet another romantic entanglement, and still keep his wits about him when the crimes of thievery, blackmail, and murder come right to his doorstep in *Season of Blood*.